The Guardian's Light

The Guardian's Light

Oliver Crane

First published in 2024 by TBLOD
publishing@tblod.com

This book is a work of fiction. Names,
characters, businesses, places, events and
incidents are either the product of the author's
imagination or used in a fictitious manner. Any
resemblance to actual persons, living or dead,
or actual events is purely coincidental.

ISBN: 978-1-7397969-5-2
eBook: 978-1-7397969-6-9

Guardian
*One who looks after, protects,
or defends*

(Collins Dictionary)

This book is dedicated to people of principles whose sense of duty holds our society together.

Such a person was John, my dad.

My thanks to the wee team who helped deliver this project: Amanda, Georgie, Thatsany and JJ.

And to Chamonix for being the amazing place you are.

Early April, Chamonix, France

On a sheer rock face, one hundred metres above the Mer de Glace and teetering on a tiny stance, Cal attached himself to a sling he'd placed over a flake of rock and unclipped from the ropes he'd descended on their route off the mountain. He looked up and shouted, 'Safe.'

The rope twitched as Knox retrieved a handful to attach himself.

A distant rumble quickly became an approaching roar. Cal instinctively drew himself hard into the face as a WHOOSH of snow and rock cascaded past, thrashing against his rucksack and chilling him in its shadow.

He hugged the face closer, clinging on for life as the turbulence threatened to buffet him off. Ominous shapes flashed by. Stones the size of tennis balls, and boulders resembling full-blown TVs. Projectiles that should one strike … End of—

The torrent eased then petered out, leaving solitary rocks that whizzed by, ricocheting off something further down and sending up the smell of cordite as they shattered and burnt.

The rope hung limp, and fearing for his friend,

Cal leant out and looked up, squinting against the sun to where the rock disappeared over a bulge. He then looked down to the bottomless bergschrund between the rock and the glacier, but no sign of Knox.

His stomach churned and his breathing quickened as the gut-wrenching despair they felt with the death of their friend, Connor, in Edinburgh came flooding back.

A voice shouted down, 'Bloody hell, Cal, what was that about?' and the ropes sprung to life as Knox appeared over the bulge and zipped his way down, landing on the stance beside Cal. Cal shook his head and removed his sunglasses to expose a round face, panda eyes from wearing sunglasses, and a rough fringe of blonde hair that drooped under his helmet.

'I thought I'd lost you,' said Cal, wiping his eyes with the back of his hand.

Knox could see Cal on the edge of tears and reached out, hugging his friend as best he could on their precarious perch. 'We're both fine, Cal, and here for each other.'

Cal nodded, sniffed and replaced his sunglasses. 'I'll bang in a piton for us to abseil off,' he said, selecting one of the steel wedges from his collection. He placed the wedge into a crack, and burning the adrenaline that still coursed through him, he hammered it home. The piton sang the song of a solid placement, its pitch elevating with each hammer blow, ringing across the valley like a cathedral bell celebrating, 'We're alive! We're alive!'

A few more pitches and they reached the glacier. The snow and rock fall that had nearly taken them now played to their favour; its debris having filled enough of the bergschrund to give a passage across. Such were the absurdities of mountaineering.

They moved to a safe open area, removed their helmets, stripped down to their T-shirts and rubbed sunscreen into their faces and arms, drawing in its flowery fragrance. Cal took a bag of boiled sweets and the last of their cereal bars from his pack. He handed a share to Knox who was now lying on his back, his eyes closed and his head with its long hair tied back, propped up by his rucksack. 'Thanks, mate,' said Knox, keeping his eyes shut as he stuffed a cereal bar into his mouth and gulped down water from a SIGG bottle. He rested his scuffed hands on his chest.

'How are you feeling, Cal?' he asked as he dozed in the sun's heat.

Cal sat with his knees drawn, marvelling at the 3754 metres of Aiguille du Dru, its faces scribed with the routes of alpine legends. To the south at the head of the glacier, Mont Blanc du Tacul stood sentinel with its fearsome Gervasutti Couloir beckoning the fearless.

'I'm good,' Cal said as his eyes roamed the view. 'It's weird how when I'm climbing, I feel confident. But when it comes to everything else …'

Knox lay as he was with his eyes still shut. He scratched at two days' worth of stubble. 'Don't beat yourself up, Cal. It's society,' he said. 'It messes with your head.'

They fitted their crampons, and in case one of them broke through a snow bridge into a crevasse, they attached themselves, 15 metres apart, to their rope and slung the excess coils over their shoulders. Cal went in front, and with their axes in hand, they trudged off down the glacier, crampons crunching as they bit into the ice.

Cal felt at home on the glacier. Pathfinding through its lurking perils was a risk in life he could mitigate, and should the worst happen, being the lightest and the better ice climber would make it easier to retrieve him.

He chose carefully, finding firm areas where the wind had scoured the ice clear of fresh snow and patches of névé that had stood the test of time.

They skirted around, scurried under and skilfully crossed crevasses, overhanging seracs and snow bridges, working their way towards the airy steel ladders up from the glacier to Montenvers and the quaint rack and pinion train down to Chamonix.

They paused on a flatter section and looked ahead at a two-metre-wide crevasse running off in both directions.

'I can jump it,' said Cal.

'Are you sure?' asked Knox.

'Yeh, man. But I'll check it first.'

Knox braced himself – just in case – and Cal inched forward to get a better look. He peered down.

From his crouched position with the shaft of his axe pushed into the snow, Knox called over, 'What's keeping you, Cal?'

'There's something down here,' Cal replied as he tried to get a better look.

'Like what?' asked Knox.

'A ski. A good ski.'

'Just one?'

'Yeah.'

'And nothing else?'

Cal shook his head. 'Nope. Only one ski stuck on a snow shelf about 10 metres down. I can't see any further because of a kink in the crevasse.'

They swapped places and Knox took a look. He switched his avalanche transceiver to receive and held it out over the abyss.

'Anything?' shouted Cal.

Knox shook his head. 'Nah,' and retreated from the edge.

They regrouped and looked around for skiers – a guide maybe, who could contact the right people in Chamonix. But the weather was closing in and they were alone.

They moved well away from the crevasse, took off their packs and donned down jackets against the cooling air.

Knox looked up at the Aiguille du Goûter now capped with a telltale cloud signalling a storm approaching.

'The weather's crapping out,' he said.

'Aye, earlier than we thought. We should beat it out of here,' said Cal, looking up the glacier to where the Tacuil was disappearing into cloud.

He looked again at the crevasse. 'But if someone is down there, we can't just leave them.'

Knox's thoughts returned to Connor dying alone in his flat, and he nodded his agreement. 'No, that's not what we're about,' he said.

Like a man on a mission, Cal turned his rucksack over and removed his ice tools. 'Set up a belay. I'm climbing down.'

Knox held the rope as Cal lowered himself over the lip of the crevasse. He kicked in the front points of his crampons and worked the picks of his tools down the vertical ice to the snow shelf where the ski was sitting.

'Anything down there?' shouted Knox.

'Still looking,' Cal shouted back as he lifted the ski and inspected it. 'Keep me on a tight rope.'

Knox took up the slack, and treading lightly on the snow shelf, Cal moved forward to the edge and looked down. The crevasse narrowed and then opened up again, disappearing into darkness. Trying to accustom his eyes to the dark, he peered down to where something was wedged but it was difficult to make out.

He took his head torch from his jacket pocket and shone it down.

'Shit!' he whispered, and then called down, 'If you can hear me say something, but don't move.'

Monday, Edinburgh, Scotland

DS John Anderson boarded the number 16 bus at Church Hill. He climbed the stairs to the upper deck, and from a window seat, gazed out at all the familiar places: Bruntsfield, Tollcross, Lothian Road and Princes Street.

As Edinburgh passed by, he wondered whether he had made a jot of difference during his 25 years as a police officer, and how many people had suffered through his failures.

It wasn't only those he had seen game the system: criminals using the proceeds of crime to fund guileful lawyers adept at finding legal loopholes. It was also those of whom he was ignorant: cunning malefactors, operating under the radar to mete out suffering and despair.

As the bus stopped and started beside a contraflow of pedestrians, it occurred to John that those hundreds of shoppers, tourists, escapists and souls with nowhere else to go were merely NPCs; non-participating characters acting as a backdrop to the antagonists in his story.

Colleagues said he had a knack for spotting crime. A policeman's nose for no good.

He alighted at The Shore and paused to look around at the coffee shops and restaurants that lined the cobbled streets on either side of the old Leith docks. Today the water was calm, reflecting a grand four-storey building on Commercial Wharf opposite.

Perhaps now I have time I'll take a proper look at Edinburgh, but not here, he thought as he recounted the horrors he had seen close by.

He looked towards the Firth of Forth and tried to fathom how something that had started as a job, turned into a career and then an obsession had so quickly disintegrated.

His counsellor had been magnanimous and said it was the nature of trauma. *Don't listen to it, John. It will send you away from your purpose in life and hold you there; hostage to avoidance. It's only been three months. Give yourself time. Don't let what happened have the final word.*

But John had concluded detective work was like any other career: a lifetime developing your craft to be lost in a moment.

The irony was that he hadn't groped a woman at the Christmas bash or been found putting the cost of an extra meal through corporate expenses. He hadn't even tried to talk his way out of a speeding ticket, let alone taken cash to advocate an incredulous cause.

He had simply tried to help people. To make society a better place. But he had failed and his conscience said, *Do the right thing, son. Go.*

He tidied his scarf, checked the envelope he had brought with him was still in his pocket, buttoned his tweed jacket and headed off towards the police

station on Queen Charlotte Street: home to the Major
Investigations Team.

***

The station was part of the old Leith Town Hall,
dating back to 1827 when Leith and Edinburgh were
separate entities. It would have been a handsome
building in its day, with its short flight of steps,
sandstone columns and portico. But with an out-of-
character access ramp added to the front, the
stonework grubby and the police-blue front door
needing a fresh coat of paint, it looked the way John
felt: battle-weary.

John climbed the front steps and tapped his
warrant card on a pad beside the door. It clicked and
he entered, pulling the door closed behind him.

An ornate staircase led up to the team's office on
the first floor. He dabbed his card on another pad,
opened the door and the room hushed as heads lifted
from screens to witness his return and try to interpret
what it might mean for them.

PC Sheila Ross was first out of the box, rushing
over, reaching up and throwing her arms around his
neck. She hugged him tight. 'Hello, big handsome
fellow. We've missed you,' she said.

She let go and took his hands in hers. 'How are
you doing, John?' she asked with the compassion
expected from an officer who had served within the
domestic abuse task force.

John smiled but didn't answer. It seemed his

words were stuck.

'I understand,' she said. 'And I can't imagine what seeing that was like for you. Come and say hello to the others.'

Those who knew John well came over and shook his hand. 'Good to see you … you're looking well … didn't manage to escape, then?' All the usual banter to avoid the uncomfortable truth. Less familiar faces gave a nod or a little wave before retreating to their work.

'Is Jack in?' John asked.

Sheila glanced over to the superintendent's door.

'He came in early. Harry's in with him,' she said, referring to Inspector Harry Freeman with whom John had been partnered throughout his time in Major Investigations. 'A VIP is meant to be gracing us. He wants to discuss something about his daughter, or stepdaughter, who died in France. But I don't know the details.'

'What's his name?' asked John.

Sheila looked unsure. 'Sir Hugo something or another, if that means anything to you?'

John shook his head. 'The cause of death?' he asked, immediately regretting being drawn.

'A ski accident, I think. I've no idea what it has to do with us.'

John shrugged. 'Listen, Sheila, there's something I want to tell you—'

Jack's door opened, cutting him short, and Jack called over. 'John, a word, please.'

John turned to Sheila to finish what he was saying but Jack was standing waiting. 'It can hold until I come out,' said John.

'Sure,' said Sheila.

She watched as the big guy, who had always had such presence and held the team together in the darkest of times, sloped listlessly off, and noticed all the others in the office were doing the same. They wanted to know … they *needed* to know … 'Is John back?'

***

Jack Demsie was a cop's cop. A hard bastard of a superintendent, and his people loved him for it. Jack liked nothing better than to be out there, grabbing and cuffing the bad guys.

When John had first set eyes on Jack, he wondered whether he was the reincarnation of the George Cowley he remembered from childhood repeats of *The Professionals*: the wavy reddish hair, rugged features and matter-of-fact manner.

Legend had it that when Jack suspected a fresh-faced fiscal's depute had returned a case asking for pedantic changes to lighten their in-tray, Jack had jumped into a response car, blue-lighted his way up Leith Walk and The Mound to Chambers Street and marched into their office. It only happened once.

Jack reached out a firm hand and pumped John's. 'Good to see you back, John. Good to see you. All hale and hearty, I hope? I'm in with Harry. Come and join us.'

Jack had pre-empted the meeting with three cardboard cups of coffee-to-go from a nearby deli. 'There's no danger of scalding yourselves with these,' he said, lifting the cardboard carrier off a side table. 'But unlike that wretched machine, at least it tastes of coffee.'

He handed one each to Harry and John.

Harry turned his attention to John. 'How are you feeling?' he asked.

Harry was short, his round face, thick glasses and spiky grey hair, giving him the appearance of an academic: a mindful thinker who gathered and processed facts before reaching logical conclusions. Those who saw Harry's 'clock speed' as a weakness did so at their peril. Behind that thoughtful demeanour was a sharp mind, astute enough to win him a First in Applied Psychology at Cambridge and have him promoted through the ranks to Detective Inspector.

John was quite the contrary: a 'feeler,' running with his gut instinct, sensing the unsaid, seeing the unseen and intuiting the meaning of these ephemeral clues.

It was this contrast that made John and Harry such a great team.

'I'm on the mend,' said John. 'Weekly sessions with a counsellor and a respite in Auchterarder have helped.'

'That's good,' said Harry. 'But these things take time. It's about learning to accommodate the trauma.'

Harry returned to his seat opposite Jack, and John

took the seat next to him.

He reached into his jacket pocket, took out the envelope and put it down on the polished desk.

Jack looked at it and moved slightly back, as if it might be contagious.

He fixed John with authoritative eyes. 'I won't sit here and patronise you, John, but I want you to hear me out. I'm as unhappy about that last case as you are, but you're shouldering too much of the burden. You walk out and the bad guys have scored. You know what it's like: what it's always been like. Two steps forward and one back.'

Harry took a tissue from his pocket, removed his glasses, and as if it might help him see clearer, he wiped the lenses.

John turned to him. 'Are they any better?'

Harry shook his head. 'Not really. I've got another appointment at the Eye Pavilion. It's bearable – just.'

'I'm sorry,' said John. 'Having ammonia squirted into your eyes is way beyond the call.'

John sensed Jack staring at him and suspected what Jack was thinking. *Man up, John. You are not the only one who's suffered.*

John took a deep breath and looked across to the door.

Jack gently pushed the envelope back across his desk towards him.

'Let's have our coffee,' said Jack.

Keeping the cups held away, they carefully unclipped the lids and took a sip: lukewarm but rich in flavour.

'Small pleasures where you can find them, isn't that right?' said Jack.

He returned to John. 'We've been asked to look into something. It's a bit left field to our stock-in-trade and we could turn it down. But I think it's a straightforward brief that could win us some brownie points, and it would give you two a few days out of the heat to think things through. Time to reacclimatise. When it's done and dusted, if you still want to discuss what's in that envelope, then you'll have my ear. How does that sound?'

'Is it to do with the fatality in France that Sheila mentioned?' asked John.

'It is. The deceased is a young woman called Freya Rowden-Mott. She's the stepdaughter of Sir Hugo Rowden-Mott, or HRM as the press like to abbreviate the name. You might have heard of him?'

'Human resources management,' said Harry.

'What?' Jack asked, looking confused.

'Oh, nothing,' said Harry. 'I'm just rambling on.'

John tried to place the man. 'He sounds familiar, but I can't say where from.'

Jack cleared his throat. 'Well, for as long as it takes to finish a decent dram at Hogmanay, he was home secretary. Part of that last shower and their revolving leadership baloney. From what I gather, the moment his arse touched the seat the music restarted, and he was churned. He's embroiled in a government procurement investigation. You know the story: helps a pal get a multimillion-pound contract for non-conforming shite that's now costing millions more to store as it rots in a warehouse.

Meanwhile, in the real world, we don't have enough to buy effing paperclips.'

'I presume he's being brought to book?' asked John

Jack made a guttural sound. 'Fat chance. A young mother who shoplifts a tin of formula milk to feed her hungry bairn would have the book thrown at her, but Sir Hugo and his kind can siphon millions from the public purse and it quietly drops off the radar.'

It was something else the officers loved about Jack: he was a man for the common people and didn't give a fuck about the establishment when it came to championing them.

'What is he doing now?' asked John.

'He's been given a cushy number with the UN in Geneva until the heat dies down. Then they'll probably bring him back onto the pitch.'

'What was he knighted for?' asked Harry.

'He was on the last PM's Resignation Honours list, which probably means they went to school together or some such hokum. That's unbridled nepotism in my playbook.'

John shook his head. 'You couldn't make this stuff up, could you?'

'Indeed not,' said Jack as he referred to a piece of paper on his desk. 'Sir Hugo's wife, or should I say second wife, is called Astrid and is connected to Swedish nobility.'

'How do you know that?' John asked.

'Sir Hugo told me so,' said Jack. 'He made quite a point of it.'

John raised an eyebrow.

'Exactly what I thought,' said Jack.

'Anyway, that aside, his stepdaughter, Freya, was spending the winter in the French Alps. Chamonix, as I understand. Two climbers found her body in a crevasse – not that I know much about crevasses. Sir Hugo has asked us to run the slide rule over it and corroborate that it's all it seems.'

Jack then looked at Harry. 'Harry, back in the day you did a bit of mountaineering didn't you?'

Harry put his glasses back on and squinted at Jack, trying to focus on him. 'I was a member of CUMA, but our ambitions were modest.'

'That sounds painful. What exactly was it?' Jack asked.

Harry disregarded Jack's jibe and took the literal line. 'Cambridge University Mountaineering Association.'

'Ah, I'm with you now,' said Jack, with an enlightened expression to suit. 'What about you, John?'

'As kids, we played on the coal spoil heaps, if it counts,' he said.

Jack gave a satisfied smile at hearing the return of his colleague's ironic sense of humour.

John continued, 'You'd be better passing this over to someone with connections in the mountain rescue. Let them pore over the paperwork.'

Jack pursed his lips and shook his head. 'Crevasses are something we're a bit light on in Scotland. No, best keep this one in-house.'

John let out a sigh. 'Let's have a quick look at whatever you have.'

'I'm afraid we don't have much,' said Jack. 'I spoke to the commandant of the Gendarmerie in Chamonix – a bumptious fellow who goes by the name something or other de Petit.' Jack looked again at his piece of paper. 'Commandant Jean-Raymond de Petit. Sounds rather grand. He says the case is done, dusted and closed.'

'Are you sure that's France?' asked John. 'Commandant sounds more Germanic to me.'

'That's what he called himself,' said Jack, crosschecking the paperwork.

'If he says that it's done and dusted, we can talk about my resignation,' said John.

Jack sat back in his seat, clasped his hands together and put them on his stomach. 'Not quite. Rowden-Mott is making rumblings in influential places, and for whatever reason, de Petit hasn't given the big "Non" to you corroborating. All he's said is he's not happy about it.'

'Which means?' John asked.

'Which means I need the two of you to sharpen your ice picks and get yourselves to Chamonix. Bear in mind we have zero jurisdiction in France and Sir Hugo and his merry band of Brexiteers put the kybosh on any goodwill we might have curried. You'll be visiting Chamonix under sufferance, so gather the information you need to give the parents closure, enjoy the snow and get yourselves back here.'

John looked incredulously at Harry, but Harry's attention was on Jack.

'They're called ice axes, not ice picks,' said

Harry, in his usual matter-of-fact way.

'Detail noted,' said Jack, jotting something down.

Realising he had just been stitched up, John raised both his hands and shook his head. 'Whoa, not so fast. I haven't agreed to anything.'

Jack glanced at his watch. 'Listen, John, the parents will be here soon. Let's hear them out.'

***

A civilian staff member phoned from the public enquiries office. Sheila took the call and shouted over, 'John, Harry, Sir Hugo and Lady Rowden-Mott are waiting downstairs.'

Jack appeared from his office and the three of them trooped off for their meeting. As they descended the stairs, they could see Sir Hugo pacing back and forth in the manner of a man held captive. His wife had taken a seat at one side. John immediately sensed her tight demeanour – closed down as though grief had rendered the world beyond her feelings irrelevant.

They hadn't reached the bottom before Sir Hugo heard their approach and moved across the hall to stand looking impatiently up at them.

He was a tall man with a straight nose, a full head of dark hair combed to the side, brown eyes and a tanned complexion synonymous with someone fortunate enough to have the time and money to enjoy exotic locations.

The officers could smell his exclusive cologne

with its notes of bergamot, cinnamon, cedar and a price tag well beyond their pay grade. His navy sports jacket was perfectly tailored, his white shirt starched, his black trousers pressed, and his brown Italian shoes immaculately polished. Replete with trophy wife, he looked like a noughties caricature used to advertise executive cars or first-class business lounges: a staid representation of masculinity and success.

Sir Hugo sensed who was superior among the three officers. He put his hand out for Jack to shake, revealing a jewel-encrusted watch and gold cufflinks.

'Sir Hugo Rowden-Mott. Currently attaché to the UN,' he said, in a half-hearted attempt to downplay his status. However, his overweening need for aggrandisement shone through, and after their conversation in Jack's office, all three officers knew what the others were thinking. *Pompous prick.*

Knowing he had just lost a loved one, it was a thought that didn't sit well with John.

'Jack Demsie and my colleagues, Detective Sergeant John Anderson and Detective Inspector Harry Freeman,' said Jack.

John raised his hand but quickly realised that other than a nod, Sir Hugo didn't intend to engage with him or Harry.

Sir Hugo turned to his wife, who was looking at them with a lost expression.

'Astrid, darling ...' he said.

Astrid stood up, and clutching her bag, walked slowly over. She was a striking woman, middle-aged with shoulder-length blonde hair and Scandinavian facial features of blue eyes and high cheekbones. Her soft pastel-blue bouclé cropped jacket with a matching knee-length skirt over a white silk shirt, and a heavy gold necklace oozed affluence to equal her husband's arrogance.

John wondered how many hungry mouths her necklace, matching bangle, Cartier watch and conspicuous rings would have been able to feed.

Yet when he looked into her blue eyes, he knew that all her finery was futile against her grief.

Sir Hugo glanced at his watch. 'We were staying with friends in their Sutherland shooting lodge when the tragic news of Freya came through. We have a plane to catch back to London this afternoon and are running late, so if you don't mind ...' he said, shifting impatiently from one foot to the other.

Jack led the way to a conference room situated off the public area, well away from the operationally sensitive 'shop,' as the team called it.

Unlike their uber-modern office, the conference room, with its ornate cornices and sash windows, was in keeping with the original build and was dominated by an oak table to suit. The only concession to modernity was the video conference equipment.

As Jack anticipated, Sir Hugo migrated to the power position at the head of the table.

'If you'd like to sit here, Lady Rowden-Mott,' said Jack, with enough of a show to emphasise her husband's indifference towards her.

'Please, call me Astrid,' she said in a quiet voice

as she moved to the seat.

John and Harry sat opposite her and Jack sat in the seat opposite her husband.

Jack clasped his hands, put his forearms on the table and leant forward.

It was a display of his childhood 'Cowley' that John had seen many times, and each time he smiled inwardly. He'd miss these little charades.

'How do you think we might help you?' asked Jack, making it clear that he saw this as a request for consideration and nothing more.

Sir Hugo took out a small notebook held in a silver cover and a Mont Blanc pen from inside his jacket. He flicked a page and wrote something down. But Jack knew his game: write something down to unsettle the away team. Something you know but they don't. Lawyers did it all the time to try and wangle an edge.

He closed the notebook, returned the pen to his pocket and looked at Jack. 'The brief is straightforward. As you can imagine, my wife ...' He paused, glanced across at his wife and corrected himself. '*We* are devastated by what has happened to Freya. It looks like a terrible accident, and I'm sure that is the conclusion you'll draw. But understandably, Astrid is struggling to come to terms with it. I would like you to confirm that all is as it seems and sign it off as quickly as possible whilst maintaining the utmost tact and discretion.'

The three officers offered nothing of their thoughts and then looked at his wife. She seemed oblivious to her husband's presence. Dislocated almost. As she stared at the spider microphone in the centre of the table, the officers knew her mind was anywhere but here.

Jack put his index fingers together and touched his lip before speaking. 'Sir Hugo and Lady Rowden-Mott, our thoughts are with you and your loss. But what makes you think we can add value? Do you suspect criminality? Without a crime or the clear intent to commit a crime, this falls outside of our remit. Furthermore, we have no powers in France. The French are competent, so let them get on with their job. If you are London-based, then you could get an opinion from the Met.'

Sir Hugo wagged his index finger and shook his head. 'Absolutely not. The Met are too tied in with the Westminster village and I don't want word of police involvement getting out. As I said, this is a straightforward request to give my wife closure. Twenty-four hours will see the whole thing wrapped up, I'm sure.'

With their suspicions validated, John and Harry looked astutely at Jack and Jack could see they had lost interest. Sir Hugo's only objective was to appease his wife and was using them to those ends.

'Sir Hugo, we're going to turn this down,' said Jack. 'But now you've asked for our involvement I'll have to send a report upstairs. I'm sure our masters will be in touch with you.'

Sir Hugo's face reddened, and he leant forward. 'I suggest you reconsider our request, Superintendent Demsie. I have connections in high places.'

Whilst Astrid looked questioningly at her

husband, Jack abruptly stood up to conclude the meeting, his chair scraping the floor as he did so. John and Harry followed suit.

Jack fixed Sir Hugo with a steely gaze. 'Your last remark could be construed as a threat or an abuse of power, but under the circumstances, I'll let it pass.'

They were about to leave when Astrid took something from her bag: a photograph.

She homed in on John, and with a trembling hand, slowly held out the picture for him to see. In a quiet singing voice, almost slurred with its Swedish accent, she spoke. 'Please, Sergeant, this is my daughter, Freya, and me.'

John hesitated so Astrid offered the photo a little further and repeated, 'Please …'

He moved around the table to look at the picture. It was of a woman and a young girl dressed in ski gear and surrounded by spectacular mountain scenery.

'When was this taken?' asked John.

Astrid offered a sad smile. 'It was taken when Freya was twelve. We visited Chamonix together and skied the Vallee Blanche with a guide. It was a wonderful day. One of those magical days that stay with you forever.'

John could sense her husband's impatience even before he spoke. 'Astrid, dear, I'm not sure that this is relevant.'

John passed him an admonitory stare. 'Let your wife have her say,' he said, pulling up a chair next to her. She handed John the photo. 'So, this was taken 10 years ago?' he asked.

'Exactly. Freya is twenty-two now. *Was* twenty-two,' she corrected, as the finality of her situation once again hit home. 'Last summer, she completed her digital sciences degree in Stockholm and wanted to do something different for a year. Bali, Chamonix: all the places that we would have loved to go to at that age had we been a little braver.'

'Indeed,' said John, but his mind wandered to how different his life had been from Freya's. The oldest boy in a family whose coal miner father had died from an industrial disease, he had little choice but to abandon dreams of university and earn a wage to help his mother.

'I take it Freya was a good skier?' he asked.

Astrid nodded keenly, glad of the opportunity to ennoble her daughter. 'Oh yes. She could ski as soon as she could walk. In Sweden, many children can. She adored everything to do with snow. But she didn't take risks. She loved life too much. It's why I don't understand any of this. Why would she go on to the glacier alone? Where were her friends?'

'Do you have a more recent picture?' John asked.

Astrid went into her bag and took out a clutch. 'Freya loved photography. Her father is a photographer, so she probably got it from him.'

From somewhere down the table came the sound of a throat being cleared and a caustic retort. 'He is an *amateur* photographer.'

John chose to ignore it.

Astrid seemed not to have heard either. 'Freya always had her favourite photos printed. She said it made them more "real". Especially after her degree.'

'What difference did the degree make?' asked John as he studied the picture.

Astrid looked hard at him. 'She didn't like the digital world, Detective Sergeant. She said it was a dark place where your soul hung over an abyss; although I've learnt through life that malevolence comes with many faces. I think that's why Freya wanted to travel: to prove to herself that the world wasn't like that. I can let you have digital copies, but they're not the same,' she said.

John looked carefully through the photographs of a beautiful blonde girl – a younger facsimile of her mother. Some were selfies, some taken using a timer, but others he wasn't sure about. Were they taken by someone else? Some were in the mountains with Freya walking or standing with her skis in hand. Others were in ancient towns with narrow roads and simple houses with unrendered stone walls. A few were set in tropical locations: beaches and grass huts with tanned young people, their hair sun-bleached, smiling at the camera. The girls wore bikini tops and sarongs wrapped around their waists, and the boys wore flip-flops, long floral shorts, and seashell necklaces over their bare chests. Colourful surfboards were propped vertically behind them. Life looked good. A few were taken in clubs and bars, the subjects, drinks in hands, huddling close and making faces under garish multicoloured lights.

'Freya seemed to be a happy young woman,' said John.

'Most of the time,' replied Astrid, shifting her eyes and fiddling with her bag. 'But I should tell you that the last weeks were difficult ones. Freya was angry with me.'

'What about?' asked Harry.

Astrid looked awkwardly at her husband and then at Harry. 'About Hugo. She didn't like me marrying him.'

Sir Hugo shifted awkwardly in his seat. 'Let's not drag this up again. You know you didn't love Anders.'

'That's not true …' said Astrid.

'Who is Anders?' asked John.

'My ex-husband.'

John could tell there was so much more Astrid wanted to say, but it seemed beyond her and she returned to the subject of her daughter.

'How did Freya communicate this? Did you speak with her?'

Astrid shook her head. 'We tended to use WhatsApp.'

Harry moved around the table to stand beside where John was sitting.

'May I?' he asked, indicating the photographs.

Astrid nodded, and Harry picked up the photos and inspected them.

Whereas John sought to feel the atmosphere, body language and emotions, Harry was clinical in gathering facts.

'Do you know her friends?' asked John.

'Some,' said Astrid. 'This is probably the most recent photo.'

She handed John a picture of Freya with another girl. They were smiling, their heads close together in a crowded bar. From the après-ski clothing – alpine jumpers, body warmers and bright fleece jackets – John deduced it was taken in a winter resort.

'Chamonix?' John asked and Astrid nodded.

He handed the picture to Harry and Harry's eyes roamed the detail.

'Do you know the girl she's with?' Harry asked.

Astrid shook her head. 'No, just that she's a friend.'

'May I take a picture of this?' asked Harry.

'Of course, but you can borrow the photograph.'

Harry put the picture on the table, took out his phone and opened the camera app. He zoomed in and took a photo, and then, using his thumb and forefinger, he further expanded the image. 'I'm struggling with my eyesight. John, what can you see written on the girl's necklace?' he asked, handing John his phone.

John looked closely. 'It says "Amy". Her friend is wearing a signature name necklace with Amy written on it. Does the name mean anything to you, Lady Rowden-Mott?'

'Please, call me Astrid,' she repeated. 'No, the name means nothing to me, only that she and Freya were friends.'

John and Harry looked at Sir Hugo to see if he knew of the girl, but he shook his head and returned a blank expression.

John glanced at Sir Hugo's right hand, its thumb and forefinger plucking the hem on the left sleeve of his jacket.

Sir Hugo noticed John's attention, stopped and

looked at his watch. 'Look, time is pressing on and I have a cabinet briefing to deliver in London. Perhaps we should leave this.'

But John was now curious. 'What social media, if any, did Freya use?'

'Sergeant—'

Sir Hugo didn't get off first base before Jack jumped in. He had heard that weary tone too many times before; the antecedent to something like, 'My client doesn't need to answer that.'

Jack riled against the man. 'If there is something you're not disclosing, Sir Hugo this is the time to come out with it.'

Astrid looked up at John. 'She was never keen on social media, but I can let you have other pictures if that helps?'

'Thank you. That *would* be helpful.'

'Does this mean you'll help me?' she asked.

John turned to Jack and Jack nodded.

'We'll take this a bit further,' said John.

As if a great burden had been lifted from her, Astrid let out a breath of relief. 'Thank you, Sergeant. I'm flying to Geneva in the morning to identify Freya's body. I will of course keep you updated.'

'Thank you, Astrid,' said Jack. 'We'll need to take individual formal statements. I'll get PC Sheila Ross to join John with Astrid. Harry, we'll work with Sir Hugo. We'd better push on if you have a plane to catch,' he said, stemming further debate.

Tuesday

The Edinburgh to Geneva flight boarded on time. Once airborne, Harry settled into his 1950s novel, *The Cone Gatherers*, and John flicked through the previous day's Metro freesheet he'd picked up.

A refreshment trolley arrived and John bought them both coffee.

'What's the book about?' John asked, whilst squirting himself with a non-compliant milk stick.

Harry looked at the cover with its picture of a WW2 hand grenade. 'I first read this at school and thought it was about two lads gathering pine cones, a nasty piece of work of a gamekeeper and a woman who thought herself above the hoi polloi.'

'And now?' asked John.

'Good versus evil, if there is such a distinction,' said Harry. 'At least that's what I see in it.'

'It's strange how the simple answers we once had have become so abstract,' said John as he used the wooden stick to stir what was left of the milk into the lukewarm coffee. 'And what are your thoughts about this job?' he asked, adopting an off-track tone to obscure the topic.

They were used to that: communicating through

nuance and relying on common understanding so anyone earwigging would think they were chit-chatting about everyday trivia.

'I'm still mulling that over,' said Harry. 'It's obvious that his nibs is using us as an artifice to keep his wife happy. He was nonplussed when the boss and I started probing. All we got was a set of monosyllabic retorts. What are your thoughts?'

'I'd wager a month's pay he didn't expect us to buy into his request,' said John

'Your reasoning?' asked Harry.

'Set aside that I don't trust him an inch, look at how he behaved. A man who is used to schmoozing and cajoling his way to what he wants comes in and starts throwing his weight around … Come on Harry, he's not just an arse, he's a smart-arse.'

Harry scoffed into the coffee he was sipping, sending it splattering over the back of the seat in front.

John smiled and used his napkin to wipe off the worst of it.

'You're making a good point there,' said Harry.

'And there's something else,' said John. 'What his wife said when we agreed to take this further. She said, "Does this mean you'll help *me*?" Not us, *me*. She knows her husband doesn't give two hoots about the loss of her daughter.'

'So why is she still with him?' asked Harry.

'Because right now that suits whatever agenda she has.'

The plane banked right, revealing a snow-covered landscape of gentle hills crisscrossed with tracks.

Shortly afterwards, it banked right again over Lake Geneva and touched down.

They disembarked through an air bridge overheated by brilliant sunshine, and wheeled their rolling luggage through a labyrinth of corridors, moving walkways and escalators. The walls were adorned with wallscapes for private banking, hand-crafted watches and resplendent hotels with beautiful people swaddled in luxurious white bathrobes, living the life fantastic.

'A bit different to Newtongrange,' said John, harking back to the Midlothian once-was pit village where he'd spent his childhood.

'Or Aberdeen, for that matter,' said Harry. 'Although Union Street is looking better than it did.'

They joined a line of Brits meandering through a taped queue barrier at All Other Passports, and a gun-toting immigration officer with a deadpan face and an eagle eye thumbed through their passports and thumped down her date stamp, reminding them of the 90-day rule, courtesy of Britain's maladaptive Brexit mindset.

A little further on they passed through baggage reclaim and double doors swished open, exposing them to 6 metres of no-man's-land, delineated at the far side by a refulgent floor light strip. Behind stood a wall of faces anxiously awaiting arrivals. A few dressed in shabby suits held forth pieces of torn cardboard bearing unpronounceable names written in an amateur hand.

'Follow me,' said John, leading off into the melee

of the Geneva airport arrivals hall.

***

They reached the pop-up kiosk of their transfer bus company and a chummy Aussie youth checked their names against a laptop and asked them to wait for the Chamonix bus to be called.

'I doubt this is how the jet set do it,' said John, as they perched their bums on a small plinth at the foot of a roof support pillar.

An hour later, Dimitri, their Greek driver, led his silent flock across the carpark to a minibus. The passengers consisted mainly of singles bearing ski bags and rucksacks with helmets swinging wildly from side to side. They exuded palpable excitement for the start of their adventure, tempered by the uncertainty of not yet knowing the social codes of their travelling companions.

John was sceptical about whether the collection of outdoor equipment and a full complement-plus of passengers would fit into the bus.

Two excitable girls in their late teens or early twenties with identical bob haircuts, and wearing similar ski jackets were heaving what John assumed were snowboard bags. 'Let me help you, lass,' he said.

'We can manage, thanks,' said one of the girls who carried a slight squint. Although both were cutely pretty, the imperfection somehow added to this one's charm. The other girl made a show of lifting John and Harry's bags and adding them to the heap in the back.

Impressive, thought John at her display of confidence. But he wondered whether behind their bravado was a naivety he knew could walk them into trouble.

'You've lucked out,' said Dimitri, ushering John and Harry to the two front seats next to him.

The minibus headed off to join the after-work exodus, making its laborious way through the douane into France.

'The money is good in Switzerland but it's expensive to live here, so people commute,' explained Dimitri. 'But if that means suffering this every day … Still, we have a proverb in Greece: "The one thing I know is that I know nothing".'

John smiled. 'I can concur with that. Have you been doing this job long?' he asked.

'For a year,' replied Dimitri. 'It used the Brits driving these buses.'

'Don't tell me. Brexit: the gift that keeps giving,' said John.

Dimitri laughed. 'Something like that. But it's not Brexit that brought me here.'

'What was it that made you leave the sun-kissed shores of the Aegean?' John asked.

'The same thing that brought all of us here,' said Dimitri.

'Which is?'

Dimitri seemed surprised. 'The magic of the mountains, of course.'

They reached Border Control and Dimitri

concentrated on navigating the bus through a tortuous chicane and past an apathetic border officer.

Once across, they picked up speed and headed southeast under overhead gantries marked *A40 Autoroute Blanche and Mont Blanc Tunnel.*

Dimitri filled the bus with vivacious Greek wedding music and the passengers went for their phones, turning up the volume on their earbuds to drown it out.

The scenery turned to a mix of fields, small towns and glass-fronted production facilities in which perfectly choreographed robots were adroitly doing whatever robots do in such places.

They stopped at the train station in Saint-Gervais-les-Bains and John looked out at an old rack and pion train on display. A few passengers got off, lugging their luggage with them, and the bus continued its journey.

Ahead were heavily wooded hills with wide gaps to accommodate ski runs, but nothing to indicate what was to come!

The road started to ascend, supported by impossibly slender pillars as it snaked up into the mountains.

John was looking down 200 feet to a grim industrial complex when a collective gasp sounded. He looked up and joined the other passengers in awe at their first glimpse of the mighty Aiguilles basking in the late afternoon sun.

'That view gets me every time,' said Dimitri. 'The magic of the mountains.'

They continued through a short tunnel. At the far

end, a UK-registered black Passat estate overloaded with passengers and luggage laboured past them.

'We call those coffin carriers,' said Dimitri, gesturing to the vehicle's black roof box, and reminding John and Harry why they had come to this place.

***

The so-called 'studio apartment' consisted of white breeze block walls, two single beds minus linen, a bathroom cubicle, and a small sink beside a solitary hob described as a kitchenette. Harry took several photos, as he would a crime scene, ensuring all angles were covered. With Dimitri's parting words echoing in his ears, *I see you're on the economy package,* he paced out the dimensions: 5 x 6 metres.

John returned with clingfilm-wrapped linen packs.

'What did he say?' asked Harry, referring to another Aussie larrikin this time covering the reception desk whilst watching cricket from Edgbaston on his phone.

'He said "India are still not out," and linen wasn't requested on our booking form, "But no worries, mate".'

'Makes sense,' said Harry, with a knowing look. 'India are the better side this season.'
John let out a laugh. 'Seriously, Harry, whoever booked this for us is taking the piss. The cells in custody are bigger – and better appointed.'

'Let's see what Jack says,' replied Harry, squinting at the screen of his phone as he typed an email and attached the photos.

Like two new kids arriving at boarding school, they opened their linen packs and made their beds. 'We had to do this as cadets at Tulliallan,' said John, as he tried to remaster his hospital corner folds.

He stood back and looked at his handy work. 'Not bad, but could be better. Anyway, I'll go over to that convenience store on the other side of the square and get us some grub.'

John returned 15 minutes later, holding a bag laden with bottles of cold beer, filled baguettes, crisps and biscuits.

They buttoned their coats, moved out onto the poky balcony and settled down in the deck chairs. The square below had been cleared of snow except around the edges, where heaps had thawed and refrozen into icy mounds, exposing all manner of dirt and detritus as it receded. People dressed for the piste and carrying snowboards or skis arrived and others left hurriedly, dressed for work or a night out in Chamonix town centre.

The surrounding apartments looked equally shabby, their balconies crammed with skis, bikes and all manner of junk that the apartment couldn't house. Some of the balcony woodwork was damaged, as though it had been kicked or had a heavy item bashed against it.

John and Harry opened their first bottles of Peroni.

'Is this Italian?' asked Harry, as he inspected the label on the bottle.

'We're pretty close to the border, aren't we?' replied John.

'True.'

They looked up at the mountains, spectacular in the evening light, and agreed that as long as they kept their eyes cast outwards, even this part of Chamonix had something magical about it.

The red sky slowly disappeared, and a youth dressed in cargo shorts and a black hoodie appeared, pedalling hands-free on a mountain bike. Speaking a mixture of English and broken French, he called like a hawker up to a select few apartments. John and Harry sunk a little further back into their seats and kept their gaze turned to the mountains while banter was exchanged, money dropped, and small packages were chucked up.

Despite the youth's attempt at rapport, John and Harry assumed he worked in a grubby world where an asymmetric relationship kept the cards firmly in the drug dealer's hands. He would be delivering to order. Cannabis: the gateway drug with the stench of shit when smoked. And ecstasy: the 'love drug,' up until the user's first paranoia episode. After that, there was no turning back. It was a problem they'd seen time and time again with drugs. Whatever the user did they couldn't undo.

The youth departed to his next rendezvous. John gulped from his bottle and Harry thought about the organised syndicates that drove the drugs trade. 'I doubt they'd trust him with the exotic stuff.'

John agreed. 'No, he's low level, at least for now. Back in the day, when I was in uniform, I'd have been itching to go after that tosser and the ones he supplies, but now …'

'But now, what?' asked Harry.

'But now I feel sorry for them. I remember a nurse talking to us on one of the drug prevention inputs. She presented the scenario of someone lacking confidence and with rock-bottom self-esteem. Someone who felt socially awkward up until their fix took hold and then, for a while, they were that guy or girl they had always wanted to be. Confident, outgoing and at one with themselves. She described it as a form of self-medication. It doesn't make it right, but it makes you think.'

The evening wore on and noisy groups returned from town. A few sat on the benches in the square, sharing a bottle of what John and Harry assumed to be the local equivalent of fortified wine. Some went back to apartments and continued to party, rousing shouts of protest from their neighbours.

John and Harry chatted about this and that: parted colleagues, unsolved cases and where on earth their years had gone.

'Do you regret joining?' asked John.

Harry wiped his glasses with the hem of his jersey, replaced them, and looked into the night sky and the silhouette of the mountains. 'I would like to have spent more time with Daphne and Pammy,' he said, referring to his wife and daughter. 'But Daphne has a good circle of friends and Pammy's engrossed in her PhD. As far as my police career goes, when I see what some of my Cambridge contemporaries have achieved, I wonder whether I should have chosen something different and made a bigger contribution to society. And then there's the personal impact. What type of people would we be if we hadn't been exposed to the ills of society?'

John nodded in agreement. 'Relationships seem to have passed me by. Most people in our line of work either met and married early when they were beat cops with predictable work patterns, or teamed up with another cop. That never seemed to happen for me, and when Mum was struck down with Alzheimer's, I didn't want her put in a care home, not after everything she had done for her family. As for my career, I don't think I gave it much thought. When you're seventeen and the only experience of life you've had is poverty, it's difficult to see alternatives. Perhaps if I'd gone to university, it would have opened my eyes to opportunities.' He looked at Harry. 'I know Jack is hoping this little jaunt will change my mind about leaving, but after that last case …'

Harry didn't need to see John's face to know that even touching the subject was unbearably painful. 'Listen John. I've run through it time and time again. We shut down what was probably the worst crime syndicate we'll see in our careers. We directly saved three lives at the bothy and we rescued numerous victims of trafficking and prevented it from happening to many others. I know we didn't save them all, but that's the nature of the work.'

'It doesn't make it easier to live with,' said John.

'Seeing those women like that …'

'No, it doesn't,' said Harry. 'Have you thought about what else you might do?'

John shrugged. 'I guess the same as most escapees. Find a humdrum job that requires trustworthiness, reliability and not much else.'

Harry shook his head. 'I'm not buying that, John. Not from you. Two weeks of mindlessness and you'd be climbing the walls.'

John returned to the mountains where a full moon had appeared behind a needle-like peak. 'We'll see,' he said.

Wednesday

They breakfasted at a pâtisserie on the already busy
Rue du Docteur Paccard: orange juice, coffee and
croissants with butter and jam.

The couple seated next to them were New
Zealanders taking a year's sabbatical from their
teaching jobs to tour Europe in a camper van.
Chamonix was high on their bucket list and from all
accounts living up to their expectations.

Harry looked at his watch, and keen to be on time
for Commandant de Petit, he and John wished the
Kiwis well and left.

'Mooching about in a camper van sounds
appealing,' said John as they made their way.

The gendarmerie was a three-storey building with
a box profile steel roof and wet dash finish. Whilst a
public building in Scotland would be an ugly-as-sin
concrete monstrosity, the gendarmerie looked as
though the architects had at least partial sympathy
with the neighbours. With a change of signage and
the removal of the coat of arms, it would have passed
for a three-star hotel.

They entered the building and approached the
public enquiries desk manned by an officer with

black hair and a chevron moustache. From the epaulettes on his navy V-neck jumper, they could see he was the French equivalent of a sergeant.

He gave a knowing smile to say he was expecting them, and Harry made their formal introduction.

'I'm Detective Inspector Harry Freeman and my colleague is Detective Sergeant John Anderson. We're from Police Scotland and have a nine o'clock meeting with Commandant Jean-Raymond de Petit.'

'I'm Guillaume. Welcome to Chamonix. I'll let the commandant know you are here,' he said in reasonable English. 'If you could please complete the *livre d'or*,' he said, pushing the visitor's book towards them.

John and Harry heard Guillaume pass their details to someone on the other end of the phone and he gave them each a clip-on ID badge.

'Commandant de Petit knows you are here. Please, take a seat,' he said, indicating the plastic chairs opposite.

They took a seat, and under the gaze of a corner-mounted CCTV camera, they waited, filling time browsing the French equivalent of police information posters. Lock up your possessions, don't drink and drive, keep off the drugs and away from people trafficking. Edicts that everyone except the originators of such posters would think obvious.

As time passed, the sergeant looked increasingly uncomfortable.

John asked Harry, 'Do you think the commandant has forgotten about us?'

Harry shook his head. 'He won't have forgotten,

but he might be caught up in something. You know what it's like.'

John was ambivalent. 'Either that or he's bloody rude.'

The sergeant made another call. 'Soon,' he said, in an awkward attempt at offering hope.

Half an hour later, a door to one side of the desk opened and a woman in her fifties and dressed in civilian clothes led them to a set of stairs and up to the first floor.

She knocked lightly on a door and after a pause, a strongly accented French voice shouted, '*Entrez.*'

Commandant de Petit's office was at the front of the building. He was sitting at a large desk with his back to a single window that looked out onto the mountains. Their escort left, closing the door behind her, and John and Harry stood waiting as the wiry little man with a tight face, thinning fair hair and silver-rimmed spectacles made a point of keeping his eyes focused on the document in his hands.

John thought how large Petit's starched white shirt seemed on his slight frame; a perception made worse by oversized multi-stripped epaulettes. It was the type of attire worn by someone afflicted by the insecurities of small man syndrome to raise their stature.

When finally ready, Petit looked up and beckoned them to the two chairs facing him. Harry thought about reaching forward to shake hands but then thought better of it and instead stuck to words.

'I'm Detective Harry Freeman and this is my colleague, Detective Sergeant John Anderson.'

'Commandant Jean-Raymond de Petit,' came the reply.

The door opened and their escort returned carrying a small tasse de café. She put it down beside Petit and left.

He took a sip, made appropriate facial gestures to show satisfaction, and reluctantly returned to his visitors.

Tipping his head, he looked over the top of his glasses. 'Inspector, Sergeant, I understand you wish to confirm the facts regarding the death of the young woman on the glacier.'

Unsure of her name, he conferred with a file on his desk. 'Freya Rowden-Mott. A Swedish national. Is that correct?' he asked, maintaining his tipped head and leaning forward as he noted one officer and then the other.

Harry nodded. 'That's what we've been tasked with, Commandant de Petit,' he confirmed, attempting deference for leverage.

Petit returned a questioning look and then sat back in his chair. 'I'm curious as to why you are *really* here. Is it normal for Police Scotland to send two ranking officers on an errand such as this? Do you do this for every foreign national involved in an overseas accident? The deceased is Swedish, is she not? So why are the British getting involved?'

'Her stepfather is British,' said John.

But he and Harry knew it wasn't much of an answer and Petit was digging a nice tidy hole for them.

Petit looked dismissively at John and then spoke

to Harry. 'And is it normal practice in Scotland for a junior ranking officer to speak on behalf of his superior, Inspector?'

'Sergeant Anderson is a respected and valued colleague, and is quite capable of answering questions without my permission,' replied Harry.

Petit circled back to his previous topic. 'I'm afraid I don't find your answer as to why you're here credible,' he said, shaking his head, leaning forward and returning to his briefing paper.

Harry gave a conciliatory smile. 'I can assure you there is no hidden agenda. Sir Hugo, Freya's stepfather, is only looking to put his wife at ease. Nothing more. We're between cases, so sending us was the least disruptive solution for our department. But if you are adamant we shouldn't be here—'

Petit interrupted. 'And what department is that?' he asked. 'Your superior officer has only a name, rank and contact details on his email.'

John wanted to shoot Harry a cautionary glance. Not only did the Major Investigations sound like overkill, but John also sensed that it would antagonise the already fractious little man on the other side of the table.

Harry was on to it. 'We're linked to Leith Police Station.'

John chipped in, 'It's just outside the centre of Edinburgh. If you visit Scotland, we'd be delighted to show you around.'

Petit murmured something and returned to their briefing. 'There is something you need to understand. We are in the mountains where sadly this type of accident is common. It has already been dealt with, and my people are extremely busy.'

'We fully understand,' said Harry, with both he and John nodding for emphasis.

Petit picked up his desk phone and said something in a hushed voice to the person on the other end.

He returned to John and Harry. 'To close this quickly I'm going to assign two officers of similar rank to you.'

Someone tapped on the door, and before Petit could answer, it opened.

A man and a woman in their late thirties entered. The man was smartly dressed in polished brown shoes, brown woollen trousers and a well-cut suede jacket. His full head of reddish-light-brown hair was neatly styled and his face carried a welcoming smile.

John was caught off guard by the woman's classically beautiful features: the slightly angular jawline, high cheekbones, graceful nose and captivating eyes. Her hair was dark brown – almost black – and set in a classic long bob, and her figure was what John's mother would have described as 'a full woman'. Wearing flat-soled black shoes, loose black trousers profiled at her hips and a button-down chemisier blanc, she looked as though she had stepped out from one of the aspirational wallscapes in Geneva airport.

John and Harry stood up to greet the newcomers, but Petit remained seated.

The male officer stepped forward and shook their hands as he introduced himself. 'Lieutenant de police Pierre Lavigne. Please, call me Pierre,' he said with a smile that put them at ease. 'I spent a year in Southampton as an exchange student. Our classes were entirely in English. Having you here will allow me to brush up again.'

'Your English sounds excellent,' said Harry. 'Sadly, the same cannot be said of our French. I can understand it but I'm lost when it comes to finding the correct words.'

Pierre agreed. 'The French word conjugation is challenging for non-native speakers.'

John sensed Petit's irritation at the display of friendliness, but the commandant kept his words to himself.

The female officer remained where she was as she introduced herself. 'Sous-brigadier de police Mathilde La Croix.'

'Please to meet you, Mathilde,' said John, assuming that Pierre's amiability was universal.

Her face stiffened. 'You may call me Sous-brigadier, or if you must Madame La Croix, but in France we reserve Christian names for friends.'

Madame La Croix's rebuke caught John by surprise, and with that surprise, he regretted the fleeting thoughts that had passed through his mind.

'As you wish, Madame La Croix.'

'Sous-brigadier ...' said Pierre, rebuffing her with his tone and look. She flinched, making it clear that Pierre was her senior officer.

Pierre returned to John and Harry. 'At least one of us will accompany you during your visit. Anything you need from us, please ask. But as you have no jurisdiction here, so you must work through us at all

times. I'm sure it would be the same for foreign
officers visiting Scotland.'

'Indeed it would,' said Harry. 'We certainly don't
want to put you or ourselves in a difficult situation.
The sooner we gather the facts needed to put Freya's
mother and stepfather's minds at rest, the sooner
we'll be out of your way.'

Pierre smiled. 'Have you met her parents?' he
asked.

Harry gestured for John to answer. 'They were in
Scotland when news of Freya arrived, so they came
to see us. It's a lot for her mother to process.'

'And her stepfather?' asked Pierre.

'I'm not sure how close Sir Hugo was to his
stepdaughter, but I'm sure he'll want to support his
wife,' said John.

Petit cleared his throat, reminding them of his
presence. 'Now, you must excuse me. I have things
to do. Pierre, please keep me updated.'

'Absolument, Chef,' Pierre said with a theatrical
bow.

John wondered whether Pierre was subtly
mocking his superior; a hunch reinforced by
Mathilde's look.

***

John and Harry followed Pierre and Mathilde
through to their office. The office looked like an
office anywhere: panel lights, MDF furniture, swivel
chairs, PCs, a stationary cabinet and not much else.

The six or so desks were unattended, their monitors scrolling screen savers, except for one where the front desk sergeant, Guillaume, was hurriedly trying to complete something.

John and Harry stood with Pierre next to his desk and Mathilde stood a little back.

Pierre took out his phone. 'We'll be together, but I think it prudent for us to share mobile numbers,' Pierre said, and the officers agreed.

Pierre and Mathilde took out iPhones, John and Harry took out their Police Scotland Samsungs and each officer called out their number for the others to enter.

Pierre had a suggestion. 'I've put together a timeline of events. It would help you understand what went on and when. Would you like me to SMS a link to you?'

'That would be useful, thanks,' replied Harry.

Pierre sent through what he had and then opened his desk drawer and removed a standard-issue SP 2022 pistol. He snapped home the pre-installed magazine and slipped the weapon into the shoulder holster under his jacket.

'Do you carry firearms in Scotland?' he asked.

Harry shook his head. 'No, we have a unit dedicated to that. John was once part of it.'

Pierre turned to John. 'Were you any good?'

'Not really,' replied John. 'My father was a miner and a staunch socialist. He believed guns were promoted by the ruling classes so that young men could be sent off to war to kill each other – or something like that. As a child, it didn't make much sense, but perhaps now …'

Pierre looked understanding. 'Your father's advice was good. As you would say, "I couldn't hit a barn door," but Mathilde has won a few competitions, haven't you, Mathilde?'

Mathilde looked dismissively at him. 'Leave it, Pierre,' she said, going to her desk, picking up the large sunglasses that were lying there and resting them on top of her head. She took the cropped duck down jacket she'd left hooked on the back of her seat and put it on. 'Shall we go?'

Pierre led them out of the station and down the hill. Mathilde hung back, making is clear to John and Harry that Pierre had touched something sensitive.

'I've booked us a table at a brasserie that I'm told was once popular with British climbers,' Pierre said. 'Now they take an early EasyJet flight into Geneva, climb a route they've rehearsed on YouTube and fly out the same evening.'

'Surely there are still old-school climbers?' asked Harry.

Pierre gave a friendly laugh. 'I'm sure there are. I was being sarcastic.'

They arrived at the centre of town and walked across to a corner brasserie with an outside restaurant separated from the street by decorative wooden barriers. Ginormous parasols covered numerous tables and chairs, all neatly set for lunch. The waiter recognised Pierre, and without fuss, led them to a table close to a patio heater and away from the tourists. They took their seats. Pierre and Mathilde sat with their backs to the pavement, and

John and Harry faced them.

The waiter efficiently took their drinks order and John and Harry soaked up the vibe as an eclectic mix of ages and nationalities, grazing on pastries, slices of pizza and quiche wandered by in both directions. The omnipresent mountains had a pull, drawing people's attention as glimpses appeared between buildings.

John thought how much healthier people looked compared to a typical Scottish high street. The Alps seemed to encourage an outdoor life, and accompanying that, a heightened state of well-being.

Mathilde put her iPhone away and turned her attention to the detectives. 'Are you short of useful work at the moment?' she asked in a tone that could have been construed as derisive.

'I've been off for three months and Harry's been supporting other cases,' said John.

'A sabbatical?' enquired Mathilde.

John shook his head. 'No. The psychologist said I was suffering from burnout.'

Harry tried to shift the subject. 'Where did you study, Mathilde?'

'I attended la Sorbonne and was then selected for the police academy,' she replied with her attention still on John and what he had revealed.

Taken by a thought, she looked at John and Harry in turn. 'And you two? Where did you study?'

'I studied applied psychology before joining the police,' said Harry.

'Where?' she asked, making it clear that the place of study was more important than the subject.

'If you mean what university, it was Cambridge,' he replied.

It wasn't the answer she expected, or from her reaction, wanted, so she turned her line of questioning to John. 'And you, Sergeant?'

He gave a wry smile. 'The university of life,' he said.

She looked unsure, so he elaborated. 'I joined the force as a cadet when I was seventeen. They've done away with the scheme now, but 25 years ago that's what I did.'

Mathilde turned to Pierre and said something in French.

Pierre shot Harry a glance to see what he had picked up and Mathilde pulled her sunglasses down over her eyes, crossed her arms and looked out across the street.

John could tell that something was amiss, so he asked Harry, 'What did she just say?'

Harry kept his eyes on Mathilde, but she wouldn't be drawn as she stared through the passing crowds.

'She just took a pop at us. I won't repeat what she said, but rest assured it wasn't particularly pleasant.'

Disbelieving, John looked back and forth between Harry and Mathilde. But from the penetrating stare Harry was giving her, he knew it wasn't a joke. It was the look Harry used when interviewing suspects to put them on the spot.

Pierre tried to intervene. 'Mathilde didn't mean it the way it came across.'

'Didn't I?' she said, looking at her colleague. 'They care even less about this case than we do.

Why are we wasting our time on it?'

John gave Mathilde an incredulous look and shook his head. It was hard to know what was going on behind her sunglasses, but he had heard enough. He stood up and turned to Harry. 'I'm off for a walk. Phone me when you're done here.'

Mathilde turned her attention to Harry. 'Was that necessary?' she asked.

'I think it's what you wanted me to do,' replied Harry.

'Don't be ridiculous,' she said, folding her arms.

But Harry could see through her façade: she was seeking attention in the only way she knew how.

Pierre tried again. 'We're under a lot of pressure at the moment. Commandant de Petit is here temporarily and is trying to make his mark. Having a case put in doubt and the involvement of the English doesn't look good for him.'

Harry corrected him. 'Scottish. And yes, there's a difference.'

'Indeed,' said Pierre, lifting a hand of apology.

But Harry wasn't seeking an apology. 'If your Commandant wants us out, he can give us what we need and we'll be done.'

'He can't,' said Pierre.

'Why?'

'Pride. Or I should say, false pride. He's what we call a *de, de, de.*'

'You'll need to explain that to me,' said Harry.

Pierre cleared his throat. 'It's how we describe people who use their name to assert an inflated sense of superiority or *amour propre*. The prefix 'de' means 'of' and is a prefix used by the aristocracy. In his case, it's quite apt. De Petit means *of the small*. He's from Provance, where he has an ancestral family home. A château, as he keeps reminding us. But it's not the Palace of Versailles. I hear that it's quite shabby. I take no pride in telling you that my commanding officer is a jumped up little bureaucrat. The French government is full of pen pushers who do little more than add complication to our lives and increase the tax burden. He'll have used his connections to get a posting here, but will likely be gone soon.'

Harry saw Mathilde shoot Pierre a glance as though questioning the wisdom of his openness, but Pierre didn't seem bothered as he sat confidently back in his chair and touched his fingertips together.

'Not exactly Liberté, Égalité, Fraternité,' said Harry.

Pierre smiled. 'All animals are equal, but some are more equal than others. Is that not what George Orwell wrote?' he asked. 'And is it not why you are here?'

Pierre was alluding to something that sat uncomfortably with Harry and John. Jack had his ulterior motives for sending them to Chamonix, but they couldn't deny that Rowden-Mott carried influence. He was able to get an audience with the superintendent and have his case heard. Would an everyday citizen have been able to pull that off? True, having listened to the pompous prick, but for Astrid's intervention, Jack would have sent him packing. But the bottom line was Rowden-Mott wanted them to pacify his wife, and they were here doing his bidding.

Harry leant forward and looked at Pierre and Mathilde in turn. 'I'm going to level with you,' he said. 'And then we'll decide where to take this. It's true, neither John nor I are in great shape.'

The waiter returned, put the drinks down, and took out his order pad. Pierre said something to him and the waiter left to attend to another table.

Mathilde and Pierre's attention returned to Harry.

'For eighteen months, we were working on a case concerning an East European network involved in drugs, people trafficking, prostitution, extortion and all manner of other horrors. We and our Europol partners struggled to make headway. It seemed that Vlatko, the head of the crime group, was always a step ahead of us. We found out that he'd tried to intimidate members of our team. We took them off the case, but we're pretty certain there were others too frightened to speak up. Eventually, our hand was forced. Vlatko went after the daughter of a woman in witness protection and he was shot dead. That's when the real horror show began. We moved quickly: making arrests and closing down his operations. As we did so, we unearthed something we knew nothing about. People started to talk about a place of no hope and no return. A place in which people – women mainly – just disappeared. There were no names for those who'd gone, but those under Vlatko's tyranny knew about it because its existence had been used to intimidate them. Finally, we got a break and John moved in on a derelict flat in a part of Edinburgh called Leith.'

Harry paused, looked into the distance and then returned to Pierre and Mathilde. 'It was a building due for demolition. The first floor was occupied by Vlatko's henchmen and the top floor was used to imprison trafficked women. When John entered that squalid hell hole, he found three women handcuffed to their bed frames. They had all been abused and, in their panic, Vlatko's people had injected them with heroin. Killing witnesses wasn't new to his organisation, and these women were nothing more than a commodity from which to make money through prostitution. But it was the sheer inhumanity of what they had done. The place was a death factory. Two of the women were dead – choked on their vomit. The third was barely alive. When I arrived, John was standing at a window holding the dying woman in his arms. At the time he couldn't speak, but when he eventually found his voice, he said the woman had asked if she could finally see Edinburgh. She had been trafficked in the belief of a new life. She died that night in hospital, but not before she incriminated those involved. Once she had said her piece, it seemed her will to live was finally extinguished. John blames himself. He carries a feeling of despair that comes from knowing he was too late to save them. He feels he let those three women down, but he also feels compromised.'

'Why?' asked Pierre.

'Because he wants to resign, but having seen what those women went through, he also feels that leaving is a cop out. He feels it's taking the easy path.'

Harry took off his glasses and wiped them.

When he placed them back on his face, he could see that Pierre was stirred by what he had heard.

'I feel for John, and that sense of helplessness must be terrible,' said Pierre.

'Yes, it's a difficult thing to carry,' replied Harry. He then looked straight at Mathilde. 'Madame La Croix, say what you will about us. We'll be gone soon enough, but don't accuse John, my friend and colleague, of not caring. He's a bloody good police officer – one of the best I've met – despite having never attended some jumped-up university.'

Mathilde rose abruptly to her feet. 'I'm going back to the station,' she said, leaving her drink untouched.

As she strutted off towards Place de l'Église, Harry took out his phone. 'I'll give John a call. He won't be far.'

'Do that,' said Pierre. 'I'll order lunch. They do an excellent *plat du jour* for the locals. This afternoon, we'll visit the rescue base and put your minds to rest.'

***

John returned to the table and Pierre apologised for Mathilde's outburst.

'It's not acceptable. I'll speak to her,' he said, but John asked him to let it go.

'Are you sure?'

'I am,' replied John. 'We all have bad days and I

probably overreacted.'

Mathilde wasn't mentioned again as they ate lunch and John and Harry's spirits were lifted when Jack called to say he had read the riot act to Business Support and they'd blown the next few years' accommodation budget on something more fitting.

Pierre knew the hotel and reassured them they wouldn't be disappointed. He said that he had transferred from Lyon to Chamonix the previous summer. His work in Lyon had been with what he called an audit team, but he didn't elaborate.

They finished lunch. Pierre collected an unmarked Peugeot from the car pool and drove them out of Chamonix to the rescue base.

Pierre explained, 'The service was formed in the late 50s following a tragic accident on the Mont Blanc. They are world-class at what they do and extremely busy, but Florent who was involved in recovering Freya should be back soon,' he said.

The base was a straightforward affair, consisting of two purpose-built helicopter hangars with what appeared to be administrative blocks on either side, all clad in wood. In front was the large 'H' marked circle of the helipad and an apron with enough space for two or three other helicopters. The complex was surrounded by security fencing and to the right was a large bank on which members of the public sat with cameras at the ready.

Pierre parked outside, and they entered on foot through the large gates and made their way to stand by the hangar. Someone came over. Pierre spoke to them, showed his warrant card, and they left.

'The helicopter is on its way back from the Hôpitaux du Pays du Mont Blanc in Sallanches, so won't be long,' said Pierre.

Shortly afterwards, they heard the fast *frappity-frop* sound of rotors and a blue helicopter with white flashes appeared over the trees. It flared its nose, came to a hover above the helipad and touched down lightly in the centre of a marked circle. The two turbines powered down, and the helicopter settled. The side door slid open and a fit man uniformed in various blues and wearing an orange helmet got out, retrieved a rucksack and ducked to avoid the winding down rotors. He was making towards the offices when Pierre called out, 'Florent.'

As if suddenly remembering they were there, Florent lifted a hand in recognition and came over. He was tall, with the athletic physique of a runner, dark, neatly cut hair and a welcoming smile. His friendly demeanour would have lent itself to the hospitality industry had he not decided upon a career rescuing people from perilous situations.

Pierre introduced John and Harry, and as he did so, Florent shook their hands.

'I visited Scotland with my girlfriend two years ago. We were climbing on Ben Nevis. It wasn't high, but very technical,' said Florent.

'I hope we looked after you,' said John.

Pierre smiled. 'Very much so. The Scottish people gave us what you call a warm welcome.'

John and Harry immediately took to Florent, with his professional but open and friendly manner and readiness to help even though he was busy.

'Pierre says you have some questions about the casualty we recovered from the Mer de Glace. I'll assist in any way I can, but it's all in the report,' said Florent.

'What report?' asked Harry, as he and John looked questioningly at Pierre.

Pierre shrugged. 'It's with Commandant de Petit. You'll need to get clearance from him.'

John returned to Florent. 'What did you see when you arrived at the crevasse?'

Florent looked over to the mountains as he visualised the scene. 'It was getting late. We arrived overhead and saw one of the climbers waving. The pilot put the helicopter down on an area of the glacier that he deemed to be safe, and then I, another team member and a doctor went to speak to the climber. He said his name was Knox and he and his partner, Cal, were Scottish. Cal had spotted a ski in the crevasse and when he investigated, he found someone trapped where it narrowed, out of sight from the surface. Cal was still in the crevasse. We set up a rope and the winch, and I was lowered in. Cal said that the person stuck lower down wasn't responding to his calls. With the winch to pull me back out, I was able to get down beside the casualty: a young woman. She had no pulse, no response and was frozen. Cal was able to climb back out. I had another rope lowered, which I tied around the casualty, and I climbed out. We then winched the casualty up. It was a difficult and distressing scene, but Cal and Knox carried themselves well. They had done everything they could for the young woman.'

Florent then looked at Pierre. 'I think your officers should have taken that into account.'

Pierre looked uncomfortable, so John asked, 'What happened when you returned?'

Florent explained, 'It was almost dark, so we brought the Scottish climbers down in the helicopter. When we arrived, two gendarmes were waiting. They interviewed the climbers,' said Pierre.

'Is that not standard practice?' asked John.

'It was the way they went about it,' said Florent.

The engines on the helicopter were coming back to life. Someone came out of the office and shouted over to Florent, and he waved back.

'I need to go, but if you want to see where we found the young woman, I'm sure we can arrange that,' he said.

Within seconds, Florent was ducking under the whirling rotors and opening the door. He was still boarding as the helicopter started to lift. The door closed, the nose dipped and off they went in a frenzy of noise and speed to help someone else in distress.

'We should speak to the Scottish lads,' said John.

Pierre shook his head. 'There's no need. I can get the transcript of their interview.'

Harry let out a false laugh. 'Can you honestly see your man Petit letting us read those transcripts this side of Christmas?'

'Then I need to come with you,' said Pierre.

***

John came off his phone and turned to Harry. 'If it hadn't been for my Scottish accent, they wouldn't have agreed to see us,' he said, referring to Cal and Knox whom he had just spoken to.

'I don't blame them,' said Harry. 'Florent was scathing of how the gendarmes had treated the lads.'

As agreed, they met Pierre at a confusing junction at the end of Avenue Ravenal le Rouge. The sheepskin bomber jacket Pierre was wearing put John's parka with faux fur hood and Harry's tweed coat to shame. It wasn't lost on John that whatever the French wore, they looked chic. In Pierre's case, he also seemed to have the budget.

'How's the new hotel?' Pierre asked.

John put on an incredulous look. 'Let's just say we're expecting a call any moment informing us of a terrible mistake and telling us to pack our bags, because in all our years policing we've never had anything as luxurious.'

'That's good,' said Pierre. 'Let's get this case closed off, and we'll find you some easy admin to give you time to enjoy it.'

Pierre led them to a bar situated on a road out of Chamonix. From the outside, it looked like any other brasserie you would see when passing through rural France: slightly rundown, with a full-width front window – in this case, opaque with condensation – and an ornate door on one side. Above were several floors with concrete balconies and balustrades of rusting ornate ironwork. They looked as if they might once have been bedrooms, but if they still were, they'd be in the below-budget segment.

Pierre entered first followed by John then Harry. The bar was rammed with people: regulars – although from the eclectic mix of languages, not locals – and knots of "visitors" with sunburned faces and still in ski gear, chatting veraciously about today's adventures.

A barman who was filling demi glasses with Kronenbourg 1664 as quickly as the faucet would allow caught their eye and nodded to a table at the far side.

John glanced around to see just how out of place they looked, but apart from the barman who had likely been given a heads up before they arrived, they were going pretty much unnoticed amongst a clientele who had little more than a shared passion for skiing in common. He spotted the two sparky girls they'd met on the minibus. They were standing at the end of the bar, beers in hand, and wearing beanie hats with pompoms, baggy snowboard trousers and tight-fitting Nike sports tops.

Pierre worked his way through the throng and arrived at the table occupied by two young men he assumed to be Knox and Cal. One was looking at the two girls, holding his stare long enough for them to note his interest. The other was slumped down in his seat, looking at something on his phone.

Whatever they had been up to that day, they were now dressed in loose jeans and T-shirts. John noticed how toned their arms were; muscled as he remembered the pit workers to be when he was a child. A fitness born of necessity.

The slumped young man with long hair looked up as they approached and took them in one by one: sussing them out, the details of their clothes, and in Pierre's case, his eyes stopping on where his firearm would be in its shoulder holster. John thought how at home the young man looked; as if whatever was happening in the bar sat with a domain he controlled. With his hair tied back by a band, and his brown eyes, there seemed something almost messianic about him.

The other lad had blonde straggly hair and a friendly boyish face.

The long-haired young man remained slumped back in his seat with his eyes fixed on John. 'Give us one good reason why we should talk to you?' he asked, leaving them standing.

'I'm John, this is Harry. We're from Police Scotland. Our colleague, Pierre, is with the Gendarmerie. You must be Knox and Cal,' he said, getting the names right the first time.

Knox kept his stare without answering.

'Do you mind if we sit down?' John asked, looking around for any free chairs. 'We are over here gathering facts for Freya's mother. Not to cause you any trouble.'

Knox laughed and looked at Cal. 'That's rich coming from them, isn't it, Cal?'

John knew it was the closest he would get to an introduction, but at least it confirmed which lad was which.

Cal gave a sarcastic grin and nodded. 'Yeh,

fucking rich.'

'What happened?' asked John.

Pierre spoke up. 'Perhaps we should leave this for another time?'

John sensed the Frenchman was reticent and wanted out of the situation, but he wasn't sure why, so he kept his attention on Knox. 'Tell us what happened.'

Knox let out a relenting sigh and Cal spoke. 'Those blonde tops over there are just about to head off. They'll give you their seats if you ask,' he said, indicating a Scand-esque group of males.

Harry worked his way to the group and returned clutching three bistro chairs. He placed them opposite Knox and Cal.

Cal made a point of ignoring the Frenchman as he looked between the Scottish officers. 'How are Freya's parents doing?' he asked.

John lifted his hands in a gesture of helplessness. 'It's tough for them. Especially her mother.'

'Figures,' said Cal, nodding his head.

'What does?' asked Harry.

Cal looked at him. 'From what Amy said, Freya was a decent girl, but her stepfather is bad news.'

'You know Amy?' asked Harry.

Knox looked hard at him. 'Sounds like you're telling us you don't.'

'No, I'm afraid we don't. We just know Freya sent her mum a picture. In it she was with a girl we think is called Amy. Can we show you?' asked Harry.

Knox nodded his agreement and Harry took out

his phone and showed him the picture of the two girls in a pub.

'That's a pub near the centre of town,' said Knox. He then tilted his head as though figuring out what was going on. 'He's holding back on you, isn't he?' he said, keeping his eyes on the Scottish officers as he gestured towards Pierre.

Knox then vented what was on his mind. 'We spent four Baltic hours on the glacier. We saw a ski in a crevasse, and Cal went down to check it out. Do you know how effing dangerous that is?'

John and Harry looked blank, and Knox continued. 'We could have made a call and reported a found ski and left it at that. But we didn't. You know why we didn't?' he asked, looking intently at John.

'Tell me why,' said John.

'We didn't do that because we felt it wasn't the right thing to do. We were concerned that someone was in trouble, so we did what we did and the helicopter arrived, and they did what they did. But it was all too late. I don't know when Freya died, but judging by her frozen body, I'd say it was way before we arrived. It was nearly dark by the time we were done on the glacier, so we hitched a ride home in the helicopter. And guess what was waiting for us?'

'I think I know,' said Harry. He looked at Pierre. 'It's what Florent was berating you about at the heliport, isn't it?'

Pierre shrugged. 'I'm going to look into it,' he said.

'Tell us the rest,' said John, knowing Knox and Cal had to get this out.

'Two cops. They wanted to go through our stuff, but when I challenged them as to what their grounds were, they backed off. They probably thought we were doing drugs or something. I mean for fuck's sake, we don't do that shit, and even if we did, what the fuck did it have to do with us reporting a casualty? They checked our passports to see if we'd been here more than 90 days. I could tell that whatever game they were playing unravelled when they saw mine.'

'Why was that?' asked Harry.

'Because my mum's French and I have dual nationality. She met my dad in Edinburgh.'

'We're based in Edinburgh,' said John. 'Leith Police Station.'

Cal seemed curious. 'We're both from Penicuik.'

For the first time, Knox looked directly at Pierre. 'I know what those flics were trying to do.'

'What?' asked John, now harbouring his suspicions.

'They were trying to intimidate us.'

Pierre shook his head. 'No, that wouldn't be the case.'

Knox looked disbelieving. 'Really? This is a cool place to live. France is great, but there was something I never understood until the helipad. My mum always said that the French had an uneasy relationship with the police. I didn't get what she meant, but now …'

Pierre cleared his throat. 'I'm sure there was a

misunderstanding, that's all. They needed a statement from you. Tomorrow I'll find out what happened and speak to the officers concerned.'

Cal let out a laugh. 'Aye, right.' he said. 'And tomorrow will be midsummer's day and we'll be skiing waist-deep powder.'

'I get where you're coming from,' said John. 'If it's any consolation to you, I'm sure Freya's mother will take comfort from knowing what you did for her daughter.'

Having had his say, Knox calmed down. 'Tell her that her daughter wasn't alone down there. Cal spent two hours talking to her.'

'But you said she had already passed away by then?' said, Harry.

'At that point, we didn't know for sure,' said Cal. 'She was about four metres below me, jammed tight. With my head torch, I could see beyond her to where the crevasse opened out again. I couldn't see to the bottom, though. It was too far. I don't like to say this, but if it hadn't been for the ski landing on the ledge, I wouldn't have gone down and found her, and if she had fallen a little to one side, she would have disappeared into the void. I didn't know if she was still alive at that time so I spoke to her so she wouldn't feel alone.'

There was silence at the table, and John could see the experience had affected Cal. He had wanted to save the girl but couldn't. His mind went back to when he was too late and had nothing but words to offer the woman who died shortly afterwards.

'Did you know Freya?' John asked.

Knox and Cal shook their heads. 'Not really,' said Cal. 'She was a blonde top, and a wealthy one, from what I've gathered. Blonde tops are what we call the Scandinavians. They're cool, but we're not part of their crew.'

'What are they like, the blonde tops?' asked John.

Cal shrugged, gave a non-committal shake of the head and looked at Knox who did the same.

'Regular dudes, I guess. But their good looks give them the edge – especially the girls. The ones with money can afford to party harder than the great unwashed. They get invites that we don't – chalet parties, that type of thing – but that's not our scene anyway.'

Knox looked over to where the two girls from the bus were now being entertained by two over-smiling boys dressed in hoodies and cargo pants. 'Oh, for fuck's sake,' he said, closing his eyes and running his hands back over his hair. 'We're about to witness a train crash.'

John, who for some reason felt a degree of responsibility for the girls, looked to see what it was. 'Are those two guys bad news?' he asked.

Cal nodded and Knox filled him in. 'They're a couple of sleekit, dope-crazed shaggers intent on increasing their body count of women. They make a living doing dodgy DIY for second-homers. Left to get on with it, they'll get those girls wired so high on something they'll have no idea what's happening to them. Then they'll fuck their brains out and dump them. I guess it's what some want, but those girls don't look savvy enough to see what's coming. The trauma of having your life trashed by two wank-pieces would take some getting over.'

At the mention of trauma, Harry looked self-consciously at John, but John's attention was on Knox.

'That sounds extreme,' said John.

'Yeah?' said Knox, his face overwritten with urgency. 'You're the detectives. How would you dress it up? Regretful sex?'

'Come on, that's not fair,' said John.

'Really?' asked Knox, now heading for a confrontation.

Cal stepped in to calm things down. 'Knox, man, let's cool it. Connor wasn't down to them.'

Pierre was curious. 'Who's Connor?' he asked.

Cal took up the aggressive stance that Knox had initiated. 'That's none of your fucking business.'

John knew from experience that 'Connor' was a trigger for the lads. Had they been cautioned suspects, he would have worked it to his favour, but they weren't and the mention of Connor was distressing them.

'He's right, it's not our business, Pierre,' said John.

The boys with the two girls were now hyper: their pupils dilated like a couple of roadrunners on an acid trip. They were moving fast, with shots of vodka lined up on the bar.

Knox turned to John and Harry. 'Listen, you dudes seem sound enough,' he said. He then turned his attention to Pierre. 'The jury is still out on Poirot here. Anyway, we've got shit to do, but you could speak to Amy. She has the apartment opposite Freya's. They were good friends, so she's pretty cut up about this whole business. Just make sure he doesn't rough her up,' he said, looking at Pierre. 'Now, unless you're going to take us into custody this time?'

Knox and Cal got up from their seats and went over to where the dope heads were encouraging the girls to down their shots in one.

Cal engaged his boyish charms to distract the girls and Knox got between the girls and their predators. Knox said something to one of them and the boy squared up to him and started to remonstrate. John heard him say, 'Fuck you, Knox, bring it on.'

But when Knox grinned and stood tall, the boy cowed.

'You can't save them all, Knox,' said the other boy as they melted into the crowd like scolded hyenas.

But now chatting to the girls with Cal, Knox was oblivious to his taunts.

Outside, Pierre looked at his watch and then asked John and Harry a question. 'Apart from the Amy girl, what did we learn from that?'

John was quick to answer. 'Thanks to your colleagues, not as much as we might have. Do you people have any idea what policing by consent is?'

'Come on John, it's been a long day,' said Harry.

Thursday

Pierre met John and Harry at the public enquiries desk and led them through to the office. He seemed to have forgotten John's jibe the previous evening.

Mathilde was also in a buoyant mood as she looked across from her desk and offered a friendly, 'Good morning.'

'Good morning,' replied John and Harry, keeping well clear of names.

She gave them a knowing smile, but otherwise, it was as if their terse encounter the previous day had never happened. 'I'm afraid I won't be joining you today,' she said. 'I have a backlog of work, but I'm sure Pierre will take good care of you.'

Harry turned to Pierre. 'Did you speak to the commandant about us seeing Florent's report?'

'I've sent him an email with your request,' he replied.

'Do you think he'll cooperate?' Harry asked.

Pierre shrugged. 'It's an internal document, but as long as Freya's mother doesn't object, I can't see why he wouldn't show you what he'll be showing her.'

John let out a sigh that Pierre picked up on.

'We have to follow procedures, John. As I told you yesterday, France is the land of bureaucracy so don't be surprised if the document first goes through Paris, Strasbourg and everyone attending the Saturday market. Now, shall we visit Freya's friend, Amy?'

They stood in the square looking around at the studio apartments. With a light on, it seemed that theirs had already been filled. 'We didn't escape this place for long,' said John as they plodded up the communal staircase of a block close to their first night's billet.

It felt damp and foreboding, reminding John of the stairways in the hastily built and now demolished tower blocks on the outskirts of Edinburgh. Schemes that had proven the utter inability of town planners to understand what made a cohesive community.

The first floor required adroit footwork to circumnavigate a bike frame, bereft of any other components, hanging forlornly off a security chain attached to the railings.

'I wonder how long that's been there,' commented Harry. 'Forever, I'd imagine.'

The second floor had remnants of the previous night's soiree: a plastic bin brimming with empty plonk and beer bottles and a black bag bursting with takeaway packaging.

On the third floor, tucked under the eaves, and according to the stickers on the doors, were the two small apartments occupied by Amy Joyce and Freya Ruuth.

Freya had drawn colourful alpine flowers in the

corners of hers, and as if making a statement, had underlined her surname, Ruuth. Amy had drawn a smiling face. The similarity wasn't lost on Harry. If the girls hadn't drawn these together, one had at least been inspired by the other.

They could see that Amy's door was damaged around the mortice lock; marks synonymous with it having been forced open and clumsily reassembled.

Pierre and Harry stood back as John knocked lightly. There was no answer, but a damp patch under the small pair of snow boots lying on their sides at the door suggested someone had recently arrived.

John knocked again. 'Amy, are you home? We'd like to have a word if we may. It's about Freya. Knox and Cal said you may be able to help us. It won't take long.'

'Why would Knox and Cal say that?' came a hesitant female voice from the other side of the door.

'They said you and Freya were friends.'

The door opened with its security chain still attached and a frightened face appeared. The same face that looked so confident and full of life in the picture Freya's mother had shown them in Leith Police Station.

'I have nothing to say,' she said. 'I hadn't seen Freya for a couple of days, and then I heard she had an accident.'

'I understand,' said John, looking sympathetically at the girl staring leerily back at him.

'You're not from France. Who sent you?' Amy asked.

'Freya's mother. We're police officers from Scotland. Freya's mum was in Scotland when she received the news about her daughter. Why don't you open the door so we can speak properly? We won't come in if you don't want us to.'

Amy looked at Pierre. Something about him told her he wasn't like the other two. John sensed it. 'Our colleague here is with the Gendarmerie. He's helping us to understand what happened to Freya.'

Amy hesitated and then closed the door. They heard the chain being unfastened and the door opened again.

They could see Amy was a pretty girl, about five foot eight inches tall with brown hair styled in a bob, a round face and freckles. She was dressed in a stone-coloured, loose-fitting tracksuit with a hooded top, thick socks and slippers.

John looked past her into the apartment where everything was lying on the floor: furniture toppled, drawers open and clothes scattered.

'Are you alright?' John asked, knowing from her face that she wasn't.

She bit her bottom lip, nodded and then burst into tears.

'There, there, lass,' he said, instructively moving forward to comfort her.

Pierre stepped forward to enter the apartment, but Harry put out an arm to stop him. 'Wait until she's gathered herself,' he said.

Amy sniffed, stood taller and with a jutted jaw took a determined line. 'This is my problem, so I'll sort it,' she said, but at the same time left the door open and moved into the bedsit apartment.

John followed her, past a pair of skis propped against the wall into the room proper, and Harry and Pierre came after, with Pierre closing the door behind him.

The main room was as they expected from their own experience – utilitarian and soulless – but Amy had done her best to spruce it up with posters and a chain of photos. They could see that they had been hanging from the exposed roof trusses but were now torn down.

John righted a couple of toppled chairs and Amy bundled stuff into a drawer.

'When did this happen?' asked Harry.

Amy sniffed and continued her tidying. 'This morning. I had something to do in town and when I came back, I found this. Whoever did it took my laptop. I just want out of here now. I want to go home to England.'

'Where in England are you from?' John asked.

'Surrey,' she replied.

What had started as a great adventure for Amy had become a nightmare. The tragedy of losing her friend and now this.

'What did you have to do in Chamonix?' asked John.

But Amy was distracted by Pierre lifting and looking at her phone. 'Do you mind?' she said, grabbing it off him. 'I wouldn't come into your house and pick up your phone. I want you all to leave. Now.'

Pierre turned to John and Harry. 'We can't force

her to talk, so let's go.'

John tried again. 'Were you meant to be meeting someone, Amy?'

'No,' she said. 'And I don't want to answer any more questions.'

'Do you want to report this?' asked Pierre.

She shook her head. 'What's the point.'

'You might get your things back,' said John.

'Fat chance. Now I want you to leave,' shooing them towards the door.

Harry stopped just over the threshold. 'One last question before we go. Do you have access to Freya's apartment?'

'I did,' said Amy. 'But I gave the key to the people her mother sent to remove her stuff. It's empty now and I don't have access.'

He could see her looking at Freya's front door: a look that said she had serious misgivings about something connected to it.

'Ah,' of course,' said Harry. 'If you need help, let us know. Here's my card. It's a UK number but I'm sure you know what to do.'

Amy made out that she wasn't going to take it but changed her mind, took the card and closed the door.

John, Harry and Pierre returned to the square where Pierre looked at his watch and then at John and Harry. 'The girl has nothing else to add. Freya went skiing and fell into a crevasse. That's the sum of it and I don't think it's in her mother's interest to make more of it than that. Is there anyone else you want to speak to before we close this off?'

Harry looked towards the Mer de Glace. 'I think

we should take up Florent's offer and visit the glacier.'

Pierre nodded slowly and pursed his lips as he weighed it up. 'We could do that, but I'm not sure how beneficial it would be. There won't be much to see except a crevasse, and the ice is always moving so it won't be as it was.'

'True,' said Harry. 'But I'm sure it would help Freya's mother and stepfather come to terms with their loss if they knew we had visited Freya's final resting place. And as you say, we need to close this off.'

Pierre conceded to their request. 'But I have a couple of things to do, so if you don't mind making your own lunch arrangements. Once I've called Florent, I'll text you a pickup time.'

'That's fine. We know our way from here,' said John.

Pierre departed and John glanced up at Amy's apartment. As he did, the curtain twitched. He turned to Harry. 'I'm not comfortable leaving her like that. She seems vulnerable.'

'What are our options?' asked Harry. 'It would be no different if we were in Edinburgh.'

'True,' said John. 'She knows we're standing here so let's talk as we walk.'

**

They made their way back towards the hotel, passing the bottom station of the Aiguille du Midi cable car with its extensive front plaza. The skiers and climbers who queued in the early hours for the first cabins were gone, replaced by milling tourists of all nationalities preparing for their vertiginous adventure: checking watches and looking up with both trepidation and excitement at a departing cable car with its futuristic red shape and smoked Perspex panels.

'Freya must have walked this route,' said John. 'There'll be cameras covering it.'

'Maybe. But that's not for us to get involved with,' said Harry. 'We're here to report back the facts as we see them – not to do the digging.'

'Are we not already digging?' asked John.

Harry put a forefinger to his lips. 'Shoosh. Perhaps this afternoon will settle it.'

'Perhaps,' said John, his voice lacking conviction. 'If it doesn't, we'll have a problem on our hands. Petit wants us out and I'm not sure how long we can keep Pierre on-side.'

'What are your thoughts about Amy?' asked Harry.

'The poor girl is scared witless,' replied John.

'And the break-in?'

John looked uncertain. 'Perhaps it was just an opportunist break-in. But why pick her apartment? Had she mouthed off about having an expensive laptop, or were they looking for something else? If she had been drawn away from the apartment and knew it, she wasn't going to tell us.'

'Freya's mother didn't say she was clearing her daughter's apartment,' said Harry. 'But let's not get ahead of ourselves. There's nothing to indicate any of this has a bearing on Freya's death.'

'No, there isn't,' agreed John. 'And like anywhere, a scumbag thief wouldn't care that Amy had just lost a friend. We should keep an eye on her, though.'

Harry nodded. 'Theoretically, that should be the role of the gendarmerie, but except for Guillaume, I get the feeling building trust isn't in their vernacular. At least not the ones we've met so far.'

'Can we say that everyone in Police Scotland fits the ideal we are setting for these people?' asked John.

It was a rhetorical question that didn't need an answer.

***

Pierre stood back as Florent briefed John and Harry. 'Have either of you flown in a helicopter before?' he asked.

With apprehension written on their faces, John and Harry shook their heads.

'I should warn you, I'm not great with heights,' said John. 'The puddle-jumper plane to Shetland was bad enough.'

'You'll be fine,' said Florent, slapping him on the shoulder. 'It only takes a couple of minutes to reach the Mer de Glace.'

He gave what they thought was his standard 'dos and don'ts' speech before leading them to the waiting helicopter where the pilot was completing preflight checks with the engines off.

Florent strapped them into minimalist canvas side seats and fitted them with headsets before taking his usual pew: the comfortably padded backwards-facing seat behind the pilot.

The helicopter was customised for search and rescue, its low rear doors giving easy entry and egress for stretchers. It was rigged for a man-on-a-wire and kitted out with an array of brightly coloured emergency equipment.

Time to ponder was short as the pilot looked back to see if they were ready. Florent gave him the thumbs up and the pilot flicked a series of switches to start the turbines. Within seconds, the rotors were turning, picking up speed to match the high-pitched whine of the two roof-mounted engines.

The pilot twisted the throttle a little further, and the helicopter twitched on its pad as the rotor blades took the load. Moments later, they were off the ground. The pilot wasted no time in pushing the cyclic forward, and with a perfect combination of throttle, cyclic and pedals they were away, simultaneously climbing and banking hard right back on themselves, and onwards towards the glacier.

Diagonal power lines with orange spherical visibility markers passed below. They banked right again and climbed hard above the steep slabby rock on which pine trees eked an existence in the fissures.

They flew over a small green lake and entered an enormous steep side valley covered in grey glacial moraine: 25,000 years of glaciation being laid bare in two generations as the ice receded.

The near-end of the glacier was a morass of tumbling ice and gushing meltwater: milky-green with the sediment formed over centuries as the ice ground its way down the underlying rock.

Now above the Mer de Glace, the helicopter levelled. A little further on they could see why the glacier was named The Sea of Ice, as a landscape of ice and snow, sparkling brilliantly in the sunlight, snaked its way into the distance.

Men not prone to show their emotions, John and Harry sat mesmerised by the awe-inspiring scale and beauty of what was unfolding ahead of them: sprawling towers of translucent ice glistening brilliantly in the sun, fields of pristine snow reaching as far as the eye could see, and all around, unworldly mountains that seemed to touch the heavens.

Florent pointed towards a cluster of buildings high above the glacier to their right. 'Montenvers,' he said in a muffled voice over their headsets. 'The ice used to reach it, but now you must take a gondola down. Global warming …'

People waved from the terraces and the pilot returned a sporty jiggle.

'For fuck's sake,' muttered John, gripping his seat.

Florent laughed. 'Everyone loves helicopters,' he said, and John reluctantly agreed there was a certain excitement to them.

Soon after, they arrived at the crevasse and set down on the ice.

They removed their headsets and Florent climbed

out and briefed them again from the door.

'Remember what I said. This is a dangerous place with lots of hidden holes and crevasses. Walk only where I walk and only when I say that it's safe to do so. If I say stop, you must stop immediately and don't move again until I give you instructions. Is that clear?'

John and Harry nodded and Pierre acknowledged that he had heard.

They climbed out, and John and Harry looked around.

'This is truly incredible,' said Harry as he pulled on a pair of cheap goggles he had bought to lessen the light.

'It is amazing,' agreed Florent. 'But as we know, it can also be unforgiving.'

Florent took his rucksack and a rope, and they followed him a short distance across old-and-sure ice to a point back from the crevasse.

Pierre put his hands in his pockets and John and Harry stood looking down the glacier.

'Where is the crevasse?' asked Harry.

'Over there,' said Florent, pointing to something inconsequential a little way ahead.

'Where were the Scottish climbers when you arrived?' asked John.

Florent indicated a point between where they were and the crevasse. 'Knox was there belaying Cal, and Cal was in the crevasse.'

'From which direction had they come?' asked Harry.

Florent pointed to a lofty peak further back on

their right-hand side. 'They said they had climbed
the Aiguille du Charmoz, so they would have come
from that direction.'

'That looks tricky,' said John, noting the seracs
looming above the ice.

'It is,' agreed Florent. 'But from where they
came, it's the logical route.'

Far off to their left, a ski guide carrying a
rucksack, and with a man, a woman and a child
following behind, stopped and waved over to them.

'Salut Florent,' shouted the guide.

'Salut Jérôme,' replied Florent. But they were too
far away for any meaningful conversation and
moved off.

John looked around again, stopped and thought. 'I
presume Jérôme's group are skiing the Vallee
Blanche?' he asked.

'Yes. They're skiing what we call the tourist
trail.'

'Is that the route Freya would have taken?'

'Presumably,' said Florent. 'But I couldn't say for
sure because I didn't see any tracks.'

'Is that usual?' asked Harry.

'Not usual, but possible. She was alone and light,
so her tracks could have filled in.'

'So, why would Freya come over here? asked
John.

Florent shrugged. 'I don't know. The weather was
settled so she wouldn't have been lost.'

Pierre looked at his watch. 'Have you seen
everything you want to see?' he asked.

'Not quite,' said Harry. 'Would it be possible for

one of us to take a closer look at the crevasse?'

Certainly,' said Florent. 'I'll put you on a rope and you can look over the edge, but you can't go down. Who would like to go?'

John turned to Harry. 'Be my guest,' he said, making it clear that his decision was final.

Harry put on a harness and Florent set up a belay.

'Ready?' asked Florent, handing Harry a torch.

'Ready,' said Harry.

Harry inched forward and Florent paid out the safety rope. As he got closer, he did as Florent had instructed and dropped onto the ice. The crevasse that had seemed indistinct from a distance was now a gaping chasm with a defined lip. Lying on his stomach, Harry looked into the abyss. There was a slight kink where it was possible to see down into never-endingness. Even with the torch, it was impossible to see the bottom. But Harry could feel it: a cold breath from deep below and the mournful groan as the ice continued its relentless journey of one centimetre per hour down the valley.

Peering into the void, Harry came to the dreadful realisation that anyone who entered that place and was unable to climb out would, to the rest of the world, have vanished without a trace.

***

The helicopter returned them to the base. John, Harry and Pierre thanked Florent and the pilot and Pierre then drove them the short distance back to

Chamonix.

As they pulled up in front of the hotel, Pierre's phone rang. It was Mathilde. She said something to him, and Pierre looked at his watch. 'I'll meet you there,' he said and hung up.

He looked concerned as he turned to John and Harry. 'Someone walking their dog has reported a body in the river Arve a couple of kilometres downstream of Chamonix. Mathilde is heading there now and I'm going to meet her. It's not something you need to be involved with, but—'

John cut in. 'Yes, we'll come.'

John wasn't sure of his rationale for wanting to be there, but his instinct said, 'Have a look,' and he was relieved that Pierre offered.

They took the minor road west out of Chamonix, negotiating numerous traffic-calming obstacles and passing a large crag dotted with early-season rock climbers.

A little further on they crossed a concrete bridge with the Arve's glacial water fast-flowing underneath, and shortly afterwards they turned right.

A snowy track led past chalets and through a wooded area to a small car park. John could see several beige signs indicating walking routes, each route with a staggered barrier to prevent vehicular access.

Mathilde had arrived in an unmarked Peugeot and was being briefed by a young, uniformed officer, dispatched in a marked car to protect the locus.

Close by stood a man in his late sixties dressed in a short dark-brown duffle coat, a scarf and a soft

Newsboy cap. He had a tan and white Braque Français hunting dog on a lead. John assumed from his pallor face and confused look that it was he who had discovered the body.

They got out of the car and Mathilde came over to them. John expected Pierre to give instructions, but Mathilde took the lead, briefing Pierre.

'The body was discovered on the other side of the river by a local man, Monsieur Lafont, or more precisely his dog,' she said, indicating the duo. 'He says he walks the route daily and had the body been exposed before today, the dog would likely have alerted him. He says he got close enough to see it was a body but didn't touch anything and alerted us. Gerbert knows where the body was found.' She nodded towards the uniformed officer. 'Pierre, would you mind taking a statement from Monsieur Lafont?'

'I'll do that,' said Pierre.

John asked Mathilde, 'Would you mind me coming with you, Sergeant?'

Mathilde thought for a moment and then looked questioningly at Pierre.

'I don't see why not,' said Pierre.

The river was flowing through a dense forest of mature pine trees. Gerbert led them across a wooden footbridge encrusted with ice. John felt a sudden drop in temperature as the already cold air was chilled further by the glacial water flowing below. He could see their breath curl and plume and noticed how fast the water was moving. *Anyone who fell into that wouldn't stand a chance.*

On the other side, they intersected a well-made path running parallel to the river and set some metres above.

Gerbert turned left, continued a short distance, and stopped. 'The body is about 20 metres further on. The easiest access is to drop to the river here,' he said.

They followed his lead, clutching onto branches to steady themselves as they descended the snowy slope to the water.

The edge of the river was shallower here, but still treacherous with large ice-encrusted river stones, rounded by millions of years of hydraulic attrition and denying a safe footing.

From a distance, John could see what looked like an abandoned piece of floral fabric caught on something, but as they got closer a human shape emerged, the cloth revealing itself to be a light-coloured dress.

Mathilde stopped. 'Wait here,' she said.

John watched on as Mathilde approached the body. She took a pair of blue latex gloves from her pocket, slipped them on, and with her right hand, reached down and touched the deceased's neck.

She stood up tall, looked around, and then gave a despairing shake of the head before carefully making her way back.

'She's a young woman, in her twenties I'd say. The cold water has preserved her, but I estimate she's been dead for several weeks.' She looked at Gerbert. 'Did you get close to the body?'

'Close enough to know she's dead,' he replied a

little too glibly.

Mathilde didn't like his tone. 'Show some respect or I'll write you up for speaking ill of the deceased. Do you understand?'

Gerbert realised he had crossed a line with Mathilde and adopted a contrite look. 'Pardon, Sous-brigadier La Croix.'

She didn't acknowledge his apology, but instead asked what he had seen when he arrived.

'The man with the dog—'

Mathilde corrected him. 'Monsieur Lafont.'

'Yes, Monsieur Lafont was waiting in the car park. He led me along the path and pointed down to what he suspected was a body at the edge of the river. I came down and confirmed it was. I then radioed in. She will have accidentally fallen into the river and drowned.'

John looked at Mathilde. 'May I ask a question?'

Mathilde nodded. 'Ask away, Sergeant.'

John turned to Gerbert. 'So we know who she is, do we?'

Mathilde knew John's train of thought and joined John in looking at Gerbert for a response.

But Gerbert seemed confused, so John offered more. 'If someone falls into a river and drowns, is it not likely that they would be reported as a missing person?'

'Not necessarily,' said Gerbert.

John had made his point so he left it at that.

Mathilde addressed the two of them. 'Until we know more, we will treat this as a crime scene. Gerbert, move those people on. I want that path closed,' she said, glancing across the river to where onlookers were congregating. She then addressed John. 'Sergeant, we should first put on forensic suits and then take a closer look.'

John and Mathilde returned to the river dressed head to toe in white zip-fronted forensic suits, double-gloved and masked. They had pulled on over-boots but knew the soles wouldn't last long.

As they approached the body, John transitioned into a role he had played so many times before, assuming a compassionate detachment, working through the evidence before him, thinking through its logic and feeling for the unseen.

He took in the locus: a young woman wearing what looked like a tattered evening dress, bare feet, painted finger and toe nails, no jewellery – not even a ring. Despite the damage to her face caused by pummelling as she was washed down the river, John could see she would have been pretty. Her high cheekbone structure and deep-set almond-shaped eyes suggested she was East European.

Mathilde examined the inside of the woman's arm. 'She's had an unhappy life,' she said, looking at the scars from where she had likely self-harmed.

John asked the question they were both forming. 'A young woman, dressed for an evening out disappears but no one reports her missing?'

Mathilde nodded in agreement. 'Trafficked – a sex worker perhaps – but that's only a working theory. We must keep an open mind. She won't be local here or we would know about her. Pâquis, the red-light district of Geneva, perhaps.'

John turned back a piece of torn fabric from the young woman's shoulder blade. 'You can see where she has had a tattoo removed. If your theory is right, she might have been what in that abhorrent business they call branded: tattooed with the name or mark of her controlling pimp or gang. It's something we see frequently in Scotland and not just with victims of trafficking. Abusers are known to do similar. She might have been seen as more attractive or compliant and sold on up the value chain. Whoever's hands she fell into would have the previous brand removed.'

Mathilde noted the nasal septum perforation damage caused by snorting. 'She was a heavy user of cocaine: possibly MDMA or ketamine.'

'It goes with the territory,' replied John. 'Another means of controlling or escaping, depending on which side of this ugly business you find yourself.'

John looked again at the young woman's face. He had seen many such faces, most recently the women killed in Leith. Early in his career, he had wondered why they didn't try to escape from the wretched lives they lived. Later, when he understood that their lives had been brutally rendered down through threats, beating, coercion and dependence into a day-by-day fight for survival, he felt ashamed of his naivety. He wondered whether this woman still bore hope, or had she succumbed to this being her pitiful lot in life.

'I know, it's heartbreaking,' said Mathilde, interrupting his thoughts.

She looked at a waterline on the riverbank and how exposed the body was. 'The water level has dropped and stranded her here. I'd say she's been washed some distance downriver. It's hard to say where she entered. The flow is powerful and fast: enough to move a body a long way quickly, assuming it doesn't get caught up on something.'

She looked again at the riverbank from where the remains of a layer of ice protruded. 'She might have been washed underneath the ice and kept submerged until the water level dropped. Air would then get in, leading to a rapid thaw and exposing her. I would say it was quite recent, otherwise we would see signs of animals scavenging. It would also account for the dog not scenting her previously.'

'Does the level change significantly?' asked John

'It does,' said Mathilde. 'I will have a hydrologist access data from the river gauges and draw up a profile with predictions. What are your thoughts on the cause of death?'

John looked up the river, down it and then at the body of the young woman. 'It would be easy to say drowning, but over my career, I've seen a lot of drowning victims, and this young woman doesn't fit that pattern.'

'In what way?' asked Mathilde.

John looked for a logical answer but nothing materialised. 'It just doesn't feel right. And there's the bigger picture: two bodies, both young women and neither reported missing. Is that a regular occurrence around here?'

Mathilde seemed sceptical. 'Freya came from a wealthy family and appeared to have a happy life: quite unlike the young woman we have here.'

'That's all conjecture,' said John.

Mathilde glanced down at the body. 'I'll push for the preliminaries.'

'Do that,' said John. 'And see if you can chase Freya's results.'

Two Renault Traffic vans appeared in the car park and Mathilde waved over to them. 'That's forensics. We'd better go over and brief them.'

Mathilde led them away from the body and then stopped, lowered her facemask and looked at John. 'Thank you for your help, Sergeant. But please don't forget this isn't your case.'

'Unless the cases are connected,' said John.

***

John and Harry ate dinner whilst watching the fading golden hour light flood the Aiguilles with pastel tones of pink, orange and eventually crimson until only the pinprick light at the top station of the Midi remained, set against the inky night.

John thought about their day. 'The young woman's body in the river seems to be one hell of a coincidence.'

Harry agreed. 'But until Mathilde comes back—'

'I know, I know,' said John with a frustrated sigh. 'We need to wait. The glacier, however, is a different story. What was an experienced skier like Freya doing there on her own? She would have known the dangers. If Knox and Cal hadn't spotted the ski, would anyone have looked down there for her? Florent said she was well off the beaten track and there was nothing to single out that crevasse from the hundreds of others, so it's unlikely she'd have ever been found, although we don't fully know the capability of the rescue services.'

'There's not much to go on,' said Harry.

John shook his head. 'Not as yet. But if Freya took the telepherique to the top station perhaps someone spoke to her. We should ask if the operators have anything on video.'

Their waiter, Antoine, came to clear their plates. In his early thirties, he was dressed in black trousers and a white shirt, and impeccably precise in all aspects of his work.

John looked up at the light on the top of the Midi, and out of curiosity asked Antoine if anyone stayed overnight up there.

'Only the Guardian,' Antoine replied as he gazed up through one of the many high windows to the mountain. 'When I was a child and had a bad dream, my mother would take me to my bedroom window and show me the guardian's light. "Look, there's nothing to worry about. The guardian is watching over us," she would say. Now I do the same for my child.'

John looked up at the light and then back at Antoine and smiled. 'Looking after all the children must be an awesome responsibility.'

'It's the guardian's purpose in life,' said Antoine as he stacked their plates on his arm. 'To serve is a privilege, is it not?'

There was something spiritual in how Antoine

told his story: as if whoever was charged with the guardianship of the Chamonix Valley acted as gatekeeper to the heavens beyond, as Janus had in Roman mythology.

'Indeed, it is. You're local, then?' asked John.

'Yes, I'm a Chamoniard. My family has lived here since before the French Revolution. Life in the valley was very different then, but its natural beauty has always drawn visitors.'

Antoine left to go about his duties and John looked at his watch. It had been a busy day but still too early for bed so he suggested they have a mooch around town.

'Sure,' said Harry. 'But let me first give Jack a quick call and update him. He might come up with something to give us leverage with Petit.'

***

The concierge bid them a pleasant evening and they walked out past a red once-was telecabin now occupied by two excited children.

They walked up the hill and turned left onto the bustling Tinseltown en Alps pedestrian precinct of Rue Joseph Vallot. Couples and groups, young and old, were strolling, browsing shops and soaking up the ambience.

A few less restrained souls, still in their ski boots, were staggering back to their accommodation, encumbered by skis, helmets, rucksacks and the consequences of overindulging in early après-ski.

Many of the shops flaunted recognisable luxury brands. John and Harry stopped to window-shop a silver puffer jacket that might have been worn by an astronaut and was now selling at an astronomical price. 'How the other half lives' said John.

'I could get used to the hotel,' said Harry. 'Someone is going to have a hissy fit when we submit our expenses.'

Another shop had grotesquely shaped saucissons hanging in the window, and behind, a full range of cured meats, gourmet cheeses, onions in strings, and an infinite selection of olive oils.

Some shops had wooden facias and quaintly painted panels evocative of traditional alpine chalets, but it wasn't hard to see the 70's concrete behind their façade.

John and Harry stepped aside to let a tall blonde male in his twenties slipstreamed by two self-conscious blonde females run past. The male bore a white towelling headband, and both women had their hair tied in ponytails that swished from side to side. Their running vests and shorts emphasised their toned and tanned physiques. But the spectacle looked contrived, and the self-conscious expressions of the women indicated they knew as much. Harry and John exchanged uncertain glances and then shrugged as if to say, 'Whatever ...'

They reached Rue de Dr Paccard, where the stores became opticians specialising in sunglasses and ski goggles, shops selling and renting out climbing and ski gear and restaurants with outside seating. They passed the restaurant where Pierre had bought them lunch the previous day, and a chemist with a window mannequin dressed in running gear and numerous orthopaedic braces and elasticated supports.

'Poor bugger,' commented John with that sense of humour that had carried him through so many awful situations during his career.

They took a seat on a wide wooden bench in the square and looked up at a magnificent mural depicting the adventurous spirit of the town.

'I read about that mural in the hotel magazine,' said Harry. 'They are all famous Chamoniards and visitors from yesteryear.'

There were images of early alpinists with wooden staffs, an expeditionary staring up at Mont Blanc through a telescope, skiers holding hardwood skis with leather strap bindings, and an aid climber cavorting precariously under a balcony.

At the top was the painted figure of a woman with a crucifix necklace, sitting at a window. Harry pointed up at her. 'Her name is Marie Paradis: the first woman to climb Mont Blanc. I read that she found it quite an ordeal, but it was subsequently the making of her.'

'Are you trying to tell me something?' asked John, not expecting an answer.

A disciplined troupe of tourists passed by: Japanese, judging by their appearance and the little Hinomaru being held aloft like a colour guard flag by their guide.

'Did Jack have any suggestions?' asked John, referring to Harry's earlier call with him.

'He has an idea, but we'll need to wait until tomorrow,' said Harry.

They both knew when to be patient. It was the nature of the job: avoid muddying the waters until *could be* was a certainty.

John waited for a group of high-spirited British teenagers in search of their next watering hole to cruise by before speaking. 'The problem we have is Petit. He's making this business more complicated than it needs to be. He wants us off his patch, but his lack of transparency is prolonging our departure. Unless, of course, he kicks us out of town.'

'My thoughts exactly,' said Harry. 'It's what I said to Jack. We either get something definitive one way or another or we're left in limbo.'

John leant forward with his forearms on his thighs and looked up and down the street. He spotted Knox, Cal and the two girls, each carrying a rucksack. The girls were dressed in leggings and trainers, and from the oversized look of them, they had purloined Knox and Cal's down jackets. Cal and Knox were wearing trainers, jeans and sweatshirts.

The girls were laughing, and the one with the misaligned eye was now hanging off Cal's arm. Cal spotted John and Harry and said something to the group and Knox steered them over.

After the previous evening's fractious meet in the brasserie, the detectives weren't sure what was coming, but the quartet seemed relaxed.

'Hi, are you enjoying your holiday?' asked one of the girls.

John looked at Knox, who winked to say, 'Best

not let on.'

'Yes, thank you,' said John. 'How about you?'

'We love it here,' she replied.

Harry looked between Cal and Knox. 'I thought you two were heading off into the mountains for a couple of days?'

Cal explained, 'Change of plan. We've been climbing – just not where we intended. Zoe and Kim invited us snowboarding today and gave us a whipping,' he said, looking at the girl holding onto his arm and then to the other to distinguish Zoe from Kim. 'So we offered a return match and took them climbing at Les Gaillands.'

'I gave them another whipping on the boulder problem,' said Zoe, and Cal did his best to look crestfallen.

'If we'd stayed any longer, we would have been stuck up there for the night,' said Knox.

Zoe gave Cal's arms a bit more of a squeeze, suggesting she wasn't wholly against the idea.

'Where are your ropes?' asked John.

'In our rucksacks' replied Cal. 'It's sus to flaunt your gear. But you don't have to look far in Cham to see a whole bunch of "all the gear and no idea" folk wearing harnesses bristling with ice screws.'

Knox looked at his watch and then at his group. 'Can you guys head down to the burger place and get our order in before they stop serving? I just want a quick word with these two.'

Cal's advocacy of 'the best burgers in town' enticed the girls away.

Knox watched them walk off, and then he turned

to the detectives. 'Where's your minder?' he asked.

'We've given him the night off,' said John. He looked up the street to where Cal, Zoe and Kim were disappearing into the burger bar. 'Have you taken the girls under your wing?' he asked.

Knox smiled. 'They're cool, and more streetwise than we gave them credit for. Who would have thought them a couple of Instagram hits? What about you? Have you made sense of what happened to Freya?'

'It's a work in progress,' said Harry.

Knox gave a scoffing laugh. 'Bollocks it is. I'd guess that wherever you look you see nothing but your reflection. Amy phoned us today. She said that someone broke into her flat and then you visited. We assured her you were only trying to help Freya's mother.'

'Thanks,' said John.

'What for?' asked Knox. 'That's the truth isn't it?'

'That's all we're here for,' said John.

'Are break-ins common around Chamonix?' asked Harry.

'Not really. Skis and bikes get stolen, and tourists' cars are sometimes broken into if valuables are left on display. But not apartments.'

'That's what we thought,' said John. 'All this will be tough on Amy. Would you mind keeping an eye on her?'

'We're doing that anyway,' said Knox. 'Here's something for you to mull over. Ask yourself why an experienced skier like Freya would go to the trouble of wearing an avalanche transceiver but not turn it on. It doesn't make sense.'

The detectives looked one to the other.

'You know what a transceiver is, right?' asked Knox.

Harry nodded. 'It's a device that sends out a signal so that you can be found if buried in an avalanche.'

'Correct. But it only works if it's on.'

'Are you sure she was carrying one, and that it was off?' asked John.

Knox nodded. 'One hundred per cent. I saw it under her jacket when Florent was looking for ID.'

'And you know it was off?'

'Well, we didn't get a signal when we tried. Unless it was damaged when she went into the crevasse,' said Knox.

'You mean when she *fell* into the crevasse?' said John.

Knox shrugged. 'Do you know that for sure? But listen, I need to shoot. Good luck with your inquiries.'

'Thanks for your help,' said John. 'If you think of anything else …'

Knox smiled. 'Sure. I can retrieve your number from when you called.'

As Knox left to join his team, the detectives saw Kim come out of the burger bar. She called out, 'Come on, Knox, we've got a table,' and beckoned him to hurry.

He waved to her and started jogging, laboured by his heavy rucksack.

'She's got him running,' said John.

'Maybe. But I also sense that that group likes being together,' said Harry. 'If what he's telling us is correct, Petit and his people have been holding back what could be crucial evidence.'

'Why would they do that?' asked John.

'If we find that out, then perhaps we'll be able to put this to rest. Tomorrow, we'll have it out with Petit, whether he likes it or not,' said Harry.

'Do you think the two lads know more than they're letting on?' asked John.

Harry wasn't sure. 'I'll have Sheila discreetly run background checks on them, but I think they'll come back clean.'

Friday

Once again, John and Harry rendezvoused with Pierre at the public enquiries desk and Harry immediately asked to see Petit.

'Not until Monday,' said Pierre. 'Petit left for Provence last night. He has builders working on that dilapidated château of his.'

'Nice of him to tell us,' said Harry, showing his irritation.

Pierre just laughed. 'Don't expect manners from the *de, de de*. To him, we are nothing but a bunch of peasants.'

A smile flickered across Guillaume's face. Pierre noticed. 'I'm right, am I not, Sergeant?'

'I couldn't possibly comment, Chef,' replied Guillaume, but Harry and John could see from the lighter atmosphere that having Petit away was a weight off everyone.

Pierre led them up to the office where Mathilde was working at her desk.

'Good morning, Madame La Croix,' said John.

She smiled – something he didn't expect. 'Good morning, Sergeant,' she replied, with an emphasis on "Sergeant" that seemed almost playful.

She continued her work and Pierre glanced curiously between John and her and then addressed Harry. 'What did you want to ask Petit? Perhaps I can help.'

'We want to know why we weren't told that Freya's avalanche transceiver was off.'

Pierre pulled up a document on his screen. 'It's on Florent's report,' he said, reading a section of the document. 'We should receive the autopsy results today. I'll personally make sure you are given copies of both.'

'Thank you,' said Harry. 'Have you got the video from the telepherique?'

Pierre dipped into his pocket, took out a USB memory stick and held it up. 'I have the files here and I've booked our AV room,' he said. 'It's our first job today, once we've had coffee.'

Mathilde's mobile phone rang. She answered, and after confirming her name she listened intently to what the speaker was saying. John saw her jot something down on a piece of paper.

'Merci. Je suis en chemin,' she said and hung up.

She quickly logged out of her computer, lifted her coat and looked over at John. 'You were right about the young woman found in the Arve. She didn't drown. Preliminary tests indicate the cause of death was ketamine. I'm going through to Annecy.'

***

The AV room looked much like one would in

Scotland: a standard room that offered privacy, and a PC with extra equipment to make the review process easier.

'How did they know where to look?' asked Harry.

'From the season pass,' said Pierre. 'But we will need to identify the exact person from the footage as they are dressed pretty much the same in their ski gear.'

They took seats huddled around the PC and popped the USB into the slot. With Pierre on the joystick, they familiarised themselves with viewing segments: advancing, rewinding, speeding up, slowing down and zooming into a frozen frame.

'This should be straightforward enough,' said Pierre.

John nodded, but his mind was elsewhere. If the young woman had died from a ketamine overdose, how did she end up in the river? Medical-grade ketamine was an anaesthetic but the street version, going by the euphemism Special K, and cut with whatever, was crude and unpredictable. Despite the risks, it had proved itself compelling for hard-core drug users seeking dreamy detachment from their real world. And then there was its use as a date rape drug. If the young woman had had a bad trip and fallen into the river, she would have drowned. But Mathilde said that wasn't the case, which meant she was already dead and someone put her there.

'Are you ready, John?' Pierre asked.

John shook himself back into the present. 'Yes, sorry. My mind was elsewhere.'

Pierre took out a photo of the clothes Freya was

wearing when her body was recovered. They had been carefully laid out on a table and images taken of the front and back.

At first, the scene on the monitors looked like a jumble of silent bodies, inching towards the camera. The throng stopped and started, proceeding in cabin-sized batches through the pass-activated turnstile to wait in a holding bay and then onto the platform ready for the next cabin. Some carried rucksacks, many wore helmets and a few were tourists wrapped up warm for the observation areas at the top.

After a couple of false sightings, they spotted a skier in the same attire as Freya, helmet on, googles down. They looked several times, slowing the image and then freezing it and zooming in. When they had finished with that view, they went to a camera monitoring arrivals at the top station and crosschecked with the timeline. It fitted perfectly with the frequency of cabins and each time showed a similar young woman carrying similar skis in the same manner.

Finally, they went through the other passengers: just to be sure.

'To think that was her last journey,' said John. 'Poor lass.'

*   *   *

They had just finished when Mathilde called Pierre to say she was on her way back from the forensic pathologist in Annecy and would meet them at the gendarmerie.

She swept into the office. 'Give me a minute to get organised,' she said. 'I need to send an urgent email.'

Once she had done what she needed to, she swivelled her chair to face them. 'I had Freya's autopsy findings printed out,' she said, holding up a thin file.

She looked at Pierre. 'I presume it's alright to let them have these?'

John detected something provocative in her tone as if informing Pierre if he was going to say no, he would have to do it publicly.

Pierre lifted the file and cast an eye over the documents inside. 'It's a summary. But it will give you what you need to complete your brief,' he said, handing the folder to Harry.

John wondered what was implied by that. Did Pierre still consider this to be an open-and-shut case? If so, the footage of Freya they had just seen played in his favour.

John returned to Mathilde. 'And the girl in the river?'

Again, Mathilde sought permission from Pierre and he nodded for her to continue.

'I sent a picture to our cantonal police colleagues in Geneva and their team in Pâquis think they recognised her. She's known by the street name Lucie, but that's all we have for now. These women are anonymised – stripped of their identity – so it will take time to find out more. They think she worked through an organised gang but hadn't been there long. They're looking into it as a matter of urgency and will come back to us as soon as they find out more. The likely outcome will be that those controlling her say she left weeks ago of her own volition and hasn't been seen since. So without evidence ...'

It was something John had seen many times: abusers securing blind allegiance by systematically coercing victims into forfeiting all vestiges of their former selves. Obliterating anything that anchored them to their past life and leaving a zombified vassal devoid of any self-determination.

Mathilde fixed John with a shrewd look. 'As I said earlier, you were right, Sergeant. Lucie didn't drown.'

John waited anxiously for more.

'The preliminaries suggest the cause of death was a ketamine overdose. And there's something else ...' Mathilde handed John a piece of paper. 'The translation isn't perfect. AI never is, but it's close.'

John's eyes ran back and forth across the page. His face visibly paled, and he sat on the edge of a neighbouring desk to steady himself. 'Bloody hell. So her injuries didn't come from being washed down the river. Are you sure about this?'

Mathilde nodded. 'As sure as we can be for now.'

John's mind fell into freefall as he tried to comprehend what kind of depraved person would do this to a woman.

With his hand wavering, he held out the piece of paper. Pierre took it, read what was written and passed Harry.

Mathilde continued. 'The person or persons who did this to Lucie were dosing her with ketamine to keep her under and either went too far or killed her as part of their plan. There's a cannula mark on the radial artery of her forearm. I'm working on the initial premise that she was dressed by a man or men and dumped in the river sometime later.'

'What makes you think that?' asked John.

'Because even without labels to guide them, women intuitively know which way out their lingerie goes.'

John could see that Mathilde was good at what she did: thorough, experienced and smart. The type of officer who could think critically, join the dots and drive a case on.

He turned to Pierre. 'I presume you are going to get a team assigned to this?'

'That will have to be authorised by Commandant de Petit. Mathilde will handle it until Monday, won't you, Mathilde?'

'I'll get the right people briefed and write up what we have so far. Then on Monday, we will take it forward. Now, if you will excuse me, I have a lot to do.'

***

John and Harry returned to the hotel armed with the folder containing the summary of Freyas's autopsy and the notes from Florent. They pulled up a couple of seats around a small table in Harry's room, and

Harry passed John one of the pages from the pathologist.

John cleared his throat and then spoke. 'Can we first discuss what we've just heard about the young woman whose name we assume to be Lucie?'

'Of course,' said Harry. 'And don't for a moment think I'm not aware of the similarities this has to Edinburgh.'

John nodded. 'It's exactly like Edinburgh …'

'And you can't stand by and let Petit brush it under the carpet,' said Harry.

'No, I can't. Mathilde appears committed and capable but Pierre seems laid back about the whole thing and happy to let Petit do whatever.'

'We don't know that about Pierre,' said Harry. 'Who's to say he isn't playing a long game with Petit, letting him hoist himself by his own petard?'

'I'm just saying …' said John.

'Why don't we look through Freya's autopsy result first?' suggested Harry in an attempt to settle his colleague. 'See what's been said.'

John gathered himself. 'Sure. Let's do that.'

Florent had been diligent in writing up what had happened: the call, what they had found on arrival at the glacier, the retrieval from the crevasse and their return to the helipad. He had noted that Freya's transceiver was off and commended the role Knox and Cal had played. He had omitted the encounter between Knox, Cal and the gendarmes, but Harry and John agreed that anyway, it was beyond the scope of an incident report.

The autopsy report confirmed that Freya had died from positional asphyxia, most likely the result of compression or constriction of her chest. It was a condition that John and Harry were all too aware of when apprehending prisoners, especially violent ones requiring higher levels of restraint.

In Freya's case, it was suggested that the constriction within the crevasse could have compromised her breathing. A footnote had been added to say the casualty would have passed out quickly and succumbed to the cold: a piece of information the officers felt had been included to offer solace to her loved ones.

Freya's clothing revealed slight quantities of cocaine consistent with her being a passive bystander, but her bloodstream was clear.

She had been dressed for skiing and was carrying her lift pass and an avalanche transceiver. She had no other emergency equipment, and her mobile phone was absent. However, one of her jacket pockets was unzipped.

John scanned the papers and then turned the pages over to see if there was something more. 'Not much to go on, is there?' he said. 'And if the timeline given to us by Pierre is correct, her phone was switched off near Chamonix the previous day.'

'But there are some pointers,' said Harry.

John nodded slowly. 'It's a bit of a stretch checking a casualty's clothes for drugs, is it not?'

'Unless someone wanted to expose something they already knew was there,' said Harry. 'A ploy to have her parents back down and preserve their dead daughter's reputation, perhaps?'

John was doubtful. 'I could see her stepfather wanting to hush it up, but not her mother. She strikes me as being a decent woman in search of the truth, whatever the cost.'

'But this is all conjecture,' said Harry. 'If we stick with facts, Freya took an early cabin to the top of the Midi. She skied down, and later that morning she fell into a crevasse.'

John looked once more at the report and then put it down. 'It's nice and neat when you say it like that. But factor in that she went alone, didn't tell her best friend, didn't appear to be properly prepared and fell into an out-of-the-way crevasse. And then there's Petit with his bizarre behaviour.'

'Maybe that's just the way of the man. Pierre doesn't seem to hold him in much esteem,' said Harry.

John drew a deep breath and blew it out. 'Either way, we need more reassurance before we can sign off Petit's version of events, and I would also like to see an obvious separation between Freya and Lucie.'

'There's nothing to connect them,' said Harry.

'Not as yet.'

John looked again at the reports, trying to find something. Anything. 'We're no further forward with most of what's here. However, there is one aspect we could delve into if we're prepared to bend the rules slightly.'

'We need to do something, and you know what they say about making an omelette. What have you got in mind?' asked Harry.

John explained his plan and Harry raised an eyebrow. 'A bit of old-school policing, is it? Seeing as we don't have any jurisdiction to prosecute and we don't intend to share our source, I can't see anyone shouting "entrapment". Let's give it a whirl.'

***

Chamonix's answer to the Royal Mile,' said John as they crossed to a ubiquitous souvenir shop selling regionally themed tacky-tat.

Display racks boasted postcards, fridge magnets, keyrings and other trinkets favoured by tourists devoid of taste.

Harry examined a cap bearing a Mont Blanc motif, and a *Made in China* label.

Beside the door sat a wicker basket containing an array of metal-tipped pseudo-walking canes, useless for anything other than cluttering the house or inadvertently poking someone's eye out.

They entered the shop and John took an interest in a male underwear mannequin bearing a racy pair of alpine-themed form-fitting boxers. 'Can I help you?' asked the assistant.

'Err, just browsing, thanks,' he said, moving uncomfortably to the T-shirts.

Harry found a cheap wallet that fitted the bill and paid at the cash desk.

They headed to a quiet side street and stuffed their purchase with pre-prepared pieces of banknote-sized paper, and for allure, added a slightly protruding twenty-euro note.

John turned the wallet in his hand. 'Looks like the real deal,' he said. 'Shall we?'

Harry nodded and the two of them returned to the area of the studio apartment complex where they had spent their first night.

They noticed how little the snow had been cleared compared to the pristine pavements of the town centre.

People were once again transitioning from returning skiers to departing night workers and revellers.

'We might be too late,' said Harry.

John checked his watch. 'It's still early for him,' noting someone sitting on a balcony, beer in hand, awaiting delivery of their weekend stash. 'We'd better find somewhere a little less conspicuous to wait.'

They settled for a dimly lit entrance on the route into the square.

Speaking as he would on a major operation, Harry commenced a briefing. 'I'll take up a position opposite and await the approaching target. You will be stationed—'

John raised a halting hand. 'Whoa there, Harry. Let's not overcomplicate this. You stand over there, I'll sit here, and you tell me when the laddie comes pedalling down the road. If the coast is clear, I'll bait the trap. If the laddie goes for it, we'll have gentle words with him. That's all we need, isn't it?'

Harry looked confused. 'Is that not what I was suggesting?' he asked.

John returned a wrinkled frown. 'Let's get this over with.'

Harry took position across the road, and attempting to look inconsequential, John sat with a hotel magazine in hand on a nearby bench. He turned up the collar of his coat against the chill and pulled his hat down over his ears.

Ten minutes later they realised their plan was flawed. From their perch on the apartment balcony, they had seen the lad arrive and ply his trade. What they hadn't taken on board were the numerous other hoodie-clad lads cutting about on mountain bikes. Some appeared at such speed that, had they been the intended subject, it would have been too late to lure them. Anything other than the rider stopping of their own volition risked drawing the attention of passersby. If they decided to get involved, it would become messy.

Harry came across to where John was sitting. 'Perhaps we should abandon this,' he said.

'Give it time,' said John. 'He doesn't know us, so if it looks iffy, I'll sit it out and no one will be any the wiser.'

Fifteen minutes later a jaunty figure on a mountain bike came into view, his hands-off-handlebars posture suggesting to Harry it was the lad they had seen.

He called over to John, 'I think this is him.'

John upped from his seat, deftly placed the wallet by the entrance and returned to his position, just as the lad appeared. He could see the lad spot the wallet as he passed, but he was too late to stop and carried on into the square. John stayed put, turned to the next page of the magazine and winced at the eye-watering price of what was described as a newly built lock-and-leave chalet near Les Praz. From the corner of his eye, he could see the lad circle slowly, the tyres of his bike crunching over some hard-packed snow that had been cleared to one side. John sensed the lad weighing up the risk versus reward as a mouse might ruminate over cheese in a sprung trap. *Come on son.*

Knowing this could go either way, John made a show of looking at his watch and then stood up, slipped the magazine into his pocket and walked away from the wallet.

Now discounting John, the lad sped around, and retracing his tracks headed towards the wallet, stopped and leant down.

John put a heavy right hand on the lad's left shoulder. 'Not so quick, son.'

With hugely dilated pupils and stinking of cheap cigarette smoke, the lad looked blankly at John, and then realising something was wrong, he tried to bolt.

John shifted his hand from the lad's shoulder to under his armpit, and in an instant had him in a firm restraining hold.

Unbalanced, the lad stumbled forward, but John steadied him. 'Easy now, son. Been smoking the stock, have we?'

Harry appeared and stood as best he could to block what was happening while John engaged with the lad.

'There's nothing to worry about. We just want to

ask you a couple of questions and then you'll be on your way.'

The lad heaved forward to break free, then flinched as John tightened his grip.

'Get the fuck off me, dude,' he demanded, in a spurious US drawl.

John could see that despite his bravado, the lad cut a pitiful figure – neglected and underweight in a threadbare hoodie and with nicotine-stained fingers. The type of young man who in Scotland might have dropped out of school, and devoid of opportunity, was now making poor life choices. He noticed the hoodie had a snowboard logo printed on it.

'When were you last out on your board?' John asked.

The lad tried to find an answer but gave up. 'I've been busy.'

Harry dipped into the side pocket of the lad's hoodie, pulled out a scrunched-up carrier bag and looked inside. He held it open for John to see as well.

'You have a decision to make,' said John to the lad. 'We can let you go, and we'll keep this, or you can calm down, answer a couple of easy questions and we'll give you back your gear to go about your business. We'll even throw in the twenty euros from the wallet as a sweetener. Bear in mind, that if we hang on to the merchandise, you'll need to explain its loss to your employers. Which do you want?'

'I don't work for anyone, and if I did I wouldn't grass them,' said the lad, lifting an indignant chin and dropping the American accent in favour of something from the south of England.

He struggled again. John re-tightened his grip, and the lad resigned himself to the only tenable offer on the table.

'You're not the gendarmerie, are you?' he asked.

'And you're not in a position to barter,' replied John.

The lad shot him a look of disdain. 'What do you want to know?'

'That's better,' said John.

Harry peered into the bag again, had a poke about and asked, 'We're interested in cocaine.'

For a moment, the lad looked hopeful, but after a reality check, he went back on the defensive. 'What about it?'

'We want to know who buys it around here,' said John.

The lad laughed. 'You want me to give you a list?'

'No, we don't have all night for that,' said Harry, with a mirth that wasn't lost on the lad. 'We want to know who the upmarket customers are. Blonde tops, perhaps?'

'Blonde tops? I don't mix with that crew.'

John released him and took a step back. 'Ah well, it was worth a try. You can go.'

'What about my gear?' asked the lad, looking keenly at the bag.

John shook his head. 'That wasn't the deal. We'll hand it into the gendarmerie as lost property and you can collect it from there.'

The lad glanced furtively around and then

lowered his voice. 'There's a dude called Adonis who buys coke for others. He hangs out with the blonde tops. That's all I know. Now give me the bag.'

'Does the guy who sells Adonis coke also sell ketamine?' asked John.

John could see the lad flip from compliant to something unpredictable and therefore dangerous.

'Fuck you and your questions,' he said.

'Give him the bag,' said John, and Harry handed it over.

John took the twenty euro note from the wallet and the lad snatched that as well.

John watched the lad pick up his bike and wheel it away in as dignified a manner as he could.

The lad then stopped and turned back to look at John. 'You think I'm a piece of shit, don't you?'

John shook his head. 'No, son. I'm not the one who thinks that of you. But you might want to consider life's about the choices we make.'

***

The Friday night party animals had left the hotel in search of Chamonix's wilder quarters. John and Harry found a secluded corner of the foyer and with beers in hand waited for Knox.

Harry could see John was lost in thought. 'You're thinking about that lad selling the gear, aren't you, John?'

John looked up at his colleague. 'Aye, I am. He

probably came to Chamonix to escape and live the dream, but ended up back where he was, dealing dope.'

'I know what you mean. The more I see and hear, the more I feel we've failed the younger generation,' said Harry.

John looked at the door and then back at Harry. 'Asking Sheila to check out Knox and Cal and then pumping them for information feels cheap; as though we're no better than the two cops who hassled them when they came off the mountain. Why could we not just trust that they were good lads?'

'It's what the job requires of us. At least we know they're clean,' said Harry. 'What Sheila said about Cal was a bit out of the blue, but I think it's best not to mention that we know unless Cal brings it up.'

'Agreed,' said John. 'If he wanted us to know he would have told us.'

Harry smiled at a distant memory.

'What is it?' asked John.

'I was thinking back to when you and that young detective had that car chop shop under surveillance. What was that cop's name you were with?'

John tried but couldn't get past the nickname they had given him: Dapper Deek

'He was Derek something or other,' said Harry. 'And obsessed with his appearance.'

John laughed. 'Aye, that he was. He must have spent a small fortune on his hair and wardrobe.'

'But it didn't make him a better cop, did it?' said Harry.

John shook his head. 'No, it wasn't the right game

for him. Last I heard he was selling pensions.'

Harry's face turned serious. 'If it wasn't for you, he would be pushing up daisies.'

John shrugged. 'The lad was careless walking in and expecting that mob to down tools and wait their turn to be cuffed. They would have thought nothing of hitting him over the head with an adjustable wrench.'

'But they didn't do that to you, did they? And you know why that was, don't you?'

John looked across to the bar and then back to Harry. 'Go on, Sherlock, spill the beans.'

'Because you have presence, John, just like the gaffer. In your vernacular, it's why people don't fuck with you.'

'So why are we sent to France to chase ghosts?' asked John.

'Do you need me to spell that out?' asked Harry.

John moved uncomfortably on his seat and took a draught of beer in lieu of an answer.

'Are you forgetting that you want to quit?' asked Harry. 'The gaffer is worried that if you walk, he'll lose the rest of the team.'

John put his glass on the table and sat back in his seat. 'He can't stall me forever.'

'He's not trying to stall you – he's trying to give you a cognitive gap.'

John looked confused. 'You'll need to translate that into something I understand.'

'Thinking time to process whether leaving the force is what you really want. We're under fire from all sides. Government cuts, the woke brigade, and you're not the only one in the department reeling from the aftershocks of Vlatko. In all my years of policing, I've never felt so unloved by all and sundry. We always put up with crap, didn't we? But we stuck it out for the wee guy; for the man, woman or child who had no one else to turn to. Now our people are wondering whether it's worth the candle. We need someone to rally around and help us re-find our purpose.'

'Is that not what you and the gaffer are paid for?' asked John.

Harry shook his head. 'Jack spends most of his time fending off the braided uniforms that sit above us, and people only come to me to get their expenses signed off and say, "Sorry, I've broken my mobile device. Can I have a new one, please?" It's you they look to when they're trying to figure out if the crap we take is worth it. It's you who gives them confidence when they're standing at the door of some shit-hole flat wondering what awaits them on the other side. And it's your experience and intuition we depend on when a case is hanging on a wing and a prayer. Look who Mathilde called into play when trying to figure out what the body of a young woman was doing in the Arve. She's a seasoned officer, John. She can read the signs. As I said, our team needs you.'

John's face tightened. 'What if I don't have it in me anymore? What then?'

'You have it in you, John. It's who you are.'

Their attention was drawn to Knox entering the foyer.

If John and Harry had been trying to keep his visit discreet, it was in vain. The barman called over, 'Salut Knox,' and Knox returned a friendly high wave.

Knox pulled up a seat opposite the officers and looked at them one at a time.

'Are you two alright?' he asked, seeing their downbeat expressions.

'We were just discussing something,' said Harry.

Knox glanced at his watch. 'Listen, it's getting late, so I need to be quick. Cal and the girls are outside. What did you want to ask?' he said as he unzipped his down jacket.

Harry cleared his throat. 'It's just a bit of local knowledge we're after.'

Knox stared across at the bar, let out a sigh, and then returned to the officers. 'The best place to start is the Office du Tourisme. It's in the Place du Triangle de l'Amitié. They'll give you all the local knowledge you need. Now, as I said, I've got stuff happening.'

He stood up and looked down at John and Harry sitting in silence. 'You two are in the shit, aren't you?'

John started to explain but Knox was in no mood to hear it. 'Cut the crap or I'm walking out of here.'

'Just sit down a minute,' said John, beckoning him back with his hand.

Knox hesitated, then slowly retook his seat.

John leant slightly forward to emphasise discretion. 'You're right, Knox. We're struggling with this one. On the face of it, there's no material evidence to say Freya's death was anything other than an accident. However ...'

'However, you're getting bad karma, right?' said Knox with an expression to say he'd thought as much all along.

'Exactly,' agreed Harry, uncomfortable knowing Freya's death had shifted from his material world of facts to the ephemeral domain of cosmic justice.

'What do you want from me?' asked Knox.

Harry waited for John to take the lead.

'What I'm about to tell you must go no further,' said John.

'Go on,' said Knox.

'Freya's mother has been told there were traces of cocaine on her daughter's clothes.'

Knox sat back in his seat and appeared to relax. 'That's no big deal. I mean in the UK there's even coke in the drinking water, right?'

John ignored Knox's flippant reply. 'We have the name of someone who mixes in similar circles to Freya and is known to buy the drug,' said John. 'But we don't know who this person is.'

'And you don't want to ask Poirot?'

Harry shifted uncomfortably in his seat and muttered, 'Something like that.'

'Don't tell me, you're going rogue,' said Knox. 'Go on, then. Give me the name.'

'It's someone they call Adonis: a man presumably.'

Knox looked incredulous, then let out a loud laugh and clapped his hands, drawing the few eyes that there were from around the room.

'Keep it down,' said John, but Knox didn't seem bothered and leant in, encouraging Harry and John to come closer. 'You're having a laugh, right?'

'No, we're deadly serious. Do you know him?' John asked.

'Yes, and so do you. He'll have made sure of that.'

'I don't think so,' said John.

'Adonis is that supremacist-looking fucker who runs through Cham each evening with gullible groupies in tow. Mostly American girls who've yet to figure out that he's a fake and dangerous fucker. He gets a bad rap in the valley for being pushy – taking things further than girls want to go. The concept of affirmative consent seems alien to him. But it's late in the season and word is out so his fuck-fest is nearing an end.'

'That's something,' said Harry.

Knox looked sceptical. 'To my mind, it makes him doubly dangerous.'

'What's his real name?' asked John.

'Jaeger Schmidt. He and Ombre are Heinz von Kesler's so-called athletes. Adonis is a freerider. Those in the know say he can't ski for shit and he's little more than Kesler's flunky.

'Whose von Kesler?' asked John.

'A German dude who has an uber-chalet up Argentière way. Adonis acts as his bitch, recruiting the anointed for parties at the chalet: young blonde tops mostly. He has a business in Germany that manufactures slop he passes off as an energy drink.'

John was keen to know more about Jaeger

Schmidt.

'I think he's from Bavaria,' said Knox. 'Apparently, he flunked university.'

'What was he studying?'

'Medicine, I think. This is his second season in Chamonix. Last year he was a regular ski bum, albeit an arrogant fucker. Then von Kesler appropriated him, and he disappeared up the valley. That's when rumours started to fly.'

'Rumours?'

'Yeah, rumours. Coke-fuelled sex parties and all that shit. But you never know how much of it is hype – the anointed trying to big-up their scene.'

'Is Ombre also a skier?' asked John.

'Nah, he gets off on paraponting. One of the guys you see floating overhead with a bright wing parachute. He's into extreme stuff like jumping off the Midi. They're quite different characters. Adonis is a control freak whilst Ombre is a fucking wild man. If you want to see them in action, go to the Festival des Sports de Montagne on Sunday.'

'What's Ombre's real name?' asked John.

'Arthur Roux – which is one hell of a dumb-ass name for a Frenchman.'

Harry nodded in agreement but John looked confused, so Knox helped him out. 'The French have a hard time pronouncing "th". It turns into "v". Feathers comes out as fevvers which sounds kind of cute, but when it comes to your name … It's probably why my mum went for Knox: both Frenchies and Brits can get their tongues around it.'

Harry elaborated. 'The French don't have "th" as

a distinct phoneme.'

But John had heard enough. 'Yes, OK. I get the point,' he said. 'Is there anything else you know about what goes on up there?'

'Only that you want to tread carefully with that fuck von Kesler and his hangers-on.'

'Why's that?' asked John.

He could see Knox seeking an answer that wasn't forthcoming.

'I just get the feeling their whole scene is bad news.'

'Just one more question,' said John. 'Is ketamine prevalent here?'

Knox's face dropped. 'Not to my knowledge. I mean, if you're talking ket, you're talking hard-core, are you not?'

'You are,' said John. 'Thanks for your time, Knox.'

Knox stood up and zipped his jacket closed, and John took out his wallet. 'Let me give you something to buy yourself and the others a drink.'

Knox looked down on him with a mixed expression of disdain and disappointment and shook his head. 'That's the whole problem, isn't it? Everything comes down to money. Cal and I are speaking to you for Freya, not to make a fast buck from her death.'

'I'm sorry, I didn't mean to be disrespectful,' said John.

Knox gave a slight nod. 'Apology accepted.'

Harry looked searchingly at Knox and then asked the question he had had hanging since they first met.

'Knox, you don't have to answer this if you don't want to, but you seem angry with the world. Is it because of what happened to your friend, Connor?'

Knox returned a hard stare 'What do you know about Connor?'

'Nothing. Only that Cal mentioned him in the bar.'

Knox shook his head. 'It's not about Connor and I'm not angry. I'm disappointed.'

'With what?' asked John.

'With this shit-show of a society that we've inherited. Now I need to go.'

They watched Knox walk out onto the street, and as he did, Cal, Zoe and Kim appeared around him like disciples.

'What do you make of him?' asked Harry.

'He's an odd lad, but I like him. He sees through the bullshit and tells it as it is,' said John. 'And like Florent, he has principles: a rare thing these days.'

'Agreed. And what do you make of these Adonis and von Kesler characters?'

John's mind trolled through a career's worth of lowlife. With each, there had invariably been a chink of hope. Something that could never be termed redemption, but a hint that buried deep within was a flicker of humanity. All except one man: Vlatko. John knew that given a second chance to go after Vlatko, all the talk of retirement would be put on hold.

His face hardened with a resolve that Harry hadn't seen in him for a while. 'If Knox's description is accurate, I'd say Adonis is a narcissist:

pathologically self-centred and acutely dangerous to anyone who gets in his orbit. And the fact that he dabbled in medicine rings alarm bells. If he's acting as a flunky, what kind of person does that make von Kesler? Could they be involved with Lucie's death?'

Harry leant forward. 'That's something we can't ignore, John, but we need to stay focused on what we are here for, verifying Freya's cause of death.'

'I am staying focused, and I'd put money on Adonis being connected and by implication, von Kesler, also,' said John. 'The cocaine link is tenuous at best, and I know you favour facts. But there's veracity to a good hunch – even if that sounds contradictory.'

'There's nothing in Freya's autopsy report to indicate a sexual angle and we can't approach Adonis directly. However, if he's linked to von Kesler, perhaps we could start with him?' suggested Harry

'That might be a battle too far with Petit,' said John.

'If it is, and he tries to send us home, then unless we can think of another way, we'll be forced to use our plan of last resort and hope it works.'

Saturday

'She's invited both of us, Harry. Not just me,' said John, rereading Mathilde's text message.

Harry looked thoughtful. 'Listen, John. I've booked my ticket for the Midi, and as polite as Madame La Croix is being, I think it's you she's invited for lunch. But if you have doubts, you can excuse yourself by saying you had already agreed to accompany me. The second cable car is breathtaking. One thousand five hundred metres of what feels like a near-vertical ascent above a precarious north face. You wonder how they engineer such things.'

'Good try, Harry, but it couldn't be any worse than another tongue-lashing from Madame Le Croix.'

Harry looked mortified. 'You'll certainly get grilling if you call her that. It's La Croix – feminine. Le Croix is masculine. The French are pedantic about these things. A bit like us Scots being called English.'

'As bad as that?' asked John.

'Perhaps worse,' replied Harry. 'But I don't think she intends to rough you up again. I think she respects you. Perhaps she wants to talk about the case or offer an apology.'

'What about Pierre? If this invite is behind his back and he gets wind of it ...'

'Mathilde is an adult. She can invite whoever she likes unless she's been told otherwise,' said Harry. 'But I wouldn't talk shop unless she brings it up and I would keep off the subject of von Kesler. We can broach that officially on Monday. Before I leave for the Midi, I'm going to email Sheila and ask her and the team to run a few discreet background checks on our principal players. She likely won't get to it until Monday, but the sooner we have some intel the better.'

**

John waited outside the hotel as he'd been instructed to. As each car approached, he evaluated the likelihood of it being Mathilde's. The Porsches, Maserati's and Ferraris of which there were plenty, and usually with Swiss or Italian number plates, were dismissed.

Then there were the legions of diesel-devouring people carriers: Citroens and Peugeots seemed to be the French family chariot of choice. But again, they just didn't seem particularly 'Mathilde'.

So, what might she drive?

He put his money on an affordably priced sports car – a Mazda MX-5 perhaps, or a Renault GTI.

A faded mustard Renault Clio with a blowing exhaust approached; the type of car that in the 80s

Papa would have bought Nicole for her eighteenth birthday. Judging by the battered bodywork, it had spent its subsequent years jostling Parisian taxis as they circled the Arc de Triomphe.

The Clio swung into the drop-off area in front of the hotel and tooted its horn. Mathilde got out wearing snow boots and jeans with a matching denim jacket. She had wrapped a long loose-weave woollen scarf around her neck, and as seemed to be the norm, her large sunglasses rested on her head.

The concierge gestured for her to move on, but whatever feminine charm she engaged worked, and the car stayed where it was.

'Madame La Croix,' said John, as he approached her.

She brushed it off with a guttural sound that only a French woman would be capable of. 'It's the weekend. Call me Mathilde.'

He smiled, and as if to start over offered a hand. 'Nice to meet you, Mathilde. I'm John.'

Proving him wrong again, she ignored his hand, leant forward, and kissed him lightly on each cheek. She smelt good – like a sophisticated floral bouquet layered with notes of wood and musk.

She took out her iPhone and looked at something on it.

'John, you'd better check your pockets.'

'Why?'

'Just check.'

He went through the pockets of his parka and then lifted his palms upwards and shook his head. 'I'm clean.'

'May I?' she asked.

'Be my guest. I've nothing sharp on my person,' he said like a suspect being taken into custody.

Mathilde checked his pockets with the diligence of a probationary officer undertaking their final Tulliallan assessment: patting down, dipping into pockets and checking underarms and garment hems and seams until she found what she was looking for.

'You know what this is, don't you?' she said, holding up a small, tagged disc she had taken from an internal pocket of his coat.

'It's an Air Tag,' said John. 'Where the hell did that come from, and why?'

She shrugged. 'It will be Pierre. He's paranoid. Harry will have one as well.'

'I'll call and tell him,' said John.

'Why? Is he going anywhere he shouldn't?' asked Mathilde.

'He's taking the cable car up the Midi.'

'That's fine. You, on the other hand, are coming to my house. I don't see why I should share my private life with Pierre.'

'Indeed not.'

'Come. I need to buy ingredients from the market for lunch,' she said, grabbing his arm and pulling him along.

The Saturday market was situated in a large communal space close to the hotel. From a distance, it looked like a bustling ramshackle mélange of people, stalls and vans. Each stall was set with a folding table loaded with produce and sheltered by either a large parasol or a colourful heavy-duty awning supported by a collapsible steel frame. The merchants' names and trades were written in various scripts on either the awning, vehicle or a name board propped close by. Most of the produce was fresh: loose vegetables, meat, cured hams, saucisson and pâté, artisan bread, numerous varieties of craft cheese and dainty patisseries, all under the glare of the spectacular mountain scenery. A few stalls carried locally produced honey, wine and herbs.

John could see that as well as being a place to shop, it was also a social venue. Traders called out to each other and took the time to chat with their customers.

Mathilde led the way through the crowd, stopping to talk with her favourite stallholders and inspect their wares: feeling the ripeness of fruit and vegetables in her hand, tasting a piece of cheese and carefully selecting what she wanted.

Stallholders watched keenly for her approval. They addressed her as Madame La Croix, and in return she replied with madame or monsieur, leaving John wondering whether he had misunderstood the whole French name thing.

He offered to carry the bags and when they were finished, he put them into the back of the Clio and climbed aboard, slamming the door several times before it caught.

Mathilde pulled a U-turn into the traffic and as John tried unsuccessfully to fasten his seatbelt he asked her, 'Does this car have an MOT?'

'I don't understand. What is an MOT?' asked

Mathilde.

'It doesn't matter,' he said.

It felt emancipating leaving town with Mathilde in her clapped-out car: reminiscent of the summer when he left school and he and his mates would chip in for petrol and spend the evenings driving around Midlothian squeezed into one of their cohort's tired XR2.

Joining the police had ended it all with the feeling he had somehow sold out to the other side. Now, the crippling insurance premiums heaped on young drivers had killed the freedoms his generation had taken for granted. He thought of Cal, Knox, Zoe and Kim and admired the effort they were making to live the dream, although, as Freya had shown, it came with risk.

He turned his attention to Mathilde. 'What did you do with that Air Tag?' he asked.

With a yelp of joy, she blasted the horn. 'Tonight it will be in a crémerie near Clermont Ferrand. At least that was the address on the trailer,' she said, seeming to take glee from this rebellious act against her colleague.

It was the first time John had seen Mathilde laugh.

Her phone rang, but she ignored it and it rang off.

'If it's important, they will ring again. People always do,' she said.

Having witnessed Mathilde's laissez-faire attitude to driving John rather hoped they wouldn't, and fortunately they didn't.

Mathilde followed a snow-lined road signposted

to Argentière. Shortly after crossing a railway line, they entered a wooded area. She turned sharply right, and dropping into second gear, they climbed a steep winding road that had been cut through the snow. The vertical walls on either side had been scored with circular marks by a rotary snow blower. Despite its winter tyres, the Clio's front wheels scrambled for traction on a surface of churned snow and grit, but Mathilde took it in her stride.

'This end of the valley is higher, so we have much more snow than Chamonix,' she said. 'It's even worse near Argentière. Some chalets there had to be dug out.'

John gripped the door grab handle as a Fiat Panda flew past them in the opposite direction, but Mathilde wasn't fazed as she gave them a friendly wave. 'They don't use much salt now,' she said. 'It's bad for the environment.'

'A couple of snowflakes and central Scotland comes to a stop,' said John, in awe of how people thrived in their niveous environment.

'The local people are used to it,' said Mathilde. 'I'm a Méridionale, but we have to adapt, don't we, John?'

The road levelled, and they came out of the woods into a hamlet of old chalets basking in the sun. A large digger with a huge front bucket and heavy chains wrapped around its tyres was parked at one side. John could see it had cleared all the minor roads that linked the chalets, heaping the snow in nearby fields.

Mathilde pulled up beside a modest chalet built

with dark timber. It had a small terrace in front, facing down the valley and catching the midday sun. 'I rent this place from a Parisian family. It was their maison de campagne, but now the parents are old and the children are focused on their careers so don't want to come here. Perhaps when they have children of their own, that will change. For now, the parents are happy to rent it to me. I think my being a gendarme gives them peace of mind.'

John was about to get out of the car when Mathilde stopped him.

'John, it's Saturday and I don't like taking work home. Let's sit here for a moment: I have an update on Lucie.'

'What have you heard?' he asked, switching to his familiar detective mode.

'Our cantonal police partners in Pâquis keep close to what's happening in the red-light district. A sex worker has come forward and claimed that a young woman known as Lucie had talked about an offer of work that would pay off her debt of bondage.'

'Did this person say what the work was or where?'

Mathilde shook her head. 'No, but it must have been a considerable sum if she thought it would enable her freedom. More likely she was being lied to – hope can blind us to reality.'

Mathilde took out her phone and opened a picture. 'The cantonal police sent me this. It's a picture taken off the dark web from what those who control her call a talent portfolio. People – men presumably – go there to select their fantasy woman for whatever perversion they have in mind.'

It was a photo of a young girl with straight shoulder-length hair wearing a white peasant shirt with long puffy sleeves, and a round collar trimmed in lace and buttoned at the top. She was a pretty country girl in front of a field of wheat, smiling at the camera, the arm of a parent or relative around her shoulder.

John took the phone, zoomed and stared into the girl's face – a lively face keen to explore the life ahead of her. 'She looks so innocent,' he said. 'That gentle smile she's carrying …'

'It's what I thought,' said Mathilde. 'That look of innocence is what her abusers are touting. Do you think she and our Lucie are one and the same person?'

'It's hard to say. Our Lucie's features are similar, but she looks older than the girl in the picture. But that's to be expected from the life she lived. Would you mind giving me a copy of the photograph?' John asked.

'Why do you need that?'

'Because she matters,' said John.

Without saying more, Mathilde took her phone and pinged John the photo.

She slipped her phone back into her pocket. 'I'm going through to Geneva on Monday morning to meet with the cantonal police. Our lab is pushing through Lucie's DNA results and the Pâquis police are looking for something from the girl in the picture to match it against. I'll keep you informed.'

'Yes, do that. And if I can help in any way …'

'Then I know where to find you.'

They got out of the car and a large fluffy cat
sauntered past. 'She's feral,' said Mathilde. 'I call
her Framboise and feed her, but I can't pick her up.
She scratches.'

Mathilde held out the back of her hand for John to
see a scar bearing testimony to her words. 'Come,
John. I have a job for you whilst I prepare lunch.'

Mathilde equipped John with a pair of the
owner's snow boots and a large aluminium snow
shovel and he set to work clearing a path from the
chalet back door to a small mazot at the end of the
garden. At first, it felt like an unrewarding task, but
soon John's coat was off, and he was refining his
technique from the use of arm muscles and bent
elbows to a straight-armed shoulder swing.
Something satisfying emerged from seeing the
immediate fruits of his labour. Shovel, shift, shape
and forwards: forging a tidy path through the snow.
Not like police work, where quick results were
seldom seen beyond the jejunity of dishing out
traffic tickets.

The more John shovelled the more familiar the
task seemed until his thoughts arrived back to the
time of his coal miner father, and how he had spent
hours stooped over in the darkness and stifling heat
of the mine gallery – backbreaking toil shovelling
spilt coal onto a conveyor or into a low wagon for
extraction. He recalled how in winter his father
would leave before sunrise and return after dark
having never seen daylight.

Yet the man never complained of his lot. Never. Even when black lung turned the tower of strength he had been into a sickly specimen gasping for air from a bottle beside his hospital chair.

'Make me proud, son,' his father had whispered, 'and look after our family.'

John stopped, looked to the mountain and wondered whether he had fulfilled the dying man's wish. *I've tried, I really have.* But what would his father think of him quitting? *Would that make him proud?*

John wiped his eyes with the back of his hand. 'Are you OK?' called Mathilde.

'Just taking a breather,' he replied, drawing in the crisp air and gazing out across the snow-topped forest.

'Don't rest for too long. Lunch will soon be ready.'

He gave Mathilde a wave and got back to his task with a renewed appreciation for his father's sacrifice and emerging doubts about his own path.

Mathilde had set a small table on the balcony. 'Beer or wine?' she asked.

'A beer would be nice.'

She brought out a glass of Kronenbourg for John and an opened bottle of chilled white wine from which she poured herself a generous glass.

John watched Mathilde use two wooden implements to turn the salad in a large bowl, lifting it gently and letting it settle again.

'It's best to do this last thing,' she said.

'Otherwise, the oil cooks the lettuce. But perhaps in winter, it's less important.'

Once it was tossed to her satisfaction, Mathilde served. 'I would normally use anchovies but thought you would prefer feta cheese.'

'It's delicious,' said John, tasting the mustard, olive oil, onion, salt and pepper dressing and biting into a piece of freshly baked baguette. 'For us, salad is an under-ripe tomato chopped in quarters, a couple of wilting lettuce leaves and a few slices of cucumber. You'd get a sachet of salad cream if you were lucky.'

Mathilde made another unusual sound that John took to be condescension. 'The British don't know how to eat.'

He laughed. 'Perhaps not, but I think for us it's less about the food and more about who is providing it. Looking back, I can't say my mother was a great cook, but we always appreciated what she put on the table.'

'You have siblings?' asked Mathilde.

'A brother in Australia, another in Glasgow, and a sister in England.'

'And your mother and father, are they still with you?' she asked.

John shook his head. 'No. My father died when I was very young. My mother brought us up on her own. She passed away a few years ago.'

'I'm sorry,' said Mathilde. 'My father is gone also, but my mother is still alive.'

'Where does she live?' asked John.

'Just outside Nice. She is still in the house I was

raised in.'

Mathilde stood up and lifted the plates.

'Let me help you,' said John.

'No. You're my guest. Sit here and enjoy the view.'

She returned wearing oven mitts and holding a Pyrex casserole. 'This is a Provencal recipe. Tomates Farcies, or as you would say, tomatoes stuffed with mince and herbs. You can only cook it with fresh ingredients.'

'What would happen if they weren't fresh?' he asked out of curiosity.

'That's inconceivable, although this isn't the season for tomatoes. These are Spanish.'

Mathilde served John two stuffed tomatoes and offered him wine. 'Just a touch,' he said.

She did as he requested and then refilled her glass and lifted it. 'Santé.'

As they ate, Mathilde told him of her love of cooking. 'It takes me back to the South of France.'

'It's delicious, as is the whole meal. Thank you, Mathilde.'

'It's nice to have time at home, and company,' she said.

John told her about Edinburgh, and as he talked about all the things that made it the vibrant, cosmopolitan city it was, he felt a love for the place he called home, and a desire to sell its virtues. It was as if, when it came to Edinburgh, he fulfilled the role of protector, as the guardian was presumed to be from his fanal atop the Midi.

'It sounds wonderful,' said Mathilde.

'It is. You should come and visit.'

'Perhaps,' she said.

It wasn't the answer that John had hoped for, but what did he expect? Only three days before she was hurling insults and he was storming off.

Mathilde cleared their plates and went through to the kitchen. As she opened the door, John could hear a song playing on the radio she had been listening to. He didn't understand the words, but he could feel the emotion they carried.

Mathilde returned with a crème caramel she had made the previous evening and a cafetiere.

'Who's the singer?' he asked.

'Charles Aznavour.'

'Ah, I've heard of him. It's a nice song.'
Mathilde agreed. 'Yes, he sings of love, lost youth and nostalgia, but also optimism for the future. In France, we have a strong lifelong attachment to our singers and musicians. It feels as though they understand our hopes and fears.'

'Like a friend?'

'Something like that,' said Mathilde. 'But I think you would need to be French to appreciate it.'

Mathilde served the coffee and as John sipped from a demitasse and returned it to its saucer, they talked about relationships.

'Do you have a partner?' asked Mathilde.

John shook his head. 'No, I don't. There was a time when I got closer to people, but I think I just lost the will. The problem with being single is that you always have time for more work, so it ends up being your sole purpose in life. What about you,

Mathilde?'

Her expression suddenly changed, and John knew he had touched something raw. 'I'm sorry. I shouldn't pry,' he said.

Framboise jumped onto his lap and Mathilde knocked the table, trying to get to her.

'Be careful,' said Mathilde.

'She's OK, aren't you Framboise?' said John, stroking the cat gently as she settled on his lap.

'She likes you,' said Mathilde, topping up her glass from the last of the wine in the bottle. 'Cats know people. They can read them. It's why she hates me.'

John kept his eyes on the cat. She was purring, enjoying his attention.

'There's something I want to tell you,' said Mathilde.

John nodded slowly. 'Ah, I wondered why you had invited me here,' he said in a low, calm voice. 'I was fairly certain it wasn't for my good looks, quick wit and repartee, and I think the snow clearing could have waited a little longer. If it's to apologise, you don't need to.'

She gave a little laugh. 'You're a handsome man, John. You must have been told that?'

He blushed and took another sip of coffee as a distraction.

'It's not to apologise,' said Mathilde. 'I was in a bad mood on Tuesday. I had been drinking the previous evening, so it's to be expected. I have a problem with alcohol.'

John let out a little laugh, which made the cat

look up and then settle again.

'To be honest, Mathilde, I hadn't noticed. I come from Scotland where it's not unusual to have more than we should. What is it you wanted to tell me?'

Mathilde looked far away and then back at John. 'John, I too have something that haunts me.'

She lifted her sunglasses so he could see her eyes. 'I'm responsible for a colleague's death.'

He looked into her eyes, wracked with anguish. 'What happened?'

'A year ago, in my previous post, I planned a raid on a gang importing a line of drugs from Syria, through North Africa to Marseille: the distribution point for Europe.'

'Captagon?' asked John.

'Yes, you know it?'

'I do. It's a frighteningly addictive amphetamine that some say is fuelling the Syrian war. It's making its way into Scotland.'

Mathilde continued her tragic story. 'I had planned the raid meticulously. The team knew exactly what to do, but I missed something, a detail that however hard I try, I can't find. On the day, when things were not as they should have been, I hesitated and one of our team was shot dead. He was "mon chef," my chief, Thierry Dubois.'

'And you blame yourself?' asked John.

Mathilde nodded and looked hard at him. 'Thierry was also my lover.'

She pulled her sunglasses back down to hide her eyes and stared out at the Aiguilles Rouges on the opposite side of the valley. 'He was married,' she said, keeping her eyes on the mountains.

'I'm sorry,' said John. 'And I think I understand how you feel.'

'I hoped you would,' said Mathilde. 'There was an inquiry, and although the report said I wasn't to blame, there's always a stigma attached to these things. Now I'm trying to hold myself together and work out how something that had been so well planned could go so disastrously wrong. I was transferred to Chamonix, but won't be here for long. They will find a way to get rid of me.'

John lifted the cat and put her gently on the ground. 'You might not find your answer, Mathilde. Sometimes the best we can do is forgive ourselves.'

She shook her head. 'It isn't that easy. That's why I never carry a gun now.'

'You would use it if you had to,' said John.

Mathilde nodded. 'That's what I'm afraid of. When I'm down and think about Thierry's death, that's exactly what I'm afraid of.'

She looked into the distance at faraway memories and then returned to John. 'But for now, I'm going to find out who did those horrible things to Lucie. I'm going to be her final voice and see justice served for her.'

It would have been easy for John to say, 'Yes, of course, that's your job.' But they both knew it ran far deeper. Lucie's death was not just an abomination, it was a challenge to see whether Mathilde still had what it took; a challenge that John recognised in himself.

She lifted her sunglasses and wiped the corners of

her eyes. 'What about you, John? Do you feel the need to atone?'

He took a deep breath and slowly blew it out. 'I'm at a loss as to what to think or feel, Mathilde. Before coming to France, I thought I had it all figured in an envelope. But now …'

There were no words necessary: John knew that she understood.

As he looked across the table at the tortured soul trying to pick herself up he saw someone quite different to the woman who had vented her self-loathing on him. And with her show of compassion and vulnerability, her beauty had returned.

Sunday

Antoine ushered John and Harry to a quiet part of the restaurant, away from the noise of nagging parents telling silent children to put phones away.

They took their seats, and with one hand behind his back, Antoine filled their cups, releasing the earthy/caramel notes of gourmet French coffee.

I could get used to this thought John, appreciating the welcome change from a teaspoonful of instant chucked into a mug before dashing out.

Antoine looked over to the breakfast buffet where a group of Koreans, some already dressed head to toe in sun-protective attire, were working their way down, assiduously inspecting and discussing each of the gastronomic offers.

'You can order from the menu if you prefer,' he said.

'We're not in a hurry,' replied John.

Antoine gave a knowing smile. 'Le temp libre est précieux,' he said before excusing himself to deal with what appeared to be a well-heeled Italian family.

'What did he say?' John asked.

'He said, "Free time is precious". It's a very

French way of viewing life, and I have to admit it's an appealing one.'

John thought back to the previous day with Mathilde, sharing her lunch table and thoughts on life. Even with her inner turmoil, she seemed to understand life's priorities. He looked around at the family tables, now settled into their breakfast and enjoying time together. 'I get the feeling that the French and Italians are more work-to-live than us.'

'No doubt about it,' said Harry. 'And they're prepared to fight for those beliefs. Look what happened when the state tried to mess with their pensions, whilst we get told to work until we drop and suck it up. Let's get breakfast and then we can swap notes.'

They waited for the Koreans to move on and cobbled together an adapted version of a full Scottish breakfast: streaky bacon, poached eggs, a variety of sausages, etc.

Once seated again, John looked at the hotchpotch on his plate. 'Perhaps we should surrender and go continental,' he said.

'Never,' replied Harry in mock defiance.

John let out a half-laugh before assuming a serious expression. 'Are we ready to share thoughts?'

Harry bit into a spicy merguez sausage, tasted it then looked curiously at what was left on the fork. 'Sure. I'll start by saying this case isn't what I expected.'

John sighed and nodded. 'I have that same feeling.'

'Did Mathilde say anything yesterday?' asked Harry.

John shook his head. 'Not about Freya. But word has come through from the Swiss cantonal police about Lucie. She was offered some sort of life-changing deal before her death.'

'What kind of deal?'

'That's not clear, but Mathilde said the word on the street is that Lucie hoped to buy her way out of whatever debt she carried. Mathilde has been sent a photograph.'

John took out his phone and showed Harry the picture. 'If the girl in the picture is Lucie – and that's still to be confirmed – she appears to come from a simple farming background.'

'I didn't get a close look at Lucie,' said Harry. 'You think, like the women in Edinburgh, this wasn't the first deal Lucie had been offered?'

John put his knife and fork down, sat back, and visibly paled. 'That's exactly what I think. I think she was sex trafficked and nobody puts their name forward for that. The deals they offer these women are never what they appear. The deal Lucie was offered would be another form of manipulation, in this instance cynically using the last thing she had – hope – against her. Mathilde has a lot on her mind: issues carried over from a past case, but she's determined to see justice done. First thing tomorrow she's going to Geneva.'

John locked eyes with Harry and Harry knew exactly what he was thinking.

'No, John. You can't go with her. It's not what

we're here for.'

'I think it is,' said John.

Harry cleaned his glasses to signal that he was about to say something profound.

'We've worked together a long time, haven't we?'

John looked to one side but didn't disagree.

'I think we make a good team,' continued Harry. 'And I think one of our strengths is that you know when to push me forward and I know when to hold you back. We need to stay focused on what we're here for.'

'And if Freya and Lucie are connected?'

'That would be a different matter. Now get back to your breakfast whilst I share some insights with you.'

Relinquishing, John picked up his knife and fork and Harry continued with his prelude.

'A case like this looks straightforward, and I think that's the premise under which the French are working. It's human nature to attribute a known cause to a familiar event. If a teenager falls off a Spanish balcony after a night on the town, it's easy to categorise it as a misadventure.'

'Cognitive bias,' said John. 'Drawing preformed conclusions from a familiar data set. If nobody is looking for evidence to the contrary, people will see what they expect to see. But in this case, we're dealing with the unfamiliar, so we're asking questions that the French might not.'

Harry nodded his agreement. 'And when we do, rather than tying up loose ends, we create more questions.'

John sipped his coffee and then spoke. 'I still can't fathom why the gendarmes at the helipad took such an interest in Knox and Cal. Were they as clumsy as Pierre seems to think, or did someone put them up to it? If they did, then it begs the questions who and why?'

'Perhaps it was Petit,' said Harry. 'Pierre seems to think the man is trying to make a name for himself.'

John looked unsure. 'I don't think Petit's as smart as we're giving him credit for. He's an obnoxious little so-and-so, and wants us out of the way, but trying to intimidate? He's too much of a windbag for that.'

'Maybe, as Mathilde thought, he believes we're a couple of hicks prepared to mindlessly sign off on whatever he puts in front of us,' said Harry.

'I don't think Mathilde ever thought that,' said John. 'I think she was trying to provoke us. A cry for help. It fits with what she told me yesterday.'

'It's common with people going through emotional distress,' said Harry.

Harry put down his knife and fork and opened the folder he had brought with him. 'There's something I want to show you, John. Something that turns this whole business on its head.'

'Go on,' said John.

'It was when I was watching skiers queuing for the telepherique, and at the top leaving to ski the Vallee Blanche. I knew there was a pattern, but it was so obvious at first I didn't see it.'

He opened the folder and handed John three

photos. They were shots Astrid had given them of Freya, taken at different times and in different places, but always in winter and with her skis. With Freya dead, they were the type of picture that in Scotland would be pinned to the wall of an incident room: human photos to remind the inquiry team why they were going to the extraordinary lengths they were.

Those images were fixed in the officers' minds long after justice had been served: a back catalogue of lives stuck where they were cruelly cut short. For John and Harry, Freya had become such a portrait: she would now always be the pretty girl with shoulder-length blonde hair, fine Nordic features, blue eyes and always smiling at them.

John looked through the photographs – one after the other – but said nothing.

Harry handed him the next batch – four photos of Freya captured from the video they reviewed: the bottom station queue, boarding the telepherique, the middle station and exiting at the top.

Again, John looked through them. He reverted to the first batch to cross-check something and then returned to the recent batch.

'Bloody hell, Harry,' he said, going through them again. 'Did you see the same pattern with other skiers?'

Harry nodded. 'Exactly the same. I wanted to be sure, so I watched a number of them progressing through as Freya had.'

John looked at Harry. 'Except it wasn't Freya.'

'No, I don't believe it was. Skis are heavy and

awkward damned things, so people carry them in their dominant hand. Freya was right-handed. Whoever that is taking the telecabin is left-handed.'

'Left-handed, but dressed like Freya, carrying the same type of skis as Freya and using her lift pass,' said John.

He looked warily at Harry. 'Are we thinking the same about who that person might be?'

'Amy is left-handed,' said Harry. 'We saw that when she grabbed her phone off Pierre and when I passed her my card.'

'Any theories on how Freya ended up where she did?' asked John.

'We still can't say for sure that she didn't ski to the crevasse, but if she didn't, then indeed, how did she get there? This is a bit of a wild card, but as I came through Chamonix, I noticed a shop offering tandem paraponting.'

John looked questioningly, so Harry elaborated. 'You and an instructor go up a mountain, strap yourselves to one of those wing parachutes we see floating about above the valley and jump off together. The instructor controls the flight. You just take photos and pray that the last few feet go to plan.'

John looked doubtful. 'Is this not getting a little left field?'

'Maybe, but a mosey around Knox's mountain festival wouldn't do any harm.'

'By rights, we should let Pierre know about the photos,' said John. 'Otherwise, it will look as if we're holding back on him. We can speak to him tomorrow, but do you agree that we keep our Amy hunch out of it for now?'

'For now,' said Harry. 'However, Petit might try to shrug us off and send us packing. We'd outstayed our welcome before we arrived.'

'If that happens, then we'll go for plan B, but if he doesn't buy it, then it's "tchao",' said John.

***

They heeded Antoine's advice about wrapping up warm for the mountain and waited patiently for a bus. Ten minutes later, a white bus with a red mountain graphic along the side stopped and opened its doors to reveal a crush of humanity staring out at them. For a moment, John and Harry considered waiting for the next one. But the passengers, with skis held vertically and backpacks at their feet to maximise the space, huddled inwards like emperor penguins incubating eggs over the harsh Arctic winter and John and Harry squeezed onboard.

The doors snapped shut, and the bus set off with passengers swaying in unison as it navigated the circuitous back road to Les Praz and the ski area. Several stops later they alighted and made their way through a carpark of creeping vehicles seeking long-since-taken spaces, to the gondola station.

They bought return tickets and headed up a ramp and through turnstiles to where the gondolas were easing slowly through the boarding bay.

With padded seats and a contemporary shape

dominated by tinted Perspex, the ten-seater cabins were luxurious compared to the standing-room-only telepherique Harry had taken to the top of the Midi the previous day.

Most passengers were skiers, well-versed in the boarding procedure: entering, taking a seat, resting their skis against a high horizontal rail and avoiding eye contact.

John and Harry stepped onboard and sat down. The cabin continued slowly through the station until the doors closed and the overhead carrier reattached to the main cable, whisking them off up the mountain at six metres per second.

Sitting opposite were two other pairs, whom they suspected were Brits. But everyone seemed to have the same idea: keep quiet lest your origin be revealed.

Through chance, John and Harry had backward-facing seats with yet another panoramic view of the valley: this time spanning from Le Tour at one end, through the sweeping vista of the Aiguilles and Mont Blanc and down to Sallanches where their transfer bus had briefly stopped.

John picked out the helipad where they had met Florent, and slightly to the left, the Vallee Blanche, once again reminding him why they were there. All this magnificence suggested an alpine version of Edinburgh. A resplendent distraction in which a malignant minority could carry out their nefarious activities, invisible behind the misbelief that "it could never happen here".

John remembered the motto on his hat badge,

Semper Vigilo – always vigilant – and how the college tutors drummed in the Police (Scotland) Act, 1967: *It shall be the duty of constables of a police force to guard, patrol and watch.*

Edinburgh was a war of attrition: day-to-day policing, relentlessly working to contain, but never able to eliminate, the evils of society. Yet it had felt honourable to be out in all weather, day or night, *Keeping People Safe*. He thought about how those basic tenets had stayed with him through his promotion to CID, and later into Major Investigations.

He looked up to the top of the Midi. *With the guardian now asleep, who will watch over his people? Perhaps it's where we went wrong with Vlatko. We were so obsessed with bringing the man to justice that we lost sight of the victims subjugated by him.*

John thought of Freya and Amy and wondered whether they had taken this cabin together and looked over the valley, wondering what life had in store for them.

He thought of Lucie. What was this life-changing offer that Mathilde said she had received? Was it what brought her to the valley? If so, it would more than likely be tied in with her death. As he scanned the valley, he wondered whether her killer or killers were still here. Her injuries were consistent with some form of extreme sadism exacted on her whilst she was sedated with ketamine. It seemed inconceivable that anyone would sign up for that. Mathilde would now be under pressure, her experience warning her that once a predator gained a taste for such crimes, they were likely to strike again.

Time to think was short as the cabin *thumpitty-thumped* over the last pylon and entered the top station. They exited, squinting in the bright sunlight reflected from all angles off the snow. Harry took out a tube of sun cream, squirted some onto his fingers and offered it to his colleague.

'I'm fine,' said John.

But Harry insisted. 'This isn't Scotland. With your complexion, you'll be like a boiled lobster in ten minutes.' John reluctantly followed Harry's example and rubbed the cream into his face and neck before putting on his sunglasses.

'What now?' asked John, looking around for the action.

Most people were clipping into their ski bindings and heading off to the next chairlift.

From behind a ridge to their right came reverberating rock music and a compere shouting in animated French over a PA system. A crowd were yelling encouragement.

Avoiding the soft snow to their left and skiers to their right, they followed a sign, *Piste de Vitesse*, until a long, steep and perfectly straight piste came into view. Spectators lined either side, many sitting in groups on the snow. A skier set off from the top, crouching into a tuck to gain terminal velocity. They shot through the bottom gate and immediately turned parallel, sending up a plume of snow and looking back at their time frozen on a large digital display. Judging by the conciliatory sighs from the crowd and the skier's woebegone gait, they hadn't set the heather alight.

'Let's take a look,' said Harry, setting off towards the spectacle.

There wasn't much for a layman to see at the bottom except skiers hurtling down at breakneck speed and coming to an abrupt stop. A few didn't get that far, losing control before the bottom, and transforming their wobbly schuss into flailing and tumbling arms, legs, skis and sticks. John was certain they would lie where they fell, but they seemed adept at walking away with only their pride injured.

Someone up the hill chose a lull in the action to make a shrill two-finger whistle. John looked up out of curiosity, but there was no one obvious. He was turning away when another whistle drew him back.

'Is that the twins with Cal and Knox?' he asked.

'It looks like them,' said Harry.

They waved politely back, but now one of the girls was on her feet and beckoning them up the slope.

Knox, Cal and the girls had made themselves comfortable by building a snow platform to sit on. Their packs and a small aluminium shovel were on one side.

Making the most of the sun, they had stripped down to ski trousers, base layers, caps and colourful sunglasses. Zoe's board was pushed at an angle into the snow. Cal was using it as a backrest, and in turn, Zoe was sitting between his knees, resting against him. With his arms wrapped around her, he leant forward and kissed her gently on the side of her head. She snuggled further back to him, making the warmth between them clear to all.

Kim was sitting next to Knox, less intimate, but equally relaxed.

'The two of you looked a bit lost down there,' said Knox. 'Do you fancy a beer?'

Without waiting for a reply, he opened the large cool box beside him and handed out an assortment of drinks.

'Are you sure?' said John, looking at the can of Kronenbourg he had been handed.

'I'm certain, but sit down man, you're blocking the rays.'

Knox pulled two pieces of dense foam from his rucksack and handed them over. 'Use these. They'll keep your bums dry.'

Sitting in the easy company of the young people, listening to their banter, dodging a snowball from Zoe meant for Kim and following Knox's comical commentary of hapless skiers whilst simultaneously cheering them on, John realised that the speed skiing was secondary. The main event was this nascent team spending time together in an environment they loved and free from the tethers of the world.

Knox stood up and surveyed the domain. Cal, Kim and Zoe looked expectantly up at him, trying to elicit a response. But Knox said nothing, and when he retook his seat, they relaxed. John could see that Knox was the "head of the family", and Cal, Kim and Zoe seemed to believe that with him on watch no harm would come to them. But as much as they needed Knox, Knox needed their followership to realise his purpose as their protector.

The dynamics didn't surprise John. He had seen it with his family. Besides the emotional bonds and mutual support, there was the informal role each member adopted. When his father died, his mother had no choice but to become the "head of the family". But the transition from caring mother hadn't sat well with her, and even before he felt capable, a sense of duty demanded that John relieve her of the burden. For John, becoming a police officer was an extension of that call to duty, just as Knox organising the team was his, and one he relished.

Reflecting on his life, John wondered whether this was something else he had got wrong from the start, and rather than his father lumbering him with the constraints of duty, the man had gifted him a meaningful purpose for his life. The chance to help and support others. Antoine's words echoed in John's mind. *To serve is a privilege.*

Knox dipped into the cool box and retrieved a bundle of film-wrapped half-baguettes.

'We have few with saucisson or ham, but only one with goat cheese,' he said. 'It seems the boulangerie had a run on them.'

The girls vied for the goat cheese.

Zoe was adamant. 'I'm the youngest, so I should get to choose.'

'Only by half an hour,' said Kim. 'But being the oldest I should decide.'

As a consolation, Knox carefully handed Kim her second choice, but the others had to work for theirs as he tossed them high in the air. 'The girls are heading home first thing tomorrow, so we thought we'd make a day of it,' he said.

Something over the PA caught Knox's attention, and he turned to John and Harry. 'This should be interesting. Your pal, Adonis, is trying his hand at speed skiing.'

They looked up the slope to the start gate where a tall individual in garish colours was preening and preparing himself. The bleeper sounded, and he was off, down into the tuck, descending the slope and through the finish gate to muted applause.

Cal stayed quiet.

'Wanker,' muttered Knox under his breath.

Kim looked disapproving. 'You shouldn't swear, Knox.'

Knox returned a questioning look. 'Is that a swear word?'

'Well, it's not nice,' she replied.

'Sorry,' he said, trying to look contrite.

As he put his arm around her, drawing her close, and she put her head on his shoulder, John and Harry wondered whether Kim knew half of it when it came to Knox's vocabulary.

Still munching on her baguette, Zoe leant forward and looked across at John.

'We had a competition last night.'

'Oh, and what was that about?' asked John.

'We had to guess what job you two did.'

John nodded slowly. 'And what conclusion did you draw?'

'I thought you were doctors and Kim thought you

were businessmen, but then Knox told us.'

'What did he say we did?' asked John, aware that Knox was now looking evasively out across the valley.

'He said that he didn't believe the girl, Freya, had died in an accident and that he told her mother. He said that you're police officers from Scotland sent to find the truth.'

Harry looked at Knox. 'I suspected that was the case.'

'And?' asked Knox.

'And I think you were right to tell Freya's mother.'

'Good. When we've finished our baguettes, we have chocolate eclairs. The girls each get a whole one and the rest of us share.'

John smiled. It was just the type of thing he would have said as a young man around their family table.

Monday

John and Harry entered the gendarmerie, prepared, if necessary, for a full-on spat with Commandant de Police Jean-Raymond de Petit.

As the previous week progressed, Guillaume hadcontinued to offer a smile and shared stories about his daughter, Émilie, and her gap year experience as an au pair in Manchester. John had asked whether the host family had looked after her well.

'As one of their own,' Guillaume had said. 'I think Émilie was disappointed when it was time to return and resume her studies at the University of Lyon. Now she's a gendarme.'

But today they could see that Guillaume had other things on his mind as he pushed the *livre d'or* over the counter for them to sign.

Harry picked up the pen and was about to make his mark when he saw the small note attached with a paperclip to the top of the page.

We are with you.

Guillaume tapped an agitated finger on the signature line. 'Please sign.'

Harry kept his eyes down, turned his back to the

camera, signed and then stepped aside to let John in. 'Keep your eyes on the page,' he murmured.

John also read the note and signed the page.

'I'll let Lieutenant Lavigne know you're here,' Guillaume said as he withdrew the book.

With any doubt that something was amiss now dispelled, they sat in silence waiting for Pierre.

The door opened and Pierre appeared wearing light woollen trousers and a herringbone tweed jacket. 'Come,' he said, beckoning them through.

As with Guillaume, the relaxed and patient manner with which Pierre carried himself the previous week had evaporated.

He looked wary. 'Commandant de Petit wants to see us immediately,' Pierre said, leading the way up the stairs.

'About anything in particular?' asked John.

Pierre gave an uncertain shake of the head. 'He's been off since Thursday, so who knows?'

Pierre knocked, and Petit barked, '*Entrez.*'

Petit was sitting red-faced behind his desk. To one side was a small China cup of black coffee. From the way his eyes roved the page he was holding, Harry could tell that whatever Petit was looking at only served to keep them waiting, although, from his flighty manner, it seemed he was impatient to address whatever was bothering him.

The three officers stood to attention like schoolboys called into the headmaster's office for a scolding. John and Harry swapped *'Shall we?'* looks, John nodded and in an authoritative voice, Harry went for it.

'Commandant, if you want to speak to us, then speak. Otherwise, we have more useful things to do with our day.'

Petit looked up, raised his fist above his head, and like a petulant child denied an indulgence, he slammed it down onto the desk, sending the coffee cup flying and a good measure of its contents onto what had been a pristine white shirt.

'How dare you,' he shouted in disintegrating English.

Whatever he lacked in stature was now amply compensated for by bulging blood vessels in his neck and forehead and a puffed red face.

John could sense Pierre wince beside him and was momentarily concerned that Petit might have a cardiac arrest, before concluding, *fuck him if he does*.

Unfazed by the theatre, Harry tossed the Air Tag he had found in his clothing onto the desk and fixed Petit with a glare.

'Explain …' he said.

Petit craned his neck forward, and as though examining a curious insect, he studied the device. He looked questioningly at Pierre.

Pierre stepped forward, picked it up and turned it over in his hand. He seemed confused and asked Harry, 'Where did you find this?'

'Tucked into one of my jacket pockets,' Harry replied. 'John found something similar.'

Petit looked again at Pierre for an answer, but Pierre just shrugged. 'I've no idea.'

Petit quickly lost interest in the tags and returned to his purpose. 'Whatever these are, we will sort it out. But the case of the Norwegian girl is now closed.'

John was quick to correct him. 'If you're talking about Freya, she is Swedish, not Norwegian.'

But if Petit thought that mattered, he wasn't prepared to show it. 'We have given you all the information you are entitled to. Anything further can be requested through your office in the UK.'

'Which means what?' asked John.

'Which means you will return to Scotland today.'

John cleared his throat. 'It's not as simple as that. There are still unanswered questions.'

'What unanswered questions?' asked Petit as he sat back in his seat, looked down at his shirt and pulled the coffee-soaked area off his skin.

'Firstly, we have doubts about Freya taking the telepherique.'

'Oh? And where is your evidence?' asked Petit as he gave up the fight with the shirt.

Harry took out a picture and put it on Petit's desk. 'Freya was right-handed. Whoever entered the telepherique was holding their skis in their left hand.'

Petit blew out air through pursed lips and made a quintessentially Gaulish *pewff*. 'That's not evidence. Lieutenant Lavigne will look at it, but you don't need to be here for that.'

'And what about the young woman found in the Arve?' John asked.

Petit turned to Harry. 'Inspector, tell your subordinate to keep out of matters that don't concern him.'

Harry gestured for John to stand down.

Petit then addressed Pierre. 'Lieutenant Lavigne, you will transport these officers to their hotel where they will collect their bags. You will then take them to Geneva airport and make sure they board a plane.'

Harry stood a little taller. 'You do not have the authority to do that, Commandant, and you know it.'

'I have all the authority I need,' said Petit. 'You have been meddling in a case and causing unnecessary distress to the parents of the victim. We were asked to share our findings with you. We have fully complied and now you must go.'

John was unable to contain himself and rejoined the fray. 'Did Freya's mother say we were causing distress, because I'm damned sure her stepfather wouldn't say it with any conviction?'

Petit didn't answer, but from his furtive look, John suspected Sir Hugo had said it, but his wife was unaware.

Harry looked coldly at Petit and held out an envelope containing a folded piece of A4 paper he had printed off that morning at the hotel reception. 'Read this, Commandant. If you have any doubts, contact your people at the Ministère des Affaires Ètrangères. John and I are now attached to the British Consulate in Paris and protected by diplomatic immunity. Are you sure you want to send us packing and trigger a diplomatic incident?'

Petit snatched the envelope, took out and unfolded the piece of paper and read what was written. For a moment, he looked flummoxed and then resorted to the only course of action he saw open to him. 'OUT!' he shouted, getting to his feet and pointing to the door.

Pierre led the way from Petit's office down to his own.

He grabbed his sheepskin jacket and scarf. 'Let's go for a coffee,' he said.

John looked over to Mathilde's desk, but she wasn't there and the monitor was off.

They left the gendarmerie and walked a short distance to a quiet coffee shop near the main Catholic church: a baroque-style edifice, framed from behind by the mighty Brégeonvent.

The outside tables were arranged to catch the mid-morning sun, and quiet except for two women doing a coffee-catchup and sharing photographs.

Pierre chose a table well away from them. The waiter arrived and Pierre placed their order. 'Deux cafés au lait et un café noir, merci.'

He then put on his sunglasses and turned his attention to John and Harry. 'That was well played with Petit. It's probably the first time anyone has ever challenged the little cretin.'

Deep in thought, Harry looked over to the church and then to Pierre. 'Do you have many senior officers like him?'

'Fortunately, not,' said Pierre. 'Compared to Britain, France is considered a formal society, but the workplace is more relaxed than it used to be. Petit is an anachronism. A frightened little man clinging on to his aristocratic title because it's all he has.'

John and Harry picked up on the vitriol in Pierre's voice: Petit was someone Pierre truly detested.

Pierre continued, 'Petit sees directness as a threat. Anyway, we need to discuss your concerns about Freya, but first, there is something I need to tell you about Mathilde. It's confidential, so I must ask for your discretion.'

'Go on,' said John, with raised interest.

Pierre nodded, acknowledging John's curiosity. 'Mathilde is a troubled person. I think you know that, no?'

John cleared his throat. 'Not exactly,' he said, failing dismally in his attempt to show separation.

'Has she told you that she feels responsible for the death of a colleague?' asked Pierre.

'She said an officer was killed and she felt that she had a part to play in it, but she didn't elaborate,' replied John.

'The operation she had planned went wrong,' said Pierre.

'Are you certain of your facts, or are you what we call the Monday morning brigade?' John asked, referring to those keen to offer unsolicited opinions in absentia.

Pierre lifted his hands and moved back in a show of submission. 'I'm not criticising, John. I'm trying to explain her situation, that's all.'

Harry stepped in. 'Let Pierre finish.'

'Thank you,' said Pierre, acknowledging Harry. 'Mathilde had become intimate with the officer. I've tried to support her, but she's in denial. She can't accept what's happened, so she's trying to invent a different narrative in which I seem to play a part.'

'And what part would that be?' asked John.

Pierre shrugged. 'The paranoid detective, perhaps?' he said, looking hard at John for a reaction.

John did his best to look impassive, trying to conceal that it was exactly what Mathilde had said.

'If she is, it's called cognitive dissonance,' said Harry, drawing Pierre's attention away from John. 'When someone is under extreme psychological discomfort, they may invent alternative scenarios or hold conflicting beliefs as an escape. It's not uncommon for victims of abuse to think the abuser loves them or that they have done something that merits the abuse meted out to them. In Mathilde's case, accepting what has happened might currently be beyond her.'

John thought about the women in the Leith flat who had died, and his subsequent inability to shake off the notion he was responsible. It felt easier to do that than to believe human beings could execute women whose lives they had already destroyed.

Pierre looked at Harry. 'You know more about these things than I do,' he said. 'But it must be hard for Mathilde. Hopefully, things will improve for her.'

'Why now?' asked John, suspecting where this was going.

'She has a problem with alcohol. This morning she didn't seem capable: her breath was tested, and she was over the limit.'

John jumped to Mathilde's defence. 'Who

authorised that?'

Pierre was blunt with his answer: 'Petit. But you'll agree in a modern police force being under the influence of alcohol can't be tolerated.'

John conceded, knowing that within Police Scotland, a dram at the back door of a pub on a cold and wet night shift was long ago consigned to the realm of nostalgia.

'I agree, but you've just discovered a woman's body in the river and found evidence of abuse while she was sedated with ketamine. Mathilde was making good progress with the case. I find it almost beyond belief that you couldn't find a way around this.'

Pierre simply shrugged. 'Not my decision.'

'What will happen to her?' asked John.

The waiter arrived and set down their coffees. 'Merci,' said Pierre, taking a sugar lump from its wrapper, dropping it into his coffee and stirring it slowly.

When the waiter had departed, Pierre answered John's question. 'I'm sure once you two have gone, Petit will calm down and see things differently. In the meantime, other officers will continue from where Mathilde left off.'

Pierre sipped his coffee and looked from Harry to John.

They suspected that if this was Petit's doing, his game was, 'Leave, and I might throw Mathilde a lifeline.'

Pierre cleared his throat and shifted in his seat to indicate he wanted to change the subject.

'Gentlemen, tell me what you learnt over the weekend.'

Harry took the lead. 'There are two aspects of the case that we think should be explored further.'

'Go on,' said Pierre.

'First, there were traces of cocaine found on Freya's clothing.'

'Yes, I read that in the report,' said Pierre. 'But there was no trace of it in her bloodstream.'

'No. But what company was she keeping?' asked John.

Pierre looked uncertain. 'From what the girl Amy said she was content to hang out with the seasonal ski set.'

Harry took it up again. 'You might be right, but we think it's worth looking further afield.'

'Do you have a lead?' asked Pierre.

Harry shook his head. 'Not a lead, but a strong hunch. Do you know a skier by the name of Jaeger Schmidt?'

'I can't say I do,' said Pierre. 'I could ask around?'

'No need,' said John. 'He's a free ride skier sponsored by a German called Heinz von Kesler to promote an energy drink he produces. Von Kesler has a chalet further up the valley. As well as skiing, Jaeger Schmidt does the weekly cocaine run to supply parties von Kesler hosts for a chosen few.'

Pierre raised a suspicious eyebrow. 'How do you know this?'

'I'm afraid we can't tell you our source,' said John.

Pierre looked from one officer to another. 'When you arrived, this was the type of thing we warned you against. Was it Cal and Knox?'

John shook his head. 'Categorically not. It was something we picked up second-hand, from a man in a pub, but we think it's sound.'

Pierre smiled and looked down at the table and then back at John. 'A man in a pub. Very good. And so typically British.'

John just smiled.

'You think Adonis invited Freya to such a party?' asked Pierre.

'We think there's a link, but we're not sure what. Parties, young people, cocaine …'

Pierre nodded slowly. 'And this business with the photo and the telepherique?'

'Again circumstantial,' said Harry. 'But Freya was right-handed and the person in the pictures appears to be left-handed.'

'It *could* be someone else,' said Pierre. 'But there are many reasons why a right-handed person might use their left hand. Perhaps she had a sprain?'

Harry agreed. 'Yes, that's possible.'

Pierre looked up at the Brevant and then back at the two officers. 'Suppose it wasn't Freya getting into the telepherique. How do you think her body ended up in the crevasse?'

'If she was dead before she got there, someone could have carried her down, but a body would be unwieldy. The flight restrictions in the Chamonix Valley make a helicopter unlikely. But a paraponter …' said Harry.

Pierre looked incredulous. 'Come on, surely you're not suggesting someone carried a body up the Midi and then jumped off with it strapped to them in tandem?'

'Courmayeur,' suggested Harry. 'Freya's body could have been taken through the Mont Blanc Tunnel. Heinz von Kesler sponsors a paraponter. A man by the name of Arthur Roux.'

John and Harry could see Pierre was sceptical. He drew air through his teeth, blew it out and then looked resigned. 'What do you want from me?' he asked.

'We'd like to visit von Kesler,' said John.

Pierre tipped his head slightly. 'We can't go dragging people into this based on a hunch. Whoever he is, I doubt he's a fool. He's going to ask why we've chosen to visit him of all people.'

'We can say that we're trying to trace Freya's last movements before the incident,' suggested John. 'Add something like we're speaking to people in the valley who host parties.'

'That would be a pretty big list,' said Pierre. 'And if the girl at the telepherique wasn't Freya, who do you think she was?'

Harry shook his head. 'It could be anyone: man or woman. We initially thought it was a female because Freya is female, but there's no evidence to support that.'

Pierre agreed. 'Confirmation bias,' he said.

'Exactly,' replied Harry. 'Looking for evidence that favours an existing hypothesis.'

'But now we've no idea who it was,' said Pierre.

'We don't,' said John. 'All we can do at this point is follow the breadcrumbs.'

Pierre looked at John and Harry. 'And we know what happened in that fairy tale, don't we? Anyway, I need to go back to the station and calm things down with Petit. I might not like the man, but he's still my senior officer. If it helps, this afternoon we can pay a visit to Herr von Kesler. I'll pick you up from your hotel at say 14.00?'

'That sounds ideal,' said Harry. 'It will give us time to write up our notes.'

Pierre called over the waiter, paid for their coffees, and stood up. 'I'll leave you here and see you outside the hotel.'

***

John and Harry finished what was left of their coffee and walked in silence back towards the hotel. As they got close, John sidled up to Harry. 'Be discreet, but the lad from Friday night is loitering on the bridge, watching us.'

'Watching or waiting for us?' asked Harry.

'Good question,' said John. 'If he's thinking of jumping us he'd better have brought some muscle with him.'

Harry took in the view of the Aiguilles and inconspicuously picked out the lad on the opposite side of the road. He was looking much the same as he had the times before and leaning against a barrier that separated the pavement from the road as it crossed the Arve.

'Yes, that's him.'

As they got closer, they half expected him to move off, but he didn't. 'Let me go and have a word,' said John. 'You can order our club sandwiches.'

He crossed the road, and the lad moved to the parapet and stared down at the cloudy water tumbling through.

John leant back against the railing and hooked his elbows over it. 'I presume you want to speak to me,' he said.

The lad glanced up at him and then back down at the river. 'And I presume you're the two UK cops people are mouthing about?'

'We might be,' replied John, evading a direct answer.

The lad shifted his eyes from the river and looked up at John. 'If you had a question for me, why didn't you just ask? Why all the Ninja crap?'

John thought for a moment and realised he didn't have a credible answer for the lad.

'I suppose we assumed—'

'Assumed what? That I'm a lowlife who's part of a big-time drug syndicate? You come here thinking you know it all, but you don't. One of the guys brings through a bit of dope and we sell it around to our mates and make a few euro, end of …. At one time, we'd have been able to do something legit, but you and your Tory pals pulled off the Brexit stunt, so now we're stuffed.'

'Steady there, son. Calling me a Tory is taking it

too far,' said John, staging an indignant expression to emphasise his words.

'Oh?'

'Yeah, oh. My dad was a coal miner.'

Being only a boy himself at the time, John was pretty sure the bitter dispute of '84-'85 that pitched miners against Thatcherism was lost on the lad, but he seemed to get the gist and returned a dutiful smile.

'Tell me that back in the day you and your pals didn't hustle,' said the lad.

John thought about the question. 'I'm afraid my career choice put the kibosh on anything like that, but car stereos were a hot item – up until they started to fit pin codes. They said that overnighting one in a freezer zeroed the code, but when they fitted removable front panels the bubble burst.'

The lad gave it some thought. 'Bummer,' he said, as though feeling the pain of a lost business opportunity.

'I'm guessing that's not what you wanted to speak to me about?'

'No, it's not. You were asking about ket?'

'We were.'

'That's not something people are into around here, but you're not the first to ask.'

'No?'

The lad shook his head. 'Word is a Russian guy was looking to buy.'

'Russian?'

'Yeh, Russian.'

'So not the same guy we talked about?'

The lad looked uncertain. 'I don't think so, but you hear these things second hand and it's wise not to seem too interested.'

'Why didn't you tell us this before?' asked John.

The lad looked incredulously at John. 'Why do you think?'

John returned an understanding nod. 'If I said we got it wrong with you, would it help?'

'It would be a start.'

John headed up to Harry's room, and they settled on the balcony.

'What did the lad want?' asked Harry.

'Respect, I think. He said a couple of weeks back someone had been in the market for ketamine. He thinks it was a Russian but isn't certain.'

'Do you think it's genuine?'

John nodded.

Harry attached the clip-on sunglass lenses he had bought to his prescription glasses.

'How are your eyes?' asked John.

'The drops are helping,' said Harry. 'I'd like to get some prescription glacier glasses, but they cost a small fortune, and I can't see us being here long enough to merit it.'

They fell silent until Harry broached what he knew was on John's mind.

'I'm sorry about Mathilde.'

'Am I that transparent?' asked John.

'No, but as we said yesterday, we've worked a long time together. I feel as though I know you better than I know my wife. If it's any help, I think she's being used, but we need to humour Pierre.'

'I was getting to know her,' said John.

'I understand,' replied Harry, filling in the blanks. 'But something's going on between her and Pierre, and we need to keep him on our side.'

'Pierre isn't on our side,' said John. 'He's running a personal agenda, but I'm damned if I know what it is. I wouldn't be surprised if he hadn't deliberately contradicted himself by saying he didn't know Jaeger Schmidt and then referring to him as Adonis. I didn't use that name and neither did you. If Pierre is bright enough to play Petit, he sure as hell isn't going to slip up with a name – Freudian or otherwise.'

'Why would he do that?' asked Harry.

'To confuse us? Or maybe it's straight taking the piss.'

'It doesn't necessarily mean he's against us,' said Harry. 'But all this might be academic. I'd say we have twenty-four hours, forty-eight tops, before our position here becomes untenable. If Petit questions our diplomatic status and cuts us off, Pierre will have to go along with it.'

John answered a knock on the door and returned bearing a tray with their club sandwiches and two bottles of Coke with accompanying glasses. He retook his seat, emptied the ramekin of tomato sauce over his chips, and then pulled the skewer from his sandwich. He bit awkwardly into it and chewed as he contemplated what the last seven days had achieved before turning his attention back to Harry.

'From the off, this assignment had the makings of

a fool's errand. The gendarmerie aren't rookies. If they have an internal issue, they should be the ones to sort it out. Jack thought by sending us here he could pull off the double whammy of appeasing Rowden-Mott and cutting us some slack. But last Monday when I looked into the mother's eyes and saw the grief she felt at the loss of her daughter, I was pulled right back to that sense of obligation that makes this job so bloody difficult. That obligation is the reason we're here, Harry. Knox and Cal know there's more to Freya's death, which is why Knox called her mother, and now on site, we know the same. And that lad outside knows why we're here and wants to bat for the right team. What will it feel like when we're forced to walk away? Do we want our legacy to be a cold case team revisiting this in 10 years and asking, "How the hell did those two miss the bleeding obvious?" We and others have invested in this physically and emotionally, and with that comes commitment. I'm just glad those two kids, Zoe and Kim, are safely out of it.'

Harry's phone rang, and he looked at the screen. 'It's Sheila,' he said, lifting it to his ear.

'Not even a hello?' asked Sheila.

'Sorry. We're having a rough day. I'll put the phone on speaker so John can hear. What have you got for us?'

'Well, I've been a busy bee on your behalf,' she said, her familiar cheery voice lifting their spirits. 'I've tracked down Heinz von Kesler's energy drink business. According to a marketing website, the drink sits with the "also-rans" for market share, but the company is offshore in the Cayman Islands, which hides the financials. There's nothing to attribute the business to von Kesler; however, the leaked Panama Files showed the energy drink finances linked to two other enterprises: a media outfit and something to do with import and export.'

'Keep digging, Sheila. Anything on Jaegar Schmidt?'

'Just what you would find yourself: an Instagram profile and a load of promotional guff, but nothing I can see as being useful.'

'And von Kesler?' Harry asked.

'Nothing on the internet.'

Harry could sense from Sheila's tone that there was something more. 'What is it?' he asked.

'Well, there's so little about von Kesler I'm wondering whether he's done a DFC: a Digital Footprint Cleanup.'

'Perhaps he's just very private,' said Harry.

'Perhaps,' she replied.

'And the others?'

Sheila's voice brightened. 'Ah, I have better tidings in that department. Whereas Heinz von Kesler hides his light under a bushel, Jean-Raymond de Petit is quite the chauvinist when it comes to his heritage. Most French nobility were given the chop – if you'll excuse the pun – during the revolution, and the remaining few ran for the hills. But in these libertarian days, de Petit et al. seem to have regained their aristocratic mojo and are quite happy to hold their heads above the parapet and wave their ancestral banners; although in Petit's case, they seem to have fallen on embarrassing times.'

'In what way?' asked Harry.

'They have a château south of Avignon: a trifling affair of fifty rooms, a moat, vineyard and even a pigeonnier. From the pictures, it looks pretty shabby. Mind you, who in their right mind would want to keep pigeons? Have you seen where pigeons live? Talk about shitting in your own nest: they're disgusting.'

'Sheila … please.'

'Sorry boss. Anyway, the château *was* up for sale. I phoned the local estate agent, or should I say the immoblier, and pleaded the case of a bored Home Counties wife tasked by her city banker husband to find a property in Provence to keep her out of mischief. The immoblier told me that the owners of Château Petit – or whatever they call it – have decided to renovate and pulled it from the market.'

'Which means Petit has either come into an inheritance, won the Lotto, or something else,' said Harry, running his free hand over his hair and staring out at the mountains.

'But don't fret, all is not lost,' said Sheila. 'I was advised that there were several better properties available. There's one I quite fancy: no pigeonnier – thank God – and an infinity swimming pool overlooking hectares of rolling vineyard.'

'Sounds idyllic, I'm sure. What about participant number 3?' asked Harry, drawing Sheila back from her dream.

'Ah, Lieutenant Pierre Lavigne. Back to ho-hum, I'm afraid. If it's the guy I found, then the usual sports club membership: a reunion club, whatever that is. He came third in a badminton tournament, but nothing to tell us about the man. If he's on social media, he'll use aliases like any other cop.'

'OK. Good work, Sheila,' said Harry, massaging his chin with his free hand to aid his thought. 'See what you can find as background to Sir Hugo and Lady Rowden-Mott and also Freya's biological father, but keep it discreet. I'll call you this evening.'

'Sure,' she said.

But the way her voice trailed off told Harry she had something else unspoken.

'What is it, Sheila?' he asked.

'I just wanted to ask, how are you doing, John?'

'I'm fine and dandy,' he said, hoping it sounded upbeat enough for her.

'Good,' said Sheila. 'And we'll be seeing you both soon, from what I gather?'

'Go on, tell us,' said Harry.

'Oh, let's just say I feel Jack thinks this one has run its course, and he wants you back earning your keep.'

'We'll bear that in mind.'

***

Pierre arrived in an unmarked Celebes blue Peugeot 308: no doubt the closest colour that the French fleet management could get to their standard marked cars.

'John, you sit in the front,' said Harry. 'There'll be more legroom.'

They climbed in and Pierre set off towards Les Praz.

John asked Pierre whether Petit had calmed down.

Pierre made a scoffing laugh, and as John suspected he would, followed it with a derogatory comment. 'Petit, or should I say, *de, de, de* Petit, is an attention seeker. But he'll be gone soon enough.'

'Do you know something we don't?' asked John, picking up on Pierre's confident tone.

'I know a lot that you don't know,' Pierre replied, glancing across at John 'But Petit's demise is inevitable, don't you think?'

'One can only hope,' said John.

Les Praz was still congested with cars searching for elusive parking bays, and frustrated bus drivers trying to find a route through them. However, the road beyond, signposted Argentière and running parallel to railway tracks, was quiet.

Pierre looked at Harry in the rearview mirror and then at John. 'When we meet Heinz von Kesler, I will take the lead. What do you want me to tease out of him?'

John spoke for the two of them. 'We need to know whether Freya was in his party circle, and if so, when did he last see her. We also need to know if Jaeger Schmidt has a part to play. Freya was friends with Amy, but Amy is a straightforward girl. I sense Freya was also part of something else, but I can't put my finger on what. The only lead we have is the cocaine on her clothing and Jaeger Schmidt being a buyer. But he's not necessarily *the* buyer, which makes the link tenuous.'

'Not much to go on, is it?' said Pierre.

'No, it's not, but it's all we have,' said John.

He wanted to mention Lucie, but with Pierre's lukewarm attitude to the Freya/von Kesler line of enquiry, he assumed Lucie would be an ask too far. It was the problem working in France: he and Harry lacked agency. Back in Scotland they would mix it up, see what emerged, and if necessary, beg for forgiveness. But Pierre seemed at best to be playing a long game, and at worst running down the clock until they had to leave. Adding to their problems, Mathilde, the only operative with a bit of va-va-voom, had been sidelined.

The road crossed the railway and ascended through a forest of mature pine trees, their snow-laden branches sagging under the weight.

They passed the road leading up the hill to Mathilde's chalet and John reflected on the Saturday they had spent together. At the time, he thought it offered hope for something more, but now he was inwardly embarrassed at his thoughts of inviting her out for dinner once the case was closed. It felt naïve – the type of thing a teenage boy would fantasise about but never find the courage to pull off. The only consolation was that he hadn't shared his hopes beyond his imagination.

'Everything all right, John?' asked Pierre, glancing at him.

'Perfectly all right,' said John, suspecting Pierre knew.

They passed through an avalanche protection tunnel and shortly after Pierre indicated right. He drove down a snow-covered road, through another wooded area, this time dotted with chalets, to reach the entrance of Heinz von Kesler's alpine retreat.

John noted a high pole-mounted security camera pointing down at them. The private drive to the property was long, flat and straight, cut through deep snow. Like the road to Mathilde's hamlet, its vertical sides were higher than a tall person could reach and scored with the circular marks of a rotary snow cutter.

The snow banks ended and the chalet appeared like a latter-day winter palace basking in sunlight. A statement of modern architecture formed with simple shapes and straight lines and constructed with traditional wood and an abundance of reflective glass; it was Bauhaus meets chic-chalet on a grand scale.

A generous driveway paved with large slabs of grey Chamonix stone skirted the building, their flecks of quartz glistening.

Seeing it perfectly dry, John asked, 'How do they keep this clear?'

'Under-drive heating,' replied Pierre. 'Expensive to run, but if money is no object ...'

Pierre parked at the front, and they climbed the short flight of steps leading to a wide terrace.

By the time they reached the heavy front door, someone had opened it.

'Good afternoon, gentlemen. I'm Heinz von Kesler. We can continue in English, or if you prefer, French or my native German. Sadly, my Italian is not to the standard it should be.'

Von Kesler was a lean-faced man in his early fifties with greying blonde hair combed back and piercing blue eyes. Dressed in black stretch trousers themed on fifties ski wear, and a loose cashmere polo-neck jumper, he clearly didn't skimp on his wardrobe.

'Lieutenant Lavigne is fluent in English and French, but sadly both myself and my colleague are monolingual.' said Harry.

Von Kesler gave an amiable smile. 'Then English it shall be.'

Pierre introduced them. 'I'm Lieutenant de Police Pierre Lavigne of the Gendarmerie, and these are my two colleagues from Scotland: Detective Sergeant John Anderson and Inspector Harry Freeman.'

Von Kesler looked each man in the eyes as he gave them a firm handshake, and then stood aside and ushered them in. 'Please, please, gentlemen.'

They stepped into a vast lounge befitting a feature in a luxury travel magazine. With marble flooring and an abundance of wood panels, stone, animal hides, glass-topped coffee tables and several sumptuous beige settees, it surpassed WOW!

Recessed LED downlighters threw beams of warm light onto various artworks. In one corner, lit from behind, was a full-sized deer sculptured from black basalt, and in another, the flames of a bioethanol stove flickered behind a glass surround. Should one tire of all this, there was a jaw-dropping view of the Aiguilles through full-height windows.

'If you don't mind changing from your outdoor shoes, you'll find these quite comfortable,' said von

Kesler, indicating three pairs of felt Hausschuhe lined up in readiness.

'We won't be long,' said John.

But von Kesler insisted. 'I'm afraid it's a house rule to keep the floors clean. But you'll be far more comfortable in Hausschuhe,' he said, directing them to the slippers.

The three officers dutifully took off their coats and sat on a large wooden bench self-consciously removing their shoes for von Kesler to place on a mat. John tried to remember if he was wearing the sock with the hole at the big toe and was relieved to see the knit was sound.

With his shoe ceremony complete, von Kesler beckoned them over. 'Come and have a seat. I'll order coffee.'

'We've just had lunch,' said John.

'Ah, in that case, it will help with your digestion. I'm assuming you take milk?'

'Please, and no sugar,' said John, succumbing to the offer, and Harry indicated the same.

'Black for me,' said Pierre.

Von Kesler picked up a phone and placed their order with 'Yan.'

They settled down, John and Harry on a settee and Pierre and von Kesler in separate chairs dressed with sheepskin throws.

Von Kesler looked from one officer to another. 'When the lieutenant called me this morning, he said you were looking into Freya's tragic death. Am I correct?'

'That's correct,' said Pierre, drawing von Kesler's

attention. 'We're trying to trace her circle of friends and acquaintances: people who might help clarify her movements before her death. Any parties she might have attended, that sort of thing.'

Von Kesler looked quizzically at Pierre. 'I'm intrigued as to how that might concern me. We're hardly of the same generation. You could speak to my athletes, Jaeger and Arthur. They sometimes host parties here for our corporate clients and associates. Jaeger and Arthur are young enough to party hard and work the next day,' he said with a mischievous grin.

'Have you held any parties recently?' asked John.

Von Kesler smiled and shook his head. 'Not to my knowledge, but I don't know all the goings on, and before you ask, no, I don't recall seeing Freya here.'

Pierre looked at John for comment.

'If you could pass us Jaeger and Arthur's contact details,' said John.

'I will ask them to contact you through Lieutenant Lavigne,' replied von Kesler, putting John back in his place.

A door at the far end of the room opened and a well-built man in his thirties, wearing black trousers and a white shirt entered carrying a tray. He appeared to be exempt from the Hausschuhe policy, opting for polished black shoes.

Von Kesler stood up and met him halfway. 'Thank you, Yan,' and took the tray from him.

Yan departed, and von Kesler handed round the coffee.

John recognised Yan's ilk: the type of butler-bodyguard favoured by corporate antagonists. 'Yan seems a handy fellow to have around. Is he local?' asked John.

'No, he's not. Now where were we?' asked von Kessler, looking to Pierre for an answer. 'Ah, yes, Freya Rowden-Mott.'

Fair play, thought John at von Kessler's brush-off, but his use of Freya's full name was interesting and the man knew it.

'As I said, I don't recall meeting Freya, but I know her stepfather, Sir Hugo, quite well, and I've passed on my condolences.'

John fought the urge to exchange a telling glance with Harry and instead looked at Pierre stirring the sugar cubes from his saucer into his coffee. He seemed unfazed by what they had just heard.

As if to say, "You may continue with your questioning," Pierre nodded toward von Kesler whilst looking at John and then Harry.

Once his initial surprise had passed, John's mind ran through the implications of what von Hesler had said and concluded that there was nothing here to triangulate von Kesler, Rowden-Mott and Freya's death. But still, it seemed at the very least, an odd coincidence.

'You're thinking ...' said von Kesler.

John and Harry sipped their coffee, both aware that von Kesler was watching for cues on their part – inadvertent or otherwise. 'I'm a little surprised, that's all,' said John.

'But on reflection, there's no reason why Hugo

would mention you to us,' added Harry.

John picked up on Harry's use of "Hugo" when talking of the man, dropping the "Sir" to imply they were close to him.

'In what capacity are you acquainted?' asked John.

'Purely business. I have an interest in an energy drink company. Let me show you.'

Before they could decline, von Kesler had risen from his seat and was heading over to a built-in cupboard. He returned with several cans, disproportionally tall for their diameter, and in various garish colours. He handed one to John.

'They seem unusually small,' said John, comparing it to a more familiar Tennant's Lager can.

'200 ml,' said von Kesler. 'We describe the container as *streamlined for convenience*. It's one of our brand differentiators.' He leant forward as though about to deliver an insight. 'Think about it, gentlemen. You're up a mountain, in a nightclub, or just chilling, as they say: do you want to carry a large can in your pocket? This is small, but it packs a punch well above its weight.'

'I'm sure it does,' said John, turning the can in his hand and seeing a lengthy list of E numbers. 'So, what is Sir Hugo's involvement? I rather thought politics was his game of choice?'

Von Kesler laughed. 'Yes, a game it is for him. One can't but wonder what goes through the minds of the electorate when they stand at the ballot box voting for their leaders. It is quite extraordinary the choices they make. Perhaps they see it as a stage for collective masochism. I care even less about politics than Sir Hugo does. But he claims to be well-connected and what they call a mover and shaker. Alas …'

'Moving and shaking what exactly?' asked Harry.

'We want to develop a media channel to promote our energy drink in the UK. For that, we need an Ofcom licence. For an outsider, it's a complex and lengthy process with no guarantees.'

'Has Sir Hugo offered his services?' asked John.

'Yes, to lobby on our behalf. All perfectly above board.'

'If it's declared,' replied John.

'Indeed,' said von Kesler.

'But you now have doubts about him?' asked John.

Von Kesler crossed the room to the window, turned and looked back at the officers in their seats. 'Sir Hugo is not making the progress he promised,' he replied, making his frustration known. 'I'm beginning to think the man has oversold his capabilities.'

Harry looked questioningly for more.

'He hasn't delivered, Inspector.'

John asked von Kesler when he had last spoken to Sir Hugo.

'A week before Freya's body was found in a crevasse. I've spoken to him once since then, on the telephone to pass on my condolences and get a progress report. Feel free to check. I'm sure you have his number.'

'How did he react to Freya's death?' John asked.

Von Kesler shrugged. 'In a manner you would expect from a stepfather.'

'Which is?' pressed John.

'Which is he thanked me for calling and used his stepdaughter's passing as an excuse for tardiness. But she wasn't his daughter, was she? She wasn't his flesh and blood.'

'No, she wasn't. But she was his wife's flesh and blood, and he'll be grieving for her loss, I'm sure,' said John.

Von Kesler gave a wry smile and then looked at his watch. 'I've never met or spoken to his wife, and as I said, I keep my relationship with Sir Hugo purely business.'

Von Kesler then looked at John and Harry in turn.

'I understand the two of you live in Edinburgh. Are you a family man, Inspector?' he asked, with a glint that said he already knew the answer.

John read the menace implicit in von Keseler's words: "I know who you are and where you live". It was a move that could have come straight out of Vlatko's playbook and as such antagonised John.

John stared hard at the man and then returned a shot designed to both tell and test.

'Mr von Kesler, a young woman has been found dead in the Arve. She too may have attended a party before her death. Have you heard of this?'

Pierre rose to his feet. 'We've taken enough of your time, Mr von Kesler. We won't keep you any longer,' he said, indicating the meeting was over.

But von Kesler didn't hear as John continued to fix him with a stare. 'That's terrible, Sergeant, but it's the first I've heard of it. If I hear anything, I'll let the lieutenant know.'

John didn't answer as he and Harry also rose to their feet.

Von Kelser looked at the can still in John's hand. 'Please, keep it.'

But John put the can down on the table.

Von Kesler led them to the door where they donned their outdoor shoes and put on their coats.

As they were leaving, Harry turned to their host. 'Is there a security issue in the valley?'

'Not that I'm not aware of. Why do you ask?'

'Because I see you have several security cameras in this room. I presume the rest of the house is the same?'

'You have a keen eye,' said von Kesler. 'Some of these artworks are quite valuable. The cameras are meant to be discreet but in your line of work you will be trained to detect such things.'

'An organised man like you will, no doubt, keep recordings,' said John.

With an expression to say he wouldn't fall for flattery, von Kesler looked at John. 'Rest assured, Sergeant, I have nothing that would be useful to your inquiry.'

'Thank you for your time. Now we must go,' said Pierre.

They drove off, and once clear of the property, John turned to Pierre. 'Why the fuck did you tell him we live in Edinburgh?'

'I didn't,' said Pierre.

'I don't believe you,' said John in a raised voice. 'You spoke to him earlier today. What did you say about us?'

Pierre remained silent. They turned onto the main road, and shortly afterwards pulled into a large layby with recycling containers at the far end. Pierre stopped, turned off the engine and looked at John then back to Harry through the rearview mirror.

'Von Kesler was warning you he's a big dog,' said Pierre.

'Which means he has something to hide,' replied John.

'A man like him always has something to hide,' said Pierre 'But it's likely to be his business dealings he wants to keep quiet.'

John shook his head. 'He was using us: telling us about Sir Hugo in the hope it would get back to him. But he didn't need to threaten us. He's hiding something bigger.'

'Why did you ask him about Lucie?' asked Pierre. 'That question was out of your remit.'

'Why didn't *you* push him about Jaeger Schmidt?' countered John. 'He brushed us off as you sat on your hands.'

'I didn't push him because all we know is that a spurious second-hand source you are not willing to divulge to me said Jaeger Schmidt bought cocaine. What's the link to von Kesler?'

The two men set each other a lengthening stare until finally Pierre spoke. 'You see, there isn't one, is there?' Pierre seemed to settle. 'I understand you're frustrated, John, but you shouldn't have mentioned the girl.'

'I mentioned her because I want him to know that we're on to him,' said John.

Pierre drew a big breath, let it slowly out and shook his head. 'I've just told you, we're not on to him. We might not like the man, but we have nothing to say he has any involvement in Freya's death.'

'Bullshit. He's connected to it and to whatever the fuck else is going on around here,' replied John. 'If he wasn't he would have asked questions about Lucie. Which reminds me you still haven't answered my question. Why did you pass him our details?'

'Listen to me,' said Pierre, raising his voice again. 'If you want to know where he got your details, look at your own force's data breach history: the ones they tell you about and the ones they don't. You Brits are famous for sharing information with the world. Laptops left in cars and restaurants, spreadsheets embedded in files and sent out under freedom of information. I even heard documents were left on a park bench. He could have easily bought your details off the dark web or from another agency if he had a route in – criminals aren't the only people who go digging for information on others, are they John?'

John could see that for the first time since they had met him, Pierre was riled. It was as though they had touched something Pierre didn't want to be touched.

'I don't believe you,' said John.

'Well, that's your prerogative,' replied Pierre as

he started the engine, looked over his left shoulder and pulled out.

***

Housekeeping had cosied up John's room for the night, with the bedding turned down, table lamps dimmed and curtains drawn, leaving a twenty-centimetre gap for that compelling view of the Midi and its light burning bright.

John stared up at it and wondered what the enigmatic guardian would make of the world. Von Kesler's blunt words had unsettled him: not the insidious threats, they only toughened his resolve. There was a noun John reserved for people who threatened others: a four-letter word too obscene to utter. No, it was von Kesler's reference to society that disturbed him: the notion that the citizens John served were being betrayed by those who were supposed to watch over them.

He had always taken the disparity of wealth as a given, but what he had heard about the ignominious Sir Hugo stuck in his craw. It seemed the man had no shame.

His thoughts turned to his mother working tough shifts as a morning-after cleaner in their local workingman's club. She would return home smelling of passive cigarette smoke and stale beer and exhausted from sweeping floors and wiping down sticky tabletops. The pay was paltry, and after deductions, she would have been better off on benefits. He recalled her words. *We're a good, honest family, John, and there are those worse off than us.*

If what Jack had said was correct about Sir Hugo's dealings, just how much of the taxes paid by those who could least afford it went into the pockets of him and his kind?

It was in stark contrast to Knox and Cal, two young men who had stood in the face of danger at the crevasse, but refused to take even the cost of a drink for their efforts.

Even the lad peddling dope seemed to have higher principles.

Harry tapped on the door and John barked an angry, 'Enter.'

'Is everything alright?' asked Harry, picking up on John's brusque tone.

'Aye, sorry boss. My mind was elsewhere.'

The two officers sat down at a small round table.

'I'm not sure your brittle exchange with Pierre was a good idea,' said Harry.

'And the alternative is?' John asked. 'We've been here a fecking week on what was meant to be a simple sign off, but as far I can see, apart from finding out it wasn't Freya in the telecabin and confirming her stepfather is a dodgy bastard we're no closer to closing this off.'

Harry looked at his watch and calculated that with the UK an hour behind they might just be on the right side of a call to Sheila.

'Let's see what Sheila has to say,' he said, putting the phone on speaker and setting it in front of them on the table.

'Sorry to call so late, Sheila. I'm here with John on the speaker. You're not in the middle of supper, are you?'

There was a pause during which they visualised her looking between her watch and whatever she had rustled up for dinner.

'No … at my desk. Are you two still living la dolce vita?' she asked, making her envy known.

'The French call it "la belle vie",' Harry replied. 'But sadly not, and the weather is due to turn for the worse tomorrow. Anything to report?'

'Quite a lot, actually,' she said, sounding a little more chipper. 'But only you two will know how useful it is. I've been digging into the murky world of Sir Hugo Rowden-Mott.'

'Oh?' said John, his ear pricking up.

'I thought that would get your attention. From what I gather, a couple of years ago Sir Hugo was reported to one of those parliamentary bodies responsible for complaints of sexual misconduct. It seems a female junior researcher accused him of something. There was an inquiry, and it was found that he had no case to answer.'

'No surprise there,' said John.

'Mm, do I detect a whiff of cynicism, Sergeant?'

'I'd call it reality,' said John 'But he certainly seems to be a busy bugger.'

'The plot thickens, does it?' she asked.

'Yes. We found out today that he's a lobbyist for Heinz von Kesler.'

'Lobbying for what?'

'An Ofcom licence.'

'That's interesting,' said Sheila. 'Perhaps there's a German connection. It turns out that the name, Rowden-Mott, was self-selected by his grandfather.'

'Did he think a highfalutin double-barrel moniker would bunk him up the greasy pole of Britain's social class structure?' asked Harry.

'I don't think the grandfather was looking to grubby his hands on a greasy pole,' said Sheila. 'He was looking to get in at the top. He had emigrated from Germany in the early fifties. I suppose he thought Rowden-Mott sounded the part and carried more clout than whatever he had arrived with.'

John wanted to know more. 'So that was the grandfather. What about Sir Hugo's father?'

'He died when the then mere Hugo was a child. Hit by a bus in central London. Hugo's mother remarried and Hugo spent most of his childhood in boarding school.'

'And his wife, Astrid?'

'Her father was honoured with membership into something called the Swedish Nobility of Dignity. Astrid studied political science at the University of Stockholm, where she met and went on to marry Anders Ruuth. They had one child, Freya. Astrid's work took her to Geneva, which is where she fell under the thrall of the soon-to-be Sir Hugo. Other than dumping her first husband, she seems like a predictable career type.'

'Good work, Sheila,' said Harry. 'Nothing more on Pierre, I suppose?'

'No. If anything, I've gone backwards with him.'

'How so?' asked John.

'Well, when I went searching again, he had disappeared. No badminton club, no nothing.'

'Did you check the cache?' asked John.

'Yup. It's showing a URL error message.'

A thought flickered through John's mind: something Pierre had said when riled in the car. *Criminals aren't the only people who go digging for information on others, are they John?*

John sat back in thought and then leant forward. 'There's something not connecting with Lieutenant Pierre Lavigne. See what else you can find, but don't go busting a gut.'

'You sound as though this one has run its course,' she said.

'I think it has,' replied Harry. 'What do you think, John?'

'We can keep turning stones and finding titbits, but there's nothing concrete enough to change Freya Ruuth's death from being anything other than an accident,' said John.

'Perhaps the strongest lead you have is in what you just called her,' replied Sheila.

'What do you mean by that?' asked John.

'You called her Freya Ruuth.'

'Yes, I did, didn't I.'

It wasn't his use of the name Ruuth, it was *why* he had used it. From their first interaction with her mother to the name on her apartment door and all the signs they had subsequently picked up, Freya and her stepfather were at opposite ends of the moral and ethical spectrum. So how would such opposites react

to each other?
'OH SHIT,' yelled Sheila.
'What's happened?'
'I've missed my effing Pilates class!'

Tuesday

John hadn't finished knocking when Harry yelled, 'Enter.'

He was impatiently waiting for his laptop to boot. He looked up at John. 'You've heard?'

'Yes, I've heard. Sheila sent us the same text. Has Jack been on to you yet?'

'Not yet,' said Harry. 'But he sure as hell will be, and before he does, we need to know what's been put out there about us.'

With his homepage now loaded, Harry googled the first tabloid he could think of; a Glasgow-based 'red top' with which he had cultivated a mutually beneficial relationship with the lead journalist.

'Two-faced bastard,' he said as the headline glared out at them.

'He wouldn't have had a say in the matter,' said John, looking at a similarly sensationalised headline on his phone. 'Once the story broke, he'd have had little choice but to join the chase. The question is, why did someone take that picture of us, and why use it now?'

'Because someone in the UK is getting unnerved by our presence here,' said Harry. 'Probably the same person who gave Petit the order to send us home.'

John moved closer to Harry's laptop and looked at the picture of them sitting outside the café on their first day. With her sunglasses, striking features and dark hair, Mathilde looked as if she had stepped off the set of *Marriage Italian Style*, Pierre was looking composed and John and Harry were smiling. The headline shouted, 'Cash-strapped cops on an alpine jaunt.'

'At least it didn't read "Piste Again",' said Harry in a rare display of humour.

But John was caught up in the irony of the situation. 'What rankles me is that two minutes later Mathilde was hurling insults at us.'

Harry's phone rang, and he looked at the screen. 'It's Jack. I'll speak to him. You might as well start packing your bag.'

***

The officers stood waiting for their taxi back to Geneva airport. It should have arrived by now, but the driver had called reception to say he was stuck in a queue near Argentière, awaiting the disentanglement of two cars that had flaunted the requirement to fit snow tyres.

Up to now, Chamonix had charmed them with its picture postcard image, but on this, the day of their forced departure, the anticipated storm painted a moribund grey scene in which wet snow fell like gloop from the skies and slush accumulated on the roads.

The roundabout had disappeared into the gloom, forsaking the chance of a final farewell to the Aiguilles. Stymied by reports of the ski stations closed, cars with ski racks and dejected-looking children staring out of misted-up windows, mooched slowly through town, and passersby cowered under their hoods as they moved guilefully from one sheltered haven to another. A snowplough came through, sending a wave of slush to the side, some of it splattering on shop windows to run down like globs of spittle.

John and Harry retreated into the hotel entrance where Antoine appeared. 'I didn't realise you were leaving today,' he said.

'Our boss has called us back urgently,' said Harry.

Apart from a knowing nod, Antoine kept his counsel as he looked into the greyness.

'Anyone still in the mountains will be in trouble unless they find a refuge to shelter in. You can't outrun a storm, only weather it out,' he said.

John thought how apt Antoine's maxim was. It was exactly what they were doing: abandoning a mother's hopes for the truth about her daughter, a week's work and all those who had stood behind them because someone was, in their case, starting to feel the heat. Fleeing an inquiry ran contrary to all he believed about police work and was sour to countenance.

Antoine's junior from the restaurant appeared

bearing a tray. Thanking him, Antoine took the tray and reached forward to John and Harry. 'Coffee and croissants to go,' he said.

The officers expressed their thanks as they took the paper cups and sipped from them, savouring the rich taste of Arabica beans, and then munched on the warm, buttery croissants.

The Celebes blue Peugeot 308 appeared, and Pierre got out looking agitated. 'Harry, John, I hear you've been stung by the press. I'm so sorry.'

'Are you?' said John.

Sensing this wasn't a place for him to be, Antoine bid them a *bon voyage* and disappeared.

John returned to Pierre. 'Hearing that Harry and I are leaving must be quite a coup for you and Petit. Your plan has delivered, hasn't it?'

Pierre shook his head vehemently. 'I knew nothing about this.'

'Really?' said Harry. 'Don't take us for fools.'

Pierre looked up and down the road and then turned to the officers. 'Listen, I'll tell you something, but it stays with you, OK?'

John shrugged. 'We'll be gone anyway once our taxi gets here.'

'OK, so I know Jaeger Schmidt and Heinz von Kesler, but don't say I didn't give you enough to realise that. The name Adonis, the sugar cubes at Kesler's, I gave you plenty of signs. Besides, can you two say that you've been completely transparent with me?'

John and Harry didn't reply, and Pierre smiled. 'See. Trust works both ways. Now come,' he said, beckoning them to his car. 'I'll run you to the airport.'

'Making sure we leave town, are you? Or is it Petit's bidding you're doing here?' asked John.

'Fuck that little *con*,' said Pierre, using the French expletive to once again show his disdain for the man.

Harry looked at his watch. 'Get in the car, John, or we'll miss our flight.'

Their arrival was a spectacular ascent into the majesty of the mountains, but their departure had disintegrated into a slow crawl through the gloom. Pierre had his wipers working hard to clear the spray from the slow-moving convoy of lorries they were following down the steep N205 from the Chamonix Valley to the plains of Sallanches below.

Leading the procession were a pair of snowploughs working in tandem across both carriageways and stamping their dominance with swishes of grit, numerous amber and blue lights and a huge tube of slush that curled its way across their blades.

'Winter's back,' said Pierre, but the officers didn't take him up on his chitchat.

'Listen, I'll make sure the two of you are briefed on any developments,' he said, trying to soothe the waters.

'We look forward to that,' said John. 'It will make a nice Christmas present when it comes.'

Pierre just smiled, and Harry and John sat in quiet awe of the Frenchman's Teflon resistance to their sarcasm.

'I heard that Arthur Roux, the paraponter is back in Chamonix,' said Pierre.

'Are you going to speak to him?' asked John.

'If we can find him. But first, I'll do a little more digging into Freya's doppelgänger.'

'I thought you didn't believe it was anyone other than Freya on the telepherique,' said Harry.

Pierre looked at him through the rearview mirror. 'I expressed an opinion, which is different from dismissing the alternative view, is it not?'

'Well, keep us posted,' said John, tiring of their spat.

John's phone rang. He sighed as he took it out of his pocket and looked at the screen, expecting to see a UK number as a prelude to more trouble.

But the number was French. 'Hello?'

'John, it's Cal. Where are you, man?' His voice was urgent.

John switched the phone to the speaker. 'We're heading for the airport, Cal. Is there something wrong?'

'There's a shitload wrong. That fucker Arthur Roux is back in town. He went to Amy's flat and now she's totally freaked.'

'What did he say to her?' asked John.

'I've no idea, but she's in a bad way. I mcan really bad. She phoned Knox, completely messed up, and saying stuff that didn't make sense. We're worried that she will do something to herself. Knox is legging it to her flat. I was meant to be collecting gear I'd left at a mate's house in Les Praz, but I'm heading back to Cham. Can you meet us at Amy's?'

'As I said—'

'Fuck what you said,' Cal shouted. 'You owe us …'

John turned to Pierre. 'Turn around now, or I'll do something we both regret.'

Pierre pulled abruptly off the main road and onto the slip down to Servoz. He turned hard left, over the bridge, and with the blue lights behind the radiator grill flashing and the siren blaring, he doubled back, up the N205 towards Chamonix.

The officers sat in silence as other drivers pulled over, allowing them to speed through.

Les Houches, Taconnaz, Les Bossons and on through the Mont Blanc Tunnel roundabout until they reached the turning to Amy's flat.

They pulled up and raced the stairs.

Knox was banging on the door. 'I've just got here,' he said.

'Amy, it's Knox. Open the frigging door,' he shouted.

'Are you certain she's in there?' asked John.

'As certain as I can be,' said Knox.

'Then stand back.'

John ran at the door, landing a foot against the already weakened area of the lock.

The door burst open, hitting the wall behind, and straight ahead, hanging lifeless from a beam in the living room was Amy, a chair toppled below her.

The officers ran through. Harry grabbed her legs to support her weight and John cut the rope, catching her as she fell forward.

They lay her on the ground and John brought his

face close to hers. 'Breathing – just – but unresponsive. Call an ambulance.'

'I'm on it,' said Pierre, already making the call.

***

Whatever Pierre said had initiated a fast response, and an ambulance was soon at Amy's apartment. The paramedics worked quickly, fitting a facemask, supplying supplementary oxygen and checking her blood gas levels.

Knox, Harry and Pierre followed as they stretchered her out of the apartment. Knox went with her in the ambulance and Harry and Pierre followed by car.

Cal and John remained in the flat.

'Best not to touch anything,' said John as the sound of the siren faded.

'Why? In case she dies?' asked Cal, challenging John on what he had implied.

Cal then sat down on the settee and put his face in his hands.

John sat beside him and took a deep breath. 'I'm sorry, Cal. That was insensitive of me. I guess I've done this job for too long.'

With his face still in his hands, Cal shook his head. 'You don't understand a fucking thing about us, do you man?'

John looked up towards the window where a chink of blue had appeared in the leaden sky. 'I used to think I knew a thing or two about most people, but not now. Do you want to tell me?'

Still leaning forward, and with teary eyes, Cal turned his head to look at John. 'Have you ever asked yourself why so many young people are in the mess they're in? Have you?'

'Because the world is in a mess and life is tough for them?'

'Jesus Christ,' said Cal. 'It's because the greed of your generation has left us a world of total fuckedupedness. You've poisoned the well that we have to drink from. Can't you see that?'

John knew this ran far deeper. He and Harry had picked up Cal and Knox's reference to something traumatic in their past. Something that had destroyed their faith in society and sent them in retreat to Chamonix. Something to do with someone called Connor.

Cal sat back in the seat and tried to find his words.

'He was our friend, John. He was one of us. A good guy who did no one any harm.'

John was gentle with his tone and the language he used. 'When you speak in the past tense, I'm assuming that something happened to your friend?'

Cal sniffed and nodded. 'His name was Connor. He was trying to make it in life and made a mistake.'

'Making mistakes is part of life. What happened?' John asked.

Cal looked fleetingly at him, checking for sincerity, and then continued. 'He started to gamble, and it got out of control. To stay afloat, he maxed out a couple of credit cards. When the letters came through the door, he borrowed from short-term lenders with exorbitant interest rates. He must have known he wouldn't be able to keep up the payments, and when they started with their demands, he moved on to loan sharks. It was a last-gasp effort of a drowning friend trying to buy some time while he chased impossible losses.'

'Did you know he was doing this?' asked John.

Cal shook his head. 'He was good at hiding it from us, but he'd changed. He lost his job in Edinburgh and stopped taking care of himself. We think that in the end, he couldn't see a way out. With lenders banging on his door and making threats, he knew soon he would be exposed. He couldn't bear the shame, so he decided to leave it all behind.'

'He took his life?' asked John.

'No,' said Cal. 'Life took him. Knox and I feel we failed our friend. We didn't see it coming and we should have. If Amy doesn't pull through …'

John knew the despair that accompanied trying but failing.

'I know what it feels like to think you should have done more, but you did everything you could for Amy, Cal.'

Cal wiped his eyes and looked at John. 'I fell out with my dad.'

The comment seemed out of context, but John sensed it was linked to the general confusion in Cal's life.

'Over the things we're talking about?'

Cal nodded. 'He's so pig-headed.'

John drew a deep breath and let it out in a way

Cal could interpret.

'You know my dad, don't you?' asked Cal.

John nodded. 'I know your dad. We were both based out of Gayfield Square for a spell. He often talked about you and your adventures.'

'Does he know you're here in Chamonix?'

'No, he doesn't.'

Cal said nothing more, so John continued. 'Your dad's a good cop. Compassionate and caring of others. The apple doesn't fall far from the tree, does it, Cal?'

Cal gave a faint smile and blew his nose. 'I suppose it doesn't,' he said.

'But you're right,' said John. 'Sometimes we wish we could have done more, and that's painful to contend with.'

John could see that at least for now, the pain Cal carried from the death of his friend and the rift with his father had stopped tearing at him.

'Anyway … did Zoe and Kim get home safely?'

'I guess so.'

'Guess so?'

'Yeah, guess so. We all decided that it was fun while it lasted, but there's enough going on in the world and relationships just add another complication.'

'I'm sorry to hear that. I thought the four of you hit it off,' said John.

Cal shrugged, but John could tell he was missing his Zoe, and from what he had seen of them together, he imagined Zoe would be missing him.

Wednesday

John stood on the balcony and looked out over Chamonix. The bright weather was back, and with it, people were cheerful, looking forward to their day on the slopes, creaming the freshly fallen snow.

But the gloom within John had turned darker. He had spent a fitful night haunted by images of Lucie staring up from the water at him and Amy hanging from the beam. There was something terrifying left within Lucie, as though her spirit had escaped its body, leaving behind whatever horrors she had endured. And Amy's face had looked distant, with bloodshot eyes and her mouth fixed slightly open. In all senses of the word, it was a look of finality.

In Scotland he and Harry would have received the standard post-trauma self-support package, and an offer of further support, "should it be deemed necessary".

But three months of listening to his counsellor's jargon around advanced empathy, and deep listening had taught John pretty much all there was to know about post-trauma counselling, and the limited outcomes to expect.

He recalled his first harrowing incident: a road

traffic accident on one of many small roads on the outskirts of Edinburgh. A young man had driven straight off a bend and into a tree. He had survived: his girlfriend in the passenger seat hadn't. There was not much left of the girl or the car, but somehow the sound system survived. John recalled the eery scene, like something from a Vietnam war movie: the distinctive smells of vapourised petrol, hot oil and mutilation, to a heavy metal backing track. He had never been keen on metal. Too much moshing, headbanging and air guitars by wannabees in need of a haircut and wearing badge-infested Wrangler jackets. That night seemed to validate his preconceptions, and however hard he tried to rationalise it, the power of association prevailed.

In those early years he expected to feel a little numb for a day or two, but nothing that gallows humour, a re-enactment with colleagues in the canteen, or possibly a skinful of beer after the shift wouldn't put right.

But he seemed to have lost the ability to bounce back, as if constant exposure to calamity had compromised his immune system and all those nameless bodies were breaking through to claim their part on his stage. Amy was a young woman he'd known was vulnerable and therefore someone else he had failed.

He shook his head, attempting to default back to "police officer doing a job", and tried to work through what they had.

He and Harry were now certain Freya's death and Amy were connected, but the how remained elusive.

Was Amy on the glacier with Freya? Or had Amy meant to be with her but cancelled, and now felt responsible for the death of her friend?

Thanks to Cal and Knox, they had got to Amy in time, but only just. Another minute or two and she would have been dead.

And what about Sir Hugo? What murky business was he involved in with von Kesler? An Ofcom licence seemed too straightforward. Was there a connection with Lucie's gruesome death?

He could hear Harry closing off his call. 'Don't worry, Jack. We'll keep you posted.'

The call ended, and Harry joined John on the balcony. 'Jack says we should stay put.'

'What about the chief constable?'

Harry shrugged. 'It seems she's changed her mind. Either that or been overruled, but I can't see who'd have the power to do that. That's all Jack had to say, apart from an expletive about the press.'

'What now?' asked John.

'I was hoping you had an idea,' replied Harry.

'We could use our well-worn strategy of revisiting everything we know so far,' suggested John. 'We might have missed a connection or the significance of something. What do you think?'

Looking for inspiration, Harry puffed his cheeks and blew out the air. 'Short of anything new, that's what we are stuck with. But I'm not happy about it.'

'I know. It's too slow,' said John. 'We need to get to the bottom of Amy's involvement. What drove her to do what she did?'

They stood, deep in thought, trying to come up

with something, but nothing materialised.

'Should we give Pierre a call?' asked John.

Harry shook his head. 'No. I think today we should let him come to us. Can you go down and grab two coffees from the restaurant? I need to phone Sheila.'

John left for the restaurant and Harry sat down at the desk and called Sheila.

Her first words were, 'How is Amy?'

Harry briefed Sheila as best he could. 'Her mother arrived last night and gave me a call. She said that Amy had regained consciousness and was talking, but as you would expect, she was very confused and distressed. The doctors gave her a sedative to help her through the night. I'll get an update shortly. What's been happening at your end?'

'A few things. First, I made an unsolicited call to your journalist friend in Glasgow. It gave me great joy hearing him grovel when I said you were going to cut him off. In a moment of contrition, he said their London bureau had sent up the picture, but he either didn't know or wouldn't tell me where or who they had received it from.'

'He knows who sent it, and he knows we know, but he's keeping schtum,' said Harry.

'A certain Sir by any chance? asked Sheila. 'I have something really important to tell you about him. It seems—'

Harry could hear the background tone of an incoming call. He took the phone from his ear and glanced at the screen. 'Sheila, I'm sorry. I need to cut you off. Amy's mother is trying to reach me.'

He dropped Sheila, accepted the incoming call and a firm female voice asked, 'Inspector Freeman?'

'Yes. Freeman here.'

'Inspector, it's Fiona Joyce, Amy's mother. You need to come here immediately. There's something Amy wants to tell you.'

***

John and Harry took a taxi from the hotel to the hospital: a modern building with a helipad at one end. The reception area was already accepting the first casualties of the day: a British boy who had taken a nasty fall snowboarding and hurt his wrist, and an Italian woman who had twisted her knee.

From their protestations, it seemed the boy was more concerned about the downtime from his boarding than the injury, and the Italian woman was nonplussed with her husband about the whole ski holiday deal.

John and Harry approached the reception desk and explained that they had come to see Amy Joyce at the request of her mother. The receptionist directed them to Amy's room on the first floor.

They ascended the stairs and followed a long, wide corridor, past a man with a flat cap and tweed jacket reading a newspaper, and on to where a female police officer bearing a sidearm was sitting outside one of the rooms. From her dark hair tied back in a bun, suntan and athletic build, John and Harry recognised her from the station.

She stood up, glanced into the room, and then back at the officers. 'I'm Émilie. You know my father, Guillaume,' she said, indicating the man sitting along the corridor.

Guillaume raised a finger in recognition and continued his unofficial vigil.

Amy's mum, Fiona, stepped out of the room to talk to them. Dressed in a pair of slim-fit trousers, a ribbed top and a cardigan, she had the look of a mother riven with concern and starved of sleep.

'Mrs Joyce?' asked Harry.

She acknowledged him but said nothing.

'You can't have slept,' said John.

She shook her head. 'How could anyone sleep through this awfulness? Amy has something to tell you.'

Harry asked, 'Are you sure it's us she wants to speak to, or would it be better for her to speak to a French police officer?'

'Amy said that she wants to speak to you. She said you came to her flat and asked about Freya's death.'

'Yes, we did,' said Harry. 'As long as you are both sure. But please remember, we don't have any jurisdiction in France.'

'Émilie does,' said Fiona, making it clear she had struck up a relationship of necessity with the French officer.

Émilie followed them into the room. Amy was sitting up in bed, propped by numerous pillows. She had a medical collar supporting her neck. Like her mother, she looked like someone living a nightmare, but in Amy's case, her face was also streaked by tears. Beside her was the usual paraphernalia associated with a hospital bed: a stand with a monitor, a drip now disconnected, and various gas fittings on the wall behind. Amy was holding a polythene face mask. On her index finger was a clip to measure her blood oxygen level.

John, Harry and Émilie pulled up chairs and Fiona hovered on the opposite side of the bed, protectively close to her daughter.

'How are you feeling, Amy?' asked John.

She sniffed, moved her neck as if to see whether it was still painful, winced and lifted the mask to take a breath.

'My head is aching and my neck is sore,' she said.

But John could tell that those physical injuries were minor compared to the turmoil inside her head.

'Your mum says you have something you want to tell us,' said Harry

Amy's eyes flitted between the officers and rested on John. 'I want to tell you what happened,' she whispered.

Whether because of what had occurred the previous day, because she had been crying or because of the intensity of what she had to say, Amy struggled to make herself heard, so John moved a little closer.

'What is it you want to tell us?' asked John in a calm, empathic voice.

'I didn't mean any of this to happen,' she said.

She looked around the room, and for a moment the officers thought she might do as she had at the flat, and decide she didn't want them there. But after a pause and gentle words of encouragement from her mother, she continued.

'It started with that guy they call Adonis. He invited me to Heinz von Kesler's chalet. I didn't want to go – they're not my scene, any of them – but Adonis said they were looking for extras for a promotional ski film they were making. I was running short of money and thought earning an extra few euro would cover me until I returned home.'

'You should have asked me,' said her mother.

Amy looked with sad eyes at her mum. 'I know you would have helped me, but I wanted to show you I could manage by myself.'

Hearing her daughter was too much for Fiona, and she leant forward and hugged her.

John and Harry knew that however untimely Fiona's hug might be, they couldn't interrupt. This had to run at whatever pace was needed and without them chivvying.

When she was ready John gently drew Amy back to what she had been saying. 'When was this, Amy?' he asked.

'About four weeks ago.'

'Freya was your friend, wasn't she?'

Amy nodded slowly. 'I didn't tell her I was going because I knew she would try to stop me.'

'Why would she want to stop you from going there?' asked John.

Amy looked at John as if questioning why he was asking such an obvious question. 'Because Freya hated him. She hated him with a vengeance.'

'Von Kesler?'

'No, her stepfather. She knew von Kesler and her stepfather were in business together. He would come through from Geneva when von Kesler held his perv-parties,' she said, in a voice spitting contempt.

'How do you know the parties were like that?' John asked.

'Everyone knows,' she said. 'People liked Freya. She was kind and didn't show off her money. They knew the whole deal with her stepdad upset her so they didn't mention the parties when she was about. But all the snow junkies knew the parties were weird and her stepfather went to them.'

'You arranged to go to von Kesler's chalet to discuss filming?'

She nodded. 'Adonis said he had stuff to do in Cham and would pick me up from the roundabout. I wasn't sure because of what I heard about Adonis, but it wasn't late at night or anything. He was friendly on the way up. I asked him about the film. He said that he and some pro skiers would be shredding down the Lavancher bowl. All I'd have to do was stand at the side with some others and give a "woohoo" as they passed. It sounded like money for having fun, but it was just a ruse to get me into von Kesler's chalet.'

She went quiet and stared down to where her toes were poking the blanket up. Émilie got out of her seat and sat on the bed beside her. 'You don't have to say anything you don't want to Amy. Maybe wait until you feel a bit better?'

'Émilie's right,' said John. 'There's no pressure

on you to say anything.'

Amy continued to stare at her toes, and then the look on her face adopted a new resolve. 'I don't want to tell you, but I have to,' she said. 'I owe it to Freya.'

John and Harry said nothing and Émilie, with the sidearm on her hip, stayed sitting on the edge of Amy's bed, as if protecting the girl. John wondered whether having the weapon so easily to hand was sensible, but from Émilie's bearing he could tell that had he said something, she would have told him where to get off: as if the weapon was telling the world, 'Just try it and see what happens to you.'

Amy looked straight at John and the words spilled out. 'When I got to the chalet, I was raped.'

John and Harry fell silent as Amy's words sunk in. Fiona became agitated and Émilie swore in French.

Harry spoke up. 'I presume you want to report this, Amy, but I don't think we are the right people for you.'

'I'll speak to my dad,' said Émilie. 'He'll arrange for female officers to speak with you.'

Amy nodded. 'Thank you.' She then looked at John. 'If I tell you what happened you'll also have to do something about it, won't you?'

'We will do what we can, Amy, but this will still be a French matter.'

'Even if the rapist is British?'

Suddenly aware of the gap in their understanding, Harry asked, 'Who raped you, Amy?'

'Freya's stepdad. Sir Hugo Rowden-Mott.'

John drew a deep breath and let it out as quietly as he could. 'Tell us what happened.'

Harry shot him a glance, but John didn't return it. 'Tell us, Amy.'

She nodded. 'I went into the chalet, and Freya's stepdad was there, sitting on a settee. There were some other people around, women mostly, but I didn't recognise them. I think they had come through from Geneva. Adonis said Heinz would be along soon to speak with me. I didn't know the man was Freya's stepdad, but he seemed to know who I was. He came over and introduced himself. I think he had been snorting coke.'

John asked, 'Did you see him do that?'

Amy shook her head. 'No. But I could see on a glass coffee tabletop someone had been cutting it and Hugo seemed excitable – the way coke-heads get.' She looked at her mum. 'Don't worry, I'm not into that. It's for losers.' She returned to John. 'I didn't want to talk to Hugo, because of Freya, but he chatted anyway. Just friendly stuff about where I came from and whether I was enjoying the skiing. It was a simple conversation, and I didn't know what else to do while I was waiting. He had a flute of champagne and offered me one. I was sipping it to be sociable, and that's all I remember.'

'All you remember?' asked John

Émilie snapped back at him, 'That's what she said.'

'I'm only trying to understand,' said John.

Émilie didn't reply and Amy tried to explain. 'I woke up on a bed feeling dizzy. Freya's stepdad was close by and Adonis was by the door. Freya's stepdad looked different.'

'In what way?'

'He looked guilty. He said I had fainted, but I'm not stupid. I knew what he had done.'

'What did you do then?' asked John.

'What could I do? I wanted to scream. I told Adonis that Hugo had been interfering with me. He said I was imagining it, but I wasn't. I could feel it.'

She looked awkwardly at Émilie for understanding and Émilie nodded to say she knew what Amy meant.

'Adonis said he had been there all the time and nothing had happened, except I fainted and they put me on the bed.'

'Why did you think it was Freya's stepdad rather than Jaeger?' asked Harry.

'Because of the look on their faces. Jaeger smirked as though he knew something, and Hugo looked as if he had a guilty secret.'

'Can I ask, were you still clothed?' asked John.

'I still had them on, except for my shoes. But they weren't tucked in as before.'

'What happened then?' asked John.

'I felt confused and sick. Adonis took me back to Chamonix. He said I was mistaken and should just forget it. He said that if I did, von Kesler would pay me for the filming anyway, but if I caused trouble for Freya's stepdad, he would deal with me. Adonis said Heinz knew influential people in the valley.'

'Did you tell Freya what happened?'

Amy shook her head. 'Not at first. I wanted to try

to forget the whole thing and make it as if it hadn't happened. I went skiing, but it just wasn't the same. I couldn't sleep and I felt scared. Freya and I always did things together, but after that, I couldn't look at her. I know she hated her stepdad, but when she was with me, it felt like I was adding more to the lies I was telling myself.'

'But she found out,' said John.

Amy nodded. 'Freya said I was acting weird, and we had a massive argument. I completely lost it. It was then that I told her.'

'When was that?' asked John.

'Two days before she was found dead.' Amy took a tissue from the box beside her bed and wiped her eyes. 'She died because I told her. I wish I'd just kept my mouth shut and gone home.'

'What did Freya do when you told her?'

Amy looked at her fingers as she twiddled them. 'She went ballistic. She said her stepfather had tried it on with her as well. Touching her and stuff. She said he was sick in the head. Freya was into IT. She said she knew things about Heinz von Kesler and his parties. People say the house is rigged with cameras and von Kesler gets off on secretly filming them having sex. Freya wanted to get the evidence and expose her stepdad. She wanted her mother to know what kind of sicko she had married and for him to pay for what he did to me.'

'So, she went back to the chalet?'

Amy nodded. 'Freya said von Kesler wouldn't keep data at the chalet in case it was raided. She said it would be cloud-based – on a server in some dodgy country. She said it would be simple enough to encrypt his data. Freya would insert a password so that only she could access it. I think she managed, but I never saw her again.'

'What makes you think she managed it?' asked Harry.

'Because she texted me and then someone broke into her flat and mine. They were looking for something, and yesterday confirmed what it was.'

'What happened yesterday, Amy?' asked Émilie.

Amy looked at Émilie and started to weep. 'Arthur Roux came to my apartment. He showed me a clip from the chalet bedroom. He said he had the whole video and that if I didn't tell him what Freya had done and give him the password, he would post the clip anonymously on social media. He said that I was also implicated in Freya's death. I didn't know what to do. That's why …'

Fiona leant over and hugged her daughter again. 'It's all right now, Amy,' she said, trying to soothe her. 'Sometimes when things happen it feels like the end of the world, but we'll manage our way through – that's what Dad would want, isn't it?'

Amy nodded and blew her nose, and Harry asked a final question.

'Was it you posing as Freya in the telepherique?'

'It was. At that point, I didn't know that Freya was dead. She messaged me saying she had managed to do what she had set out to do, but Heinz von Kesler suspected her and she needed an alibi. She said Arthur Roux was helping her. All I had to do was use her pass and take the telepherique up, wearing her ski gear over mine. I was to leave her skis and clothes with Arthur. I took my pass with me – just in case. Once I'd done that, I snuck in among the tourists and took the cabin back down. It was only when I heard that Knox and Cal had found her body that I realised Freya couldn't have sent me the text. It was Arthur Roux.'

Harry asked, 'Did you see where Roux went once you'd given him Freya's things?'

She shook her head. 'He just disappeared.'

'You've done the right thing, telling us,' said John.

Amy looked at him with hopeless eyes. 'But it won't bring Freya back, will it?'

John shook his head. 'No, it won't. But it will help bring those responsible to justice.'

***

'Would you mind if myself and Harry had a word with Mum outside?' asked John.

He could see the suggestion made Amy nervous, so he tried to reassure her. 'Émilie will be here.'

'I won't go anywhere, I promise,' said Émilie, rubbing Amy's hand.

Amy forced a thin smile. 'OK. As long as you stay here.'

'I'll be straight back,' said Mum, and John led them to a quiet spot at the end of the corridor.

Fiona looked at Harry and John in turn. 'You two won't do anything about this, will you?' she said.

'We will, but we need to gather evidence,' said Harry.

With a combined look of rage and despair, Fiona shook her head and then spoke in a hushed, biting tone. 'Someone drugged and raped my daughter, almost killing her, but you're impotent because Sir Hugo Rowden-Mott is part of the privileged elite; part of the Great British establishment, and I'm a lowly primary school teacher. He and his kind will close ranks and make this quietly go away. It's what they do, isn't it? All those paedophiles, rapists and crooks sitting in high chairs groping each other and exposing themselves, and it will never change. I ask you, who is left to look after us? Our young people come to places like this to escape the rotten society those people have perpetuated, but those vile creatures follow like predators in their wake.'

Fiona's face hardened further. 'You go off and play the charade of finding evidence, but don't think you're fooling me. I'm going to fight for my daughter. I'm going to phone the press and tell them what that man did to her, and I'll say you are a couple of corrupt cops complicit in it. Because you are, aren't you? How many other girls has he drugged and raped during his miserable life, and how many times has it been hushed up?'

'Come and sit down,' said Harry.

'Don't tell me what to do, and I swear, if you tell me to calm down, I'll—'

'Please,' said Harry, ushering her to the seat.

She hesitated and then reluctantly moved to one of three utilitarian chairs in a line and buried her face in her hands. 'This is like something from a medieval nightmare,' she said. 'Young girls sacrificed to cleanse a syphilis-riddled king.'

John tried to explain their position. 'If you go to the press, they'll first want to investigate. If they don't, they could be prosecuted for defamation.'

'I'll post it on the internet. That's what they threatened to do to Amy,' she said.

John nodded in empathy. 'They were looking to scare Amy. We believe her, but we need to get tangible proof. The last thing we want is for the man Amy is accusing to get wind of it.'

He paused, wondering if he could make this easier for the mother, but concluded she deserved the truth.

'I'll be frank with you, Mrs Joyce. He'll go on the attack and get a super-injunction served to close you down, and his expensive barristers will bay for you and Amy's blood. You're right, society isn't equal, and it's especially hard for our young people, but unfortunately, it's all we have. Give me and Harry a chance to look into this for Amy. I promise we won't walk away.'

Fiona's anger abated, and she looked dejectedly at the officers. 'You hear of things like this happening to other families, but you never believe it will happen to your child. Do either of you have a daughter?'

'I do,' said Harry. 'Her name is Pamela, and if she had suffered what Amy has, I would be beyond furious.'

Fiona then looked at John.

He shook his head. 'I don't, but I have people I care deeply for. I've spent my career seeking justice for victims and know the devastation caused by crimes against the person.'

Fiona seemed to accept this. 'I suppose I have the two of you and Amy's friends, Cal and Knox, to thank that she's still alive. But how is she going to get over this?'

Émilie was standing at the door speaking to her father, Guillaume. They could see that Émilie was angry: someone had come into her valley and defiled its sanctity. Émilie glanced along the corridor at John and Harry and shook her head as if to say, 'How could this happen?'

John turned to Amy's mother. 'Will you give us a bit of time?'

Once again, she shook her head in despair. 'What choice do Amy and I have? Amy's father, my husband, Richard, died two years ago. We were nearly destroyed by it, but Amy stuck in, passed her A Levels and secured a place at university. She kept me afloat. She had always wanted to take a year out. We're not wealthy people, so she worked hard all summer to save up for this trip. We topped it up with a little money from Richard's life insurance. Not for a minute did I suspect something like this would happen.'

***

Fiona returned to her daughter and John and Harry

made their way out of the hospital and drew a breath of cold valley air to try to clear their heads.

'The first question is how confident are we with Amy's version of events,' said Harry.

'I believe her,' said John. 'It fits with the timeline, and why would she lie? Why would she tell us her part in it? She's scared witless to the point of wanting an out. When she said she had been raped, I immediately thought of Jaeger Schmidt, but I think we both had Rowden-Mott down as a misogynist. Hearing that he believes he can do as he wants with a vulnerable young woman doesn't surprise me.'

Harry's phone rang. 'It's Sheila. I'd better take this: she had something important to tell me.'

Harry took the call, and with John looking on eagerly to know what was happening, he listened to what Sheila had to say. He ended by saying there had been a major development and he'd be calling Jack.

He came off the phone and looked gravely at John. 'Rowden-Mott has been accused of drugging women before. Sheila found out that the junior researcher who lodged a complaint against him said he had spiked her drink with Rohypnol during a post-work get-together in London. Her partner turned up as they were leaving the bar. Rowden-Mott said he was being the good Samaritan and trying to get her home.'

'Bloody close call for the woman,' said John. 'And I think Mum is bang on the money.'

'About Rowden-Mott wriggling out of it?'

John nodded. 'He'll use the power differential to crush Amy. His barristers will be straight in with an injunction and intimidate the girl with the threat of a defamation claim. How many times have we seen that done? They'll stall, frustrate, infuriate and obfuscate to beat Amy and Mum into submission. They'll bank on Amy withdrawing her complaint for the sake of her mental well-being. If she does eventually have her day in court, Rowden-Mott will relish seeing her suffer. His barristers will break her down: they'll dig up dirt from her past, or paint their client as a misunderstood surrogate father figure. They'll put Jaeger Schmidt on the stand to testify that either Amy is imagining the whole thing, or, as Knox threw at us, she consented but now regrets it. If that doesn't work, they'll use her involvement in Freya's death to make her appear like an unreliable witness. Von Kesler will say he knows nothing about it. He knows the value of his video evidence lies in dangling it over Rowden-Mott's miserable head. He can only use it once, but he can hold Rowden-Mott hostage forever. Right now, without evidence, Amy Joyce will take nothing but suffering from what happened to her. As Knox put it, her life will be trashed.'

'We could try to get our hands on Arthur Roux,' suggested Harry.

'And do what?' said John. 'You've said all along that this comes under French jurisdiction.'

'Which brings us to Petit and Pierre …' said Harry.

'I've no idea about Petit. I had him in the "not so bright" category. But now nothing would surprise me.'

'And Pierre?' asked Harry.

John took another deep breath and blew it slowly out. 'God knows. But we can't keep him out of this for long.'

'No, we can't. What do you suggest?' asked Harry.

'Amy thinks Freya got into von Kesler's system and was going to expose him and her stepfather, right?'

Harry nodded.

'It seems von Kesler either doesn't understand or isn't able to undo whatever she did. If whatever was going to happen had happened, Roux wouldn't have tried to intimidate Amy. That means it's either time-activated or, as Amy thinks, a password-protected gateway.'

'I'd go for the latter,' said Harry. 'It would be why Freya's flat was emptied and Amy's turned over. Freya was going to do something but died before she could complete it.'

'If she had the key to solve his problem, they would want her alive,' said John.

Harry looked towards where the glacier sat behind a ridge. 'Perhaps Freya's death was an accident after all, but I don't think either of us is buying that, just as her mother isn't.'

John had a thought. 'Could the answer be with her mother, Astrid? Amy says Freya wanted to save her mother from her stepfather. Didn't Astrid say she received angry messages from her daughter?'

'She did,' said Harry, taking out his phone. 'I need to brief Jack and then we need to get ourselves up the valley. Von Kesler will be trying to fix his problem and when he does, he'll move any evidence out of our reach.'

John put his hand on Harry's arm. 'No, Harry. Leave this one with me: it's what I do best. Besides, if I'm handing back my warrant card anyway, what difference will it make?'

Harry shook his head. 'It will make a difference to me and it will make a difference to Cal, Knox and all the other young people who want to see change. But Jack's been a decent gaffer and isn't one to back away from a just cause, so let's give him a chance.'

'And if he says no?'

'Then we'll go, anyway. But we can't barrel up to von Kesler's in a taxi,' said Harry as he waited for Jack to answer.

***

Guillaume rubbed his chin as he thought through the implications of what Harry and John had asked. With his mind made up, he beckoned them to follow him out one of the hospital's back doors and across to where his metallic green Dacia Duster was parked. They climbed in and sat for a moment.

John looked across at him from the passenger seat. He could see anxiety etched across Guillaume's face. 'You don't have to do this, Guillaume,' he said.

'Yes, I do,' he replied. 'I am a police officer and I'm also a father. The young woman, Amy, and her mother need our help. I presume you have a plan?'

he asked before starting the engine.

Seeking a credible answer, John twisted his head to Harry sitting in the back. But Harry looked even less certain than he was, so John tried to explain.

'We have half a plan.'

'Which is?' asked Guillaume, looking sceptically back at John.

'Which is, you get us up to von Kesler's chalet and that will be the end of your involvement. We're going to see if we can get access to his IT suite. If we can, we might be able to patch a PC through by mobile phone to our people in Gartcosh.'

'Gartcosh?' asked Guillaume.

'It's the Scottish Crime Campus an hour or so from Edinburgh where we deal with serious organised crime. The digital forensics geeks hang out there. Our boss is heading through now,' replied John.

'Can't they access the computer remotely?' asked Guillaume.

'It's not the computer we need – it's the cloud that it's connected to and that could be anywhere in the world. We're hoping a PC together with what we think are the passwords sent by Freya to her mother will give us an in. Given enough time, it might be possible to trace the cloud remotely, but if von Kesler gets access first, the evidence will probably be shifted and that will be that.'

'So you're going to break into von Kesler's chalet?'

'That's the plan as it stands … unless you have a better idea?'

Looking far from happy, Guillaume muttered something in French, started the engine and set off. 'This should be a properly authorised and planned operation,' he said. 'You don't know how von Kesler will react.'

'And you think Petit would sanction it?' asked John.

Guillaume was forced to agree. 'We know he wouldn't, which is why we are undertaking this folly. I meant it when I said we are with you. Petit's arrival has been *une catastrophe*. The man is an embarrassment to the gendarmerie.'

'I know that,' said Harry. 'Don't think you're the only station in the world to suffer an incompetent officer. We've had our share.'

'What about Pierre? What do you make of him?' asked John.

'Ah, Pierre. You've been with him for over a week, so surely you can answer that yourself.'

John gave it some thought and concluded that apart from Pierre being friendly, enjoying expensive tastes and having transferred from some or other role in Lyon, they knew little about the man.

'I'm afraid I'm still in the dark,' replied John.

'Exactly,' said Guillaume. 'Pierre is *l'homme au masque de fer*. The man in the iron mask. It's what we call a mysterious person who works alone. But he has *savoir-faire* as a detective and is prepared to stand up to Petit.'

'He certainly doesn't seem to have much time for the man,' said John.

'But you don't trust him?' asked Guillaume.

An awkward answer was avoided by an incoming call on Harry's phone. He checked the caller ID, answered and listened.

'Got it, boss,' he said and hung up.

'John, take note of the time. Jack says he'll be at Gartcosh and ready in 60 minutes. Guillaume, would you mind stopping at the hotel? We need to collect a few things.'

When John and Harry returned to the car, Guillaume was finishing a call. John sought an explanation.

'It's OK,' said Guillaume. 'Remember, we are on the same side. Have you got everything you need?'

'We've got what we've got, and it will have to do,' replied John in a manner that revealed his doubts.

Guillaume set off, went straight ahead and turned right at the junction. 'This is the back road to Les Praz,' he said.

John and Harry recognised it as the route they had taken by bus only three days before. That now felt like another age. John thought about how traumatic events did that. They fractured time into a before and after. His father's death, joining the force, the passing of his mother, the women that Vlatko's people had murdered and now Amy hanging lifelessly from a beam. But getting to Amy in time had broken the pattern and today they would try to get justice for her and Freya.

'Are you OK, John?' asked Guillaume.

'I'm fine. I was just thinking, that's all.'

It was the question Pierre had asked him on the

way to visit von Kesler, and it occurred to John that although he and Harry didn't know these people, they could see that they were caring: Pierre's concern for Mathilde, Antoine bringing them coffee and croissants for their aborted retreat from Chamonix, Émilie championing Amy and her mother and Guillaume acting as a proxy father. Knox and Cal risked their lives so Freya wouldn't be alone and Florent was fiercely protective of the lads. Fraternity: it was a refreshing way of life, and to John, reminiscent of his childhood.

Guillaume spoke. 'If you want to approach von Kesler's unseen, then I have an idea.'

'What?' asked John, but Guillaume just offered a smile.

About a kilometre further on, Guillaume pulled into layby set back from the road.

Harry looked at his watch. 'What are we stopping for?' he asked.

'Wait,' said Guillaume, looking intently for something in the rearview mirror.

A police car pulled in behind them and Guillaume got out to meet it.

The newly arrived officer didn't get out. Guillaume went to the driver's window and leant in. There was a short exchange of words and Guillaume took something from the officer, slipped it into an inner coat pocket and returned as the police car pulled away.

'Who was that?' asked John.

'You don't need to know. But we have something that will help you. Here is a security keycard for the rear door of von Kesler's chalet. He has valuable artwork, so the alarm is linked to the gendarmerie. We have the card to gain access. If it's found out that we gave you this, we will lose our jobs and likely end up in La Santé,' he said, referring to the notorious prison near Paris.

John took the card. 'Thank you, Guillaume. But it's unlikely to be that easy to access.'

'Indeed,' said Guillaume, as he handed John a small pair of bolt croppers and a piece of paper from inside his jacket. 'This is a cadastral map showing the boundaries of von Kesler's property and the chalet footprint. My colleague has pencilled in a rough layout based on what he remembers from the security survey. However, he wasn't there as a cartographer, so it may not be accurate. Now we must go or you'll be late for your rendezvous.'

They followed the road into Les Praz, out again towards Argentière and across the railway line. Once again, they started up the hill, but instead of following the main road, Guillaume turned onto the steep winding road leading to Mathilde's village.

'There's a tractor track used for taking food to the cattle in the pasture,' said Guillaume. 'As long as it's been used recently, we should be able to get you close to the rear of von Kesler's chalet. You'll need to drop through the trees and the snow will be deep, making a return virtually impossible. The alternative would be to come in from the main entrance, but that runs the risk of someone seeing your approach.'

'We'll take our chances through the woods,' said

John.

John looked for Mathilde's car as they passed her chalet. It was gone, but Framboise was basking in the sun atop the balcony balustrade. She watched curiously as they passed by. For some reason, John wanted to give her a wave, as if somehow it would reconnect him to the safer world of a lazy lunch, honest conversation, and the kindling of feelings.

He was brought back to earth with a jolt when the Duster dropped into a pothole.

'Putain,' protested Guillaume, but carried on, his tyres intermittently gripping the tractor tread pattern embossed in the snow whilst the high centre mound threatened to maroon them.

The tracks ended beside a large hay feeder where cattle had trampled the snow, making it easy for Guillaume to turn.

He stopped the vehicle. 'Perhaps I'll come with you, after all,' he said.

John shook his head. 'No. If this goes wrong, we need someone able to speak for what happened. Embellish your story as you will, and make sure you look after Amy and her mother.'

Guillaume stared out of the windscreen, trying to think of another way, but falling short and with time pressing he accepted it. 'I'll take you as far as the route down to the chalet.'

Moving briskly, Guillaume led them along the fence that separated the pasture from the trees below.

He stopped and peered down. 'This is a good place to descend from. How long do you need?' he asked.

John checked his watch and did some rough calculations. 'Give us an hour and a half and then send in the cavalry.'

'It isn't too late to do that now,' said Guillaume.

John shook his head. 'If Petit gets wind of this, he'll either close us down or go in with sirens blazing and any evidence in that chalet will be disposed of.'

Guillaume embraced John and Harry in turn.

'You make this seem final,' said John, but Guillaume didn't reply, and they set off down through the woods.

***

The ground quickly fell away, but the snow made for a cushioned slide, coating them with makeshift white camouflage.

They worked their way down, keeping trees between themselves and the chalet for cover. It didn't take long to reach the edge of the forest where they hid behind the last of the trees and looked across the 50 metres of open ground. The final section was the chalet perimeter in dressed Chamonix stone. A black 4x4 was parked in front of closed double garage doors, and to the left was the entrance described by Guillaume.

'Have you seen the film, "Too Late the Hero"?' asked Harry, as they peered across a no-man's-land of snow, metamorphosed through freeze-thaw into hard névé.

John smiled. 'Not for years. Once this is over, you can come around to my place with a six-pack and we'll watch it together.'

It was something they did when under pressure: look for a diversion: a quip or common analogy usually worked.

They looked around for security cameras and counted three PTZs: pan-tilt-zooms, capable of scanning and homing in on subjects of interest.

'I don't understand why none of those cameras are pointed this way,' said John.

'Either a lazy operator or some may be down. You know the problems we have with CCTV, so what must it be like here in winter?' replied Harry.

John looked at his watch. 'Jack should be nearing Gartcosh. Shall we make a bolt for it?'

'Roger that,' said Harry, once again attempting to lighten what they both knew was a serious undertaking.

Stooping low but unsure what difference it would make in open ground, they jogged across the snow to the back door. Harry kept a lookout while John retrieved the keycard from his pocket and unlocked it.

He turned the aluminium handle, and the door inched open. 'So, we won't be needing the bolt croppers,' he said, gently pulling the door closed again. 'But it feels too easy …'

Harry agreed. 'What choice do we have?'

'None,' said John. 'We can't go back and tell Amy and her mother that we abandoned our plan because it felt too easy.'

They brushed as much snow off themselves as they could, John opened the door again and they slipped through into a dimmed windowless corridor. The floor was plushly carpeted, and on one side were identical polished oak doors with modern stainless-steel handles and security locks. Between the uniformly spaced doors were wall insets housing tall vases on plinths and lit by downlights. It resembled a boutique hotel: chic but functional, indicating a serious purpose. John suspected that Rowden-Mott had taken Amy into one of these rooms and raped her.

They listened intently for any sounds of life, but all was quiet. John took out the pencilled sketch and orientated it with the corridor. 'It should be the second door this way,' he said, pointing to their right.

The door was fitted with a sophisticated alphanumeric keypad. Harry put his ear hard against it and after a few seconds made a facial gesture to say he couldn't hear anything.

John tried the handle, but it was locked. They looked up and down the corridor and then at the keypad. Putting his finger close to it, Harry looked questioningly at John. John shook his head. 'Get it wrong and we could set off an alarm,' he whispered.

It looked as though they had reached the end of the road but in last-ditch play, John tipped the closest recessed vase forwards on its plinth and there was someone's memory jogger.

John looked at Harry as though once again questioning the ease with which they were making progress, but with the alternative being to abort, Harry gestured for him to try it.

They expected a computer suite, but what they entered was an audio-visual room with a mixing desk and a huge wall-mounted TV screen. A comfortable recliner chair was positioned in the middle of the room.

'It looks like the rumours Amy heard were right,' said John. 'This is where von Kesler gets off on watching people.'

John looked around at the expensive equipment. 'This goes well beyond perve-parties. We know that he videoed at least one girl being drugged and raped: what else is he hiding? We'd better get on with what we're here for.'

To the right of the mixing desk was a high-end tower PC with a plethora of ports on the front. The PC was running but locked.

John realised they hadn't checked for a mobile phone signal, and this could all be in vain, but the screen read five bars.

Harry searched the PC tower for a USB Type-C port, and confirming its presence, he connected his phone and dialled the number sent by Gartcosh.

'We should have bought a burner,' he said.

'No time,' replied John.

Almost immediately, the line connected.

'We're through,' said Harry.'

John nodded and looked towards the door. 'If you want to leave now, I'll watch the phone.'

But leaving the other wasn't an option for either

of them.

John's phone lit up: a text with the prearranged digit '1' from an anonymous sender.

He turned to Harry. 'Gartcosh are connected.'

The seconds seemed an eternity as they waited for the next text. They looked about the room, trying to find something useful to divert the tension. Evidence, perhaps? But apart from the screen, the chair and the AV desk the room appeared clean.

John's phone lit up again. He looked at the screen, a French number, possibly Mathilde's.

Trying to figure it out, he mouthed 'Mathilde?' to Harry and was about to cancel the call when his sixth sense warned him to wait for it to drop off. It was something Mathilde had said: someone with something urgent to say will try again.

It rang again and John answered. 'I need to be quick.'

'John, listen carefully. I've met with the cantonal police and am driving back to Chamonix.'

'I thought Petit had grounded you?'

There was a burst of French that sounded pretty unpleasant, and then she continued in English. 'The DNA results are back. The girl in the river is not Lucie.'

'Not Lucie?' he asked.

'No, she's not Lucie. The girl in the picture is Lucie, but the girl in the river is called Anya.'

They heard urgent voices approaching along the corridor.

'I need to go, Mathilde.'

'Where are you?' she asked.

'Von Kesler's chalet.'

'Merde—'

I think the game's up,' said Harry as he hurriedly disconnected his phone.

They had a last look around for an escape, but with only one door and no windows it was hopeless: they were trapped.

'I guess it comes down to Guillaume calling the cavalry,' said John.

'What did Mathilde have to say?' asked Harry.

'She said the woman found in the river isn't Lucy. It's another woman who goes by the name Anya.'

Harry nodded, and the voices got closer. They could make out von Kesler saying something excitable in German. He called through from the corridor, 'We're opening the door and Yan is armed. Stand back so we can see you both and nobody will get hurt.'

John gave Harry a pat on the back and an apologetic smile.

Harry returned something more positive. 'Don't worry, John. We've had a good run of it, haven't we?'

'We have indeed,' John replied.

They stood back in the open, knowing that with Yan holding a weapon, any kind of resistance would make the situation more dangerous than it already was.

The door swung open and Yan walked in confidently holding a pistol, followed by von Kesler. Von Kesler grinned and glanced around to see if anything obvious had changed before turning his attention to John and Harry.

'Pierre told me to expect you. It doesn't alter the fact that you have broken into my property, but I'm hoping it will play to my advantage. Come, gentlemen, we'll wait in the main lounge until we find out.' He then turned and put a thoughtful finger to his lips and smiled. 'I have a visitor: an acquaintance of yours.'

John and Harry had never quite figured out Pierre. Guillaume's advocacy for him had offered a glimmer of hope, but von Kesler had just given them a reality check. The amiable Pierre had set them up.

They looked at Yan with his gun trained on them. John recognised it as a 9mm Russian Udav: a potent weapon with eighteen rounds designed to pierce body armour. It would have been sold from the back door of a Soviet military base or separated from its keeper in some conflict or other.

From Yan's detached look, John concluded that like Vlatko's people, Yan had long since lost any sense of morality, but whereas Vlatko's people were murderous thugs, Yan had the bearing of a professional killer. He'd have started as a teen with national service and deployed in any number of wars that had mutatcd into the state-sponsored murder of civilians. With killing becoming his trade, he'd have moved to the lucrative world of PMCs: private military companies that sat even further outside 'the laws of war.' Now he was an android dressed in designer clothes and killing on his paymaster's request, but with no motivation to go beyond. Why would he? It could only add to the risk of losing his freedom.

The real danger in the room was von Kesler. He'd proven himself capable of many things, including manipulation, cruelty, and voyeurism, and John suspected he was implicated in Anya's death.

Von Kesler sensed the officers weighing Yan up. 'You'd be unwise to test him. When it comes to dispatching problems, Yan is both capable and without compunction.'

'I'm sure he is,' said John.

Yan kept his weapons pointed at them, as he stepped forward and with an outstretched arm, patted John and Harry down. He removed the bolt croppers from John's coat, took their phones and wallets and handed them to von Kesler.

Von Kesler put the croppers to one side but retained the phones.

'Unlock these,' he said.

John and Harry hesitated until Yan lifted his gun, and with a two-handed grip took careful aim at Harry's head.

It was a tell not lost on John. Yan would know that pointing the gun at John would be futile. John would likely tell him to go and fuck himself. But pointing the gun at his colleague ... now that was a different matter. And von Kesler only needed one of them.

Von Kesler moved back, and with no choice, the officers unlocked their phones.

He beckoned a geeky-looking guy who was waiting in the wings. The man stepped forward and von Kesler handed him the phones and wallets. 'See if they have accessed the network and report back to me.'

The geek nodded obediently whilst trying to keep his face turned away.

Von Kesler led them along the corridor, past the door they had entered. 'In case you have ideas of leaving, I'm afraid it's now locked from the inside,' he said, as he carried on, and up a short flight of stairs. At the top, he opened another door, and they entered into the daylight of the large living area they had visited with Pierre.

Yan kept the gun trained as von Kesler ushered them into the centre of the room. The officers looked around. Jaeger Schmidt was sitting on one of the sofas facing them. With his blonde hair, white shorts and a sleeveless white running vest, he still looked in love with himself, but he also looked frightened.

Sitting away from him in an armchair, with his legs crossed and holding a crystal whisky tumbler, sat Sir Hugo. As on their first meeting, he was impeccably presented with his hair neatly combed, and dressed in dark trousers, a white shirt, and a navy sports jacket. And as before, the surrounding air hung heavy with the scent of his cologne. He still had that imperiously smug look, but now having heard what he had done to Amy, rather than dismissing it, John wanted to slap it off his face.

Jaeger made to move, but von Kesler snapped his fingers. 'Stay where you are, Jaeger.'

Jaeger sat back down and looked warily at von Kesler.

Unperturbed by two British police officers being held at gunpoint, Sir Hugo swirled the contents of his glass in a theatrical display of confidence and then spoke. 'You two are compiling quite a rap sheet on your little jaunt. Insulting your host Commandant de Petit, impersonating a member of His Majesty's Foreign Office, and now breaking and entering.'

Sir Hugo reached into his pocket and took out the document Harry had handed Petit on Monday.

'What is this?' he asked, putting the glass to one side and opening the paper.

'The 1320 Declaration of Arbroath,' said John.

'Ingenious,' replied Sir Hugo. 'It certainly had the commandant fooled. There's hope for you yet.'

From how von Kesler and Sir Hugo chuckled, John assumed they were once more on amicable terms.

'Is it purely coincidence that you're here today?' John asked.

Sir Hugo sipped his whisky and returned to the officers. 'I'm here on business.'

'Don't tell me, your conscience has got the better of you and you're going to give this man his money back?' John asked, glancing at von Kesler.

Von Kesler looked as though that was something he hadn't considered, but might.

'Nothing like that,' said Sir Hugo. 'We've secured a UK government grant to support Heinz in setting up an import/export business. A timely initiative to help the British economy with the post-Brexit customs issues we are facing.'

'Aye, right. There are no flies on you, are there?'

said John. 'How much are you skimming off this time?'

The smile dropped from Hugo's face. 'I find you tiresome, Sergeant, and have to say that I took a dislike to you from the start.'

'I'll take that as a compliment,' said John.

'Take it as a threat, Sergeant. The people I'm connected to would swallow you whole.'

Von Kesler glanced at his watch, and as he did so, John and Harry caught a glimpse of a dark car driving quickly by to the rear of the chalet.

Whoever it was, von Kesler seemed relieved they had arrived. 'Now we'll get this sorted out,' he said.

Yan switched position, keeping a distance from John and Harry as he also covered the door from the corridor.

Moments later, the door opened, and Pierre entered.

He looked around to see who was present.

Yan, von Kesler and Sir Hugo remained as they were and Pierre asked von Kesler, 'Have you got what you need?'

'We're waiting to find out,' said von Kesler. 'Of course, this is a fuckup of your making. If you had kept these two on a tight leash, as you were paid to, we wouldn't be in this position.'

Pierre slowly shook his head, looked at Sir Hugo and then back at von Kesler. 'These two have nothing to do with you being locked out of your digital cesspool. Your distinguished associate here drugging and raping a young woman led to this, and getting Arthur Roux to show her a clip of his depravity is beyond belief.'

Sir Hugo's face dropped. 'What clip?' he asked, looking at von Kesler and Pierre in turn.

John could see alarm bells ringing loudly in Sir Hugo's head.

'The sex tape he took of you raping the girl,' said John. He wanted to add something like, 'I thought videoing yourself in the act was the norm for you people.' But he knew with the situation escalating it would be a provocation too far.

Sir Hugo's face paled. He dropped the glass to smash on the marble floor and rose quickly to his feet. He looked at Pierre and then turned his attention to von Kesler. 'You have a video?'

Pierre looked at John and Harry and then questioningly at Sir Hugo. 'Why do you think these two are here?'

Heinz's face contorted. 'Shut up, Pierre.'

But Pierre seemed unfazed by the man.

Von Kesler glared at him and then flipped to a broad smile. 'You know me well, Pierre. But I'm more subtle than you think. Paying for sex is the norm for men like Hugo. Even their wives accept it. As long as it doesn't impinge on their expensive lifestyles, they'll pretend not to know. But rape is altogether different. No woman wants to be married to a rapist and Hugo and his kind know that society is on to them and fear the backlash.'

Sir Hugo's manner turned to rage. 'You think you can blackmail me?'

For a moment it looked as though Hugo would lunge at von Kesler, but John had heard enough and went for von Kesler first. 'You're a sick bastard, von Kesler. Someone should put you down.'

He then turned to Sir Hugo. 'As for you, you're a fucking abomination. How many other women have you drugged and raped? Perhaps the name Anya will help your memory.'

He could see Jaeger twitch uncomfortably in his seat, so he turned his attention to him. 'You know, don't you, Jaeger, because you're part of this and you're going to go down with them.'

Jaeger was about to say something, but von Kesler shut him up.

John looked at Yan for a reaction, but Yan remained impassive.

There was a timid knock on the door.

'Enter,' shouted von Kesler, and the technician appeared.

'Well? Have you resolved our problem?' asked von Kesler.

Aware he was the harbinger of bad news and unsure what that meant to his life chances, the technician shook his head. 'There's no change, Herr von Kesler, we're still locked out of the system. The phones have nothing obvious that we can use.'

Von Keseler moved towards him. 'When I contacted you in Stuttgart you assured me you were a savant in cybercrime and could sort this out, did you not?'

The man pleaded with him. 'I told you it would take time. Whoever did this was clever. If you need a quick result, we could seek help: I know people …'

'And be held hostage by a dark-web ransom

gang? Or are you in cahoots with them?' asked von Kesler.

The technician glanced at Yan and shook his head vehemently. 'I'm not.'

'It would be unfortunate for you if you are. Now get back into the studio and stay there until you've solved this.'

With sweat on his brow and shaking hands, the technician scurried off.

John was unable to resist a dig. 'Lost the keys, have we?'

Von Kesler looked at him, then turned, strode over to Harry and kicked the side of his knee.

Harry gasped in pain and crumpled to the floor. His glasses fell off and von Kesler crushed them under his shoe. 'Shut the fuck up, Sergeant.'

Von Kesler clasped his hands behind his back, went to the window and looked out as he gathered his thoughts.

Harry tried to get back onto his feet but struggled.

Keeping his eyes on von Kesler, and under Yan's scrutiny, Pierre pulled him up and then stepped away from him.

Von Kesler returned to them. 'So, this is what we'll do. Let's end this charade: we all know why you came here. You're looking to continue what Hugo's stepdaughter started. If I ask whether you succeeded, you'll say no.'

'We didn't have time,' said John. 'As your so-called "savant" from Stuttgart tried telling you, it's more complicated than we thought.'

Von Kesler looked sympathetic. 'No, of course

you didn't. I knew it was a pointless question. But I have another solution. Let me tell you what happened to the girl, Freya, and then perhaps we can come to an accommodation,' he said, looking at Jaeger Schmidt.

'That's unlikely,' said John.

Having reached the same conclusion, von Kesler nodded. 'You're probably right, Sergeant. We can but try, and if we fail Yan will finish the matter for us. Pierre will then make sure this sorry business is buried once and for all.'

Pierre offered his counsel. 'The death of two British police officers won't be a straightforward thing to cover up, especially if they've told someone they are here.'

'Perhaps they haven't told anyone. They didn't tell you, Pierre, did they?'

Pierre shook his head. 'No, they didn't.'

'I'm sure you'll find a way,' replied von Kesler. 'It's what I pay you for. So, let's continue.'

He addressed John and Harry. 'Believe me, had I known the contempt in which Hugo's stepdaughter held him, I would never have allowed this moron to lure her friend here,' he said, glancing at Hugo and then Jaeger.

John could see that he and Harry were being led further down a path of no return. Von Kesler had taken them at gunpoint and was now exposing incriminating information. It could mean only one thing: he had no intention of letting them go. And Harry was struggling with the pain in his leg and unable to see clearly.

John knew that if they were to have any chance of getting out, they needed to retake the agenda and he'd have to lead.

He stood slightly taller, and as he did so, Yan lifted his weapon in readiness. 'Careful with that, son,' said John, and then turned to von Kesler. 'Why did you kill her? Why did you kill Freya? It was him she was after,' pointing at her stepfather, 'not you. She was the one person who could solve your problem.'

Von Kesler moved towards John and looked him in the eyes. 'I didn't kill her, Sergeant. That idiot sitting on the couch did.'

John looked at Jaeger Schmidt slumped down: the self-proclaimed Adonis who Knox said forced himself on women and couldn't ski for shit. He suddenly felt a huge regard for the Scottish lads, Knox, and Cal. Throughout the sorry saga of finding the truth about Freya's death, they alone seemed able to separate good from bad. They had contacted Astrid, cast doubt on Pierre, talked of Amy's distress, warned of Jaeger Schmidt, and Knox's words of caution about von Kesler now echoed in John's ears: *Tread carefully with that fuck von Kesler.*

Jaeger Schmidt looked seriously worried. If what von Kesler had just said was true and Jaeger had killed Freya, he was publicly in the frame for murder.

'I only did what you told me to,' said Jaeger.

But from his pleading tone, it was obvious that like everyone else in the room, he knew von Kesler had just thrown him under the bus.

Pierre looked curious. 'What happened, Jaeger?'

Looking hopeful that Pierre was an ally, Jaeger tried to explain. 'Heinz told me to force the code from her, but no injuries. I used a pillow and must have held it to her face for too long.'

John felt rage building inside. 'So, you suffocated the lass, is that it?'

'No, it wasn't like that,' said Jaeger.

Pierre took an interest in his fingernails and casually asked, 'So what *was* it like Jaeger?'

John didn't give Jaeger a chance to answer. 'You say you didn't mean it, but we can see from her autopsy there was no attempt to resuscitate her, and from what I understand there wasn't an ambulance called to assist. Instead, you got your friend, Arthur Roux, to dispose of her body on the glacier. To save your miserable skin, you tried to cast that young woman into oblivion.'

John looked at Sir Hugo. 'You've just heard that someone suffocated your stepdaughter. Don't you have anything to say about that?'

Sir Hugo muttered something, but John stopped him. 'You knew, didn't you? All this time you knew …'

Von Kesler seemed to find it amusing and returned to Jaeger. 'You see, Jaeger, there's no way out for you. Especially now that everyone here knows your secret. Come,' he said, beckoning Jaeger. 'Perhaps we can get it right this time around. You see these two officers either have the solution to our problem, or they don't. Either way, we need to find out.'

Heinz walked over to Yan and reached out a hand. Yan put his free hand behind his back and retrieved another gun from where it was tucked into his trouser belt. John could see that this weapon was a rare Luger, and from its condition, likely to be part of a private collection.

Von Kesler took the gun and looked at Yan. 'Three rounds?'

Yan nodded, and von Kesler went over to Jaeger.

'Have you used a gun before?' he asked.

John could see that Jaeger was completely out of his depth.

'Once or twice,' replied Jaeger. 'In a forest in Bavaria.'

Von Kesler took off the safety catch. 'Take this. There are three rounds. Use the first on the inspector's leg. I'm sure that will help the Sergeant with his memory.'

Whether because he was frightened of the weapon, frightened of von Kesler and Yan, or scared at the thought of what he was about to do, Jaeger Schmidt held back.

'Go on, Jaeger, take it,' said Heinz. 'You're a murderer. You'll get life for what you did. Do you want that?'

As the now terrified young man took the gun, John surprised himself by feeling sorry for him. Whatever hopes and dreams he had harboured for life were now gone.

'I don't want to do this,' Jaeger said, trying to return the weapon.

Yan lifted his gun higher.

'Look,' said von Kesler. 'You don't have a choice. Your prints are on that gun. Yan will kill you in self-defence and Pierre will vouch for it. Now shoot the inspector. A leg shot is all it needs and perhaps then he or the sergeant will speak and you are free to go. Does that sound reasonable?'

Jaeger stood back from Harry and tried to aim. But with sweat from his brow stinging his eyes and trembling hands, he couldn't.

'This needs to stop,' said Pierre. 'Jaeger, you killed Freya, but you didn't mean to. Put the gun down.'

Yan was now aiming at Jaeger's head, and Heinz was berating him. 'Shoot him, Jaeger, or we'll shoot you. Now do it.'

Tears were streaming down Jaeger's cheeks. 'I can't.'

Von Kesler turned to Yan. 'Kill him.'

Jaeger lifted the gun again and half-heartedly took a shot at Harry's legs.

Harry instinctively jumped anyway, and the sound of an empty cartridge case rattled on the marble floor.

John shouted out. 'For fuck's sake, stop this. It's madness. I'll tell you what we know.'

Von Kesler lifted a hand for Yan and Jaeger to cease. 'What do you know?'

John told them what he could. 'We connected a phone to your system and our people in Scotland were trying to get through whatever gate Freya set up.'

'And did they?' asked Heinz.

John shook his head. 'I honestly don't know. We heard you coming and disconnected the line. You came in before we had a chance to call Scotland. That's the truth.'

Von Kesler pursed his lips. 'You've given me nothing here. Nothing at all. Jaeger, shoot the inspector in the stomach, and don't miss this time.'

'For pity's sake, you'll kill him,' said John. 'He's a good man with a wife and daughter. Shoot me instead. Come on Jaeger, I'm a nice big target for you.'

Von Kesler shook his head. 'No. Make it the inspector.'

'Why? Because he can't see or walk?'

Harry looked at John. 'It's OK. This isn't down to you. Keep an eye on Daphne and Pammy and tell them that it was quick.'

John looked at Pierre and gave him a look of loathing. 'You bastard. You fucking bastard,' he said. 'We're trusted to protect our citizens – it's our duty. How could you break that vow?'

Pierre just smiled. 'Life is what it is, John.'

'What's that supposed to mean?' John asked.

Von Kesler looked pleased with himself. 'So, it's settled. Jaeger, over to you. Shoot the inspector.'

John didn't see it coming. In one fluid action, Pierre's SP was out of its holster. He spun on a heel and took a shot at Yan. Yan's gun clattered to the floor and Pierre stepped back. With a twitch of his gun, he indicated for Yan to join the others. Yan raised his hands slightly and looked at the gun on the floor.

'The next shot will kill you, Yan,' said Pierre.

From what he had witnessed, Yan seemed to accept this, lifted his hands higher and moved lightly across the room.

So much for can't hit a barn door, thought John.

Jaeger was still holding the Luger and with the dynamic in the room changed, Sir Hugo and von Kesler were looking warily at him.

'It's over, Jaeger. Put it down,' said Pierre.

But Jaeger lifted the gun and pointed it at von Kesler.

'Don't do that,' said John. 'It won't fix anything.'

Pierre's phone rang. He took it from his pocket, held it up to his ear, listened and then hung up.

He suddenly looked transformed: as though something significant had changed in his favour. 'Heinz, my people and the British have accessed, decrypted, downloaded and deleted your cloud. Captagon, bank accounts, your sex tapes and your esteemed colleague's rape. Everything.'

Von Kesler went a light shade of grey and Yan looked furtively to him for direction.

Von Kelser turned on Pierre. 'You set me up, Pierre. You had me let these two enter the chalet to access the system for your ends. I should have gone with my instinct: you're not Gendarmerie, are you?'

John could see the genial smile that had been Pierre's signature throughout their time in Chamonix return to his face.

'Mossad, Shin Bet or DGSI?' asked von Kesler.

If Pierre was in one of those shadowy

organisations, he would never admit it.

Pierre was still looking at Jaeger. 'Put the gun down, Jaeger. There's nothing more to be gained.'

Jaeger shook his head as tears streamed from his crazed eyes, down his cheeks. 'I didn't want to kill anyone,' he said. 'I didn't mean to kill Freya, and he made me inject the girl,' he said, glancing at Sir Hugo.

'What girl?' asked John, already knowing the answer.

'Anya. He was abusing her; doing terrible things while she was sedated. She was coming around and I knew the pain she would be in so I gave her a bit more ketamine and she faded away. I tried to bring her back, but her heart had stopped.'

John could see that Jaeger was having a breakdown as the enormity of what he had been a party to overwhelmed him.

'There's another girl, Lucie, locked in the basement – that's why Hugo's here,' he said, reaching into his shorts pocket, retrieving an access card and chucking it towards Pierre.

Sir Hugo exploded into a rage and ran at Jaeger. 'You bloody—'

But Jaeger swung the Lugar and shot him square on.

In a world that now seemed to run in slow motion, John saw Sir Hugo's face implode as the bullet entered through the bridge of his nose and exited from the rear of his skull, taking the contents of his head with it.

Jaeger then turned the gun on himself and looked

at von Kesler. 'Betrüger,' he said.

Again, the sound from the Luger filled the room and Jaeger Schmidt fell to the floor.

Yan seized the moment to retrieve his weapon and dive behind the settee.

Pierre took a shot in Yan's direction to hold him at bay and shouted to John and Harry, 'Go to the basement and see if Lucie is still alive.'

***

John grabbed the card and made for the door, pulling Harry behind him.

As they headed down the corridor, they could hear the occasional shot and shouting from the main room. Von Kesler was trying to negotiate, but Pierre was no fool.

John looked at the map they had been given by Guillaume.

'This way,' he said, moving in the direction of a door marked cave in pencil on the plan.

He opened the door and an automatic light came on. 'Wait here, Harry.'

Harry stayed at the top and John descended. At the bottom of the stairs were two doors facing each other. He opened the first and saw what looked like a makeshift surgery with towels, syringes and drug vials set out. He pulled it closed and moved to the one opposite.

The room was sparse except for a bed, and sitting on the end of the bed dressed in white running shoes and a loose jogging suit was Lucie.

She looked vacantly up at John, barely able to move her head. 'No, no,' she said, trying to move it from side to side.

With any resistance to her fate spent, her head fell forward again.

John could see there wasn't much of anything left in her: quite different from the happy-looking girl in the photo, but written in her face he could still see a flicker of innocence.

'It's alright, lass. I'm not going to hurt you,' he said in a calming voice.

He swung her arm over his shoulder. At first, she tried to fight him off but then capitulated and he supported her out of the door and up the stairs.

'She's heavily drugged, Harry, but we must take her with us. If Pierre loses the day they'll kill her. I'll support her and you help as best you can.'

Jaeger's key got them back outside.

'I can't see a thing,' said Harry, trying to shield his eyes from the bright light.

Pistol shots sounded from inside the chalet.

John moved them over to Pierre's car, but the keys weren't in it.

'We need to get clear of here,' said John.

'But which way?' asked Harry. 'We can't go back the way we came, and the snowbanks on the drive will hem us in.'

John looked around for an escape, but the only obvious way was around the front and down the drive. 'We need to get to the drive and hope we reach the end before someone comes out.'

'Perhaps we should wait it out here,' said Harry.

John shook his head. 'No way. One of those loons will kill us. Let's move.'

With Lucie slung between them, dragging her feet, they staggered around the granite slabs and onto the snow-covered drive with its vertical sides honed by a season of snow clearing.

More gunshots. 'We need to move faster,' said John, as they stumbled and staggered on the slippery surface.

'We won't make it,' said Harry.

But John persisted. 'We're going to make it and make it together. Nobody gets left behind.'

The shooting diminished to sporadic shots … and then stopped.

They heard the throaty howl of a powerful car's exhaust.

'Pierre has either taken a bullet or run out of ammunition,' said Harry.

John glanced back and could see Pierre running towards them.

Pierre shouted, 'Keep moving, von Kesler will run us down.'

Unfettered by a casualty, Pierre caught up and John could see he had been shot in the arm. Blood was dripping from his sheepskin jacket to form crimson blotches on the snow.

'John, you take Lucie and I'll support Harry,' said Pierre, taking Harry's arm over his shoulder.

They moved as quickly as they could, but it was obvious they weren't going to make it. The vehicle's deep exhaust note was now reverberating down the snow-sided cutting. They were trapped.

John glanced back as the large black 4x4 appeared, its tyres throwing up snow and its engine howling as it went up through the automatic gearbox.

'Keep moving,' shouted Pierre.

Ahead, into the sun, they could see the end of the lane, but they would never reach it in time.

'For god's sake leave me,' said Harry.

But Pierre was resolute. 'If we go down, we go down together. We're a team, are we not?'

The two pairs stumbled on, but Pierre's stoicism couldn't give them the boost they needed.

More shots rang out, this time from ahead, and they could see someone standing in the middle of the road firing towards them. A shot whizzed past Johns's head, and another missed Harry by millimetres. The shots kept coming, and John faltered, fearing for Lucie as they faced the barrage of fire.

'Better to take a bullet than be butchered under von Kesler's car,' said Pierre, encouraging them on.

But something had changed … all they could hear was their heavy breathing and snow crunching under their feet.

A voice shouted out, 'You're safe,' and John looked back to see the 4x4 had rolled over. Yan was hanging lifeless out of the smashed windscreen, and Heinz von Kesler was climbing out through a side window to make off.

Ahead, the shooter was still pointing a gun towards them.

A man stepped out. It was Guillaume. 'It's over,

Mathilde,' he said, and she gently lowered the weapon she was clutching.

With John still supporting Lucie, and Pierre holding Harry, they waited passively with their backs to the wall of snow as several dark-blue Peugeot vans with blacked-out windows arrived. Heavily armed officers wearing green combats, balaclavas and helmets spilt out and ran forward to saturate the locus. One of them checked Yan's corpse. Another released an enthusiastic German Shepherd dog, and not long after, barking and von Kesler's shouts sounded from the rear of the chalet.

John asked Pierre if he knew who the armed officers were.

'Guillaume's cavalry: GIGN,' said Pierre.

Before Pierre could say more, a heavy-set officer with cropped hair and wearing winter boots, jeans and an expensive brown leather jacket arrived.

He stood aside as a female and a male officer came forward and took Lucie to one of the vans. He then looked at them and smiled. 'I'm Colonel DeValle.'

'Harry Freeman and John Anderson, Police Scotland. Could we use your phone to make a call?' asked Harry.

***

Harry checked in with Jack and then hung up.

'Jack says they've got enough information, but my phone had been hacked.'

'I'm sure whoever did that was acting in everyone's best interest,' said DeValle as he looked sideways at Pierre.

John shook his head in disbelief. 'And the tags were just to distract us?'

'Something like that,' said Pierre.

They watched in silence as a handcuffed von Kesler was put into the custody cage of a van.

Pierre looked at DeValle and gestured towards the chalet. 'Make sure everyone knows that's a major crime scene. One of von Kesler's IT people is in there somewhere.'

There was something in the way Pierre spoke to DeValle that left John wondering who was senior.

DeValle shouted orders in French and several of his people made off towards the building. 'We have Arthur Roux in custody, his vehicle triggered an ANPR camera en route to Belgium, and Commandant de Petit is at the station awaiting the arrival of internal affairs,' he said.

An Eclipse Blue Peugeot 508 with blackout windows and a driver dressed in civvies pulled up across the entrance.

'Pierre, that's your car. Now if you'll excuse me,' said DeValle.

DeValle headed off to join his officers and John turned to Pierre. 'Did Petit know what was going on?'

Pierre shook his head. 'No, but he was too fixated with his career and status to be curious. As you said, John, police officers are trusted to protect their citizens. He failed to live up to that, and now his career will end in ignominy.'

Mathilde and Guillaume arrived.

Mathilde looked at Pierre's arm. 'Are you alright?' she asked.

'Yes, it's only a nick.' He turned to Guillaume. 'Thank you for your help, Guillaume. You and your daughter are fine police officers. Now, could you please excuse us?'

John had something to ask Guillaume. 'Would you mind going to the hospital and reassuring Amy and her mother?'

'I'll do that,' said Guillaume.

He made off towards the gate, leaving Pierre with John, Harry and Mathilde.

Pierre looked back at the chalet. 'I have mixed feelings about the way this ended for Jaeger. He was right about von Kesler: the man deceived him. Jaeger was never going to make the grade as a professional skier, but von Kesler strung him along for his ends.'

John agreed. 'Von Kesler offered Jaeger the world ... but when Jaeger realised the price he had paid ...'

'Indeed,' said Pierre. 'Anyway, I need to leave so the real Lieutenant de Police Pierre Lavigne can return from Reunion and continue with his badminton competitions and duties in Lyon. And you, my dear colleagues, will be left with a memory.'

'Can you tell us your real name?' asked John.

Pierre smiled. 'I am Pierre. Pierre Traves. My family are from Provence.'

He turned to Mathilde. 'You're a good officer,

Mathilde. You did nothing wrong in Marseille: you were let down. The truth will now come out, but you need to put what happened behind you.'

'Did you have me transferred to Chamonix?' she asked.

'As I said, Mathilde, you did nothing wrong, and coming to the valley has given you space. Can we leave it at that?'

John moved uneasily on the spot, and Mathilde's face tightened to mask her emotions. But torn between keeping a professional distance and expressing her gratitude to Pierre for the faith he had in her when she was so full of doubts, she lowered her guard, stepped forward and embraced him with a hug of kindness and thanks.

'Fraternité,' he said, holding her tight.

'Fraternité,' she replied.

He then turned to John and Harry. 'What can I say? We have only known each other for nine days, but I feel we are family. I'm sorry I held back on you, but as you know, undercover operations are complex, and less is a good thing. If I had told you everything, you wouldn't have been able to play your part with the conviction that you did, and von Kesler would have seen through it. But be assured, as Guillaume's note said, "*We are with you,*" and always were.'

'Unbelievable,' said John, again shaking his head and wondering how much more they had missed.

Pierre just smiled and continued. 'When Freya was killed, von Kesler became suspicious of everyone, and I believed we would have to abort.

With your arrival, he became even more reliant on me. You and your people were also able to complete Freya's work and uncover von Kesler's Captagon distribution operation, which was my main purpose.'

'All that stuff Rowden-Mott was saying about a UK government grant for import/export – was he in on that, also?' asked John.

Pierre shrugged. 'That was breaking news to me, but if it's as it sounds, it would have flooded the UK with the drug. Freya wouldn't have known it, but her work has saved a lot of lives, and you, my friends, have brought justice for Freya, Amy, Anya and others. We couldn't be in the right place all the time, but we did our best.'

'Sometimes that's all we can do,' said John.

Pierre hugged John and Harry in turn and then headed for the car.

They stood watching it drive off.

'He took a bullet for us,' said Harry.

John nodded. 'And was prepared to give his life.'

Two Weeks Later

From a fast ground idle, the helicopter's turbos rose in pitch, bringing the rotor blades back into a whirling frenzy. From inside, Florent shouted out,

'We'll be about half an hour.' He pointed his thumb towards John and Harry whilst looking at Cal and Knox. 'Make sure you look after these two.'

The door then slid shut and the helicopter lifted, pivoted and sped off down the Mer de Glace, leaving the four of them standing in silence.

'Follow me,' said Cal, leading the way.

With their boots crunching the ice, Harry still encumbered by a knee brace and Knox humping his cool box, they reached a safe area dotted with rocks and each found an uncomfortably cold one to sit on.

But a little discomfort didn't matter. The day was what they had hoped for; sunny and still, and with the Vallee Blanche relatively free of skiers.

From their snowy amphitheatre, John looked up at the towering mountains, down the glacier with its expanse of glistening snow, and further back to magnificent ice formations.

'All this makes you feel insignificant.'

Harry agreed. 'It's why skiers and climbers come to these places. The mountains bring perspective.'

'An escape from this upside-down world we've found ourselves in,' said Knox, as he stared up at a route on the Dru.

Cal nodded in agreement. 'This is our happy place.'

'What are you lads planning for the summer?' asked John.

Cal, with his dishevelled blonde hair flopping down over his eyes, spoke first. 'I'm going home for a few days to patch things up with Dad – maybe drag him up the odd hill – and then I'm visiting Zoe in

England. She's having her eye sorted and is pretty freaked out about it, so I'm going to support her. They have to detach and reattach muscles behind her eyeball.'

'Gruesome,' said Knox. 'But kudos to Zoe. I'd sooner climb a north face bollock naked than go through that.'

Cal laughed and then looked at John. 'Has Astrid told you she's asked me to help her set something up?'

John shook his head, so Cal elaborated. 'It's no secret. She wants to establish a charity in memory of Freya. It's to help young people better manage their relationships with the digital world. It's what Freya had wanted to do. Zoe knows loads about that stuff and she's keen to help. Once her eye is sorted, we're all coming back here for three months, and we'll work remotely.'

'I think that's great,' said John. 'We have a team that collaborates with other agencies in that type of work. If you need an introduction, just ask.'

'Thanks, we'll probably take you up on that.'

'Do. But you gave me the impression that the four of you agreed relationships were too complicated?'

'They probably are,' said Knox. 'But we did a Snapchat video call with the girls to let them know everything was cool and two hours later we'd planned the next six months together. I guess we decided to give "complicated" a go.'

'And what's next for you, Knox?' asked Harry.

Knox sighed. 'Pierre asked me the same thing.'

'Oh? He wasn't trying to recruit you, was he?'

Knox bit on his bottom lip and looked again at the Dru. 'If he was, I wouldn't tell you, would I?'

John suspected Pierre had made overtures to Knox. Pierre was an enigma: a determined warrior for his cause and a master at deep cover. He would see the potential in a young man like Knox. Perhaps he already had and Knox was part of his charade, playing a blinder when looking dissociated from him. And there was the matter of what Cal and Knox lived on. They never mentioned work, but Pierre would have access to discretionary funds and could easily keep the boys in a base, beer and baguettes. But that was their business.

'You could join us,' said Harry. 'Police Scotland are looking for good people.'

'Aye, right, and give this up?' said Knox, taking in the magnificence surrounding them. 'Besides, I'm not the type to take orders. But I am considering how to be a bigger part of the cure for this fucked-up society.'

'Harry and I think you're already a big part of the cure,' said John. 'You both are. We've been humbled by everything the two of you have done. You guys, Florent, Amy, Émilie and Freya have renewed our faith in humanity. You're the next generation, and we think something better.'

'Yeah, yeah, yeah,' said Knox.

But John and Harry could see that Knox and Cal had taken their words on board.

Cal looked at John. 'Are you still thinking of jacking?'

John shook his head. 'No. I've decided to stay

with the programme – at least for a while.'

'What made you change your mind?' asked Cal.

'As strange as it sounds, it was the guardian's light on the Midi that swung it.'

Cal looked curiously towards the Midi and then back at John. 'What difference did the light make?' he asked, trying to figure it out.

'A sense of duty,' said John.

'Yeh, I get that,' said Cal. He then adopted a mischievous look. 'Hey, the word in Cham is that you and that bad-ass cougar, Mathilde, have something happening?'

John looked to Knox for help. 'For goodness' sake, Knox, tell him to wind it in, will you?'

But Knox was grinning ear to ear.

Still enjoying the novelty of the prescription glacier glasses he'd treated himself to, Harry leant forward and spoke to John. 'He's figured you out, my old son,' he said, slapping John on the back.

The sound of the returning helicopter thwarted any more awkward questions and John, Harry, Knox and Cal rose to their feet in readiness for what they knew would be difficult, but necessary.

The rotors slowed, and Florent opened the door, jumped out and pulled a large rucksack after him. He then held out a hand to help Astrid and Amy disembark.

They moved away from the helicopter and it departed.

Astrid was wearing sunglasses and dressed in sheepskin boots, stretch ski trousers and a light-cream puffer-type jacket. Amy was dressed in her ski trousers and jacket.

Astrid looked across and gave a brief, courteous wave, and Cal, Knox, John and Harry waved back. Amy seemed to falter, but Astrid said something to her, and Florent led them over.

Amy stood a little behind as Astrid took off her sunglasses and shook hands with John and Harry in turn. 'Hugo underestimated you two, but I didn't. I knew you would find the truth. Thank you for coming to our aid. I owe a debt I can never repay.'

Cal could see that Amy was uncomfortable, her eyes cast down. He stepped forward to her. 'How are you doing, Amy?' he asked.

'A bit better,' she said, but her eyes filled with tears. 'I'm not going to let what happened beat me, Cal. I'm going to university and then I'm coming back here. It's what my dad would have wanted me to do.' She then looked Cal in the eyes. 'Freya was my friend ...'

'We know she was,' he replied. 'None of this is your fault. You're a victim and we're here for you.'

Astrid broke off and put a comforting arm around Amy. 'Freya knew you were her friend. She was a friend to all of us ... she was our saviour.'

Amy gave a weak smile and wiped her tears.

Astrid then turned to Cal and was about to say something, but as had happened to Amy, her words failed and Cal threw his arms around her. She clung to him in a tight embrace, and when her emotions allowed, she whispered. 'Thank you so much for finding my daughter, for staying with her and bringing her back to me.'

Finally, she reached Knox. Facing him, she took each of his hands in one of hers and looked him straight in the eyes, pinched her mouth closed and nodded as if to say there were no words worthy.

'You don't need to say anything. I know,' said Knox.

'And I know you know,' she replied. 'You and Cal are the best.'

She then turned to Florent. 'May I see, now?'

'Of course. Cal, you'll accompany Astrid.'

Knox and Cal helped Astrid into a harness and Cal donned his. As they had planned, Knox and Florent belayed Cal and Astrid as they walked to the edge of the crevasse.

They stood there for a while, Cal doing most of the talking, and then returned to the group.

'It was important for me to see the crevasse,' said Astrid. 'Thank you.'

Knox helped Astrid out of her harness and then made a suggestion.

'Freya loved this place. We've brought some cakes and soft drinks with us. We thought maybe we could chill out here for a while with her?'

'I think that's a lovely idea.'

Astrid turned to John. 'Would you mind if I had a word with you, Sergeant?'

'I'll go with Florent and help the young team set up,' said Harry, leaving Astrid and John alone.

Astrid stared into the distance and then turned to John. 'Sergeant, you must have seen some terrible things during your career.'

'I have,' he said, looking back at her.

'Seeing all that awfulness, how do you keep your faith in humanity?' she asked.

John thought for a moment. 'It's not always easy, and believe me, I have my wobbles.'

He looked over to where Knox was up to his old tricks: holding a cake high in the air for Amy, egged on by Cal, to try and retrieve. Each time she jumped he lifted it a little higher, and each time she laughed at her failed attempt and tried again.

'But when I look at them, falling down, getting back up and dusting themselves off, well, what's there not to hope for?'

The End

OTHER BOOKS BY THIS AUTHOR

The 'Nicholas' trilogy:

A Boy in a Storm

Set in Edinburgh and the Highlands of Scotland, this is a tale of adventure, friendship, and hope. An abusive father hiding behind an affluent Edinburgh address. A mother haunted and manipulated by secrets from her past. A young man brought up never to speak about what he has witnessed … and a storm on the mountain that changes everything.

Past, Present, and Hope

Bereft of purpose, Londoner, Gary Hughes, returns to the Highlands of Scotland in search of the boy he once was. But returning reawakens long-buried feelings and deeds that force him to confront the reality of what happened all those years ago. A story of how what was once, threatens what life could be.

A Girl and her Compass

Set in London, Edinburgh, the Western Isles, and the Highlands, this is a tale of adventure, self-discovery, and resilience. Faced with living a lifetime of regret, or, overcoming your greatest fear, what would you choose?

ABOUT THE AUTHOR

Oliver's journey began in Edinburgh, where at a young age he discovered his love for Scotland's rugged terrain and outdoor adventures. After studying Outdoor Education he pursued a career as an outdoor instructor.

His career has been anything but ordinary. From ventures in business and policing to working in academia and chalet construction, he's embraced diverse experiences.

Now settled in Perthshire, Scotland, Oliver spends his days climbing the odd hill, sailing, kayaking, and sharing his knowledge, experiences, and adventures through writing and lecturing.

Printed in Great Britain
by Amazon